THE BEST SCIENCE FICTION OF E. C. TUBB

E. C. Tubb

GW00775658

WILDSIDE PRESS

THE BEST SCIENCE FICTION OF E. C. TUBB

Published by:
Wildside Press

www.wildsidepress.com

Cover painting by Sydney Jordan.

Acknowledgements:

"Fallen Angel" first published in *Fantasy Annual #3* in 1999. "Death-wish" first published in *Authentic Science Fiction* in 1955. "The Ming Vase" first published in *Analog Science Fiction—Science Fact* in 1963. "The Beatific Smile" first published in *Nebula Science Fiction* in 1958. "When he Died" first published in *Authentic Science Fiction* in 1956. "Read Me This Riddle" first published in *New Writings in SF #30* in 1978. "Logic" first published in *Authentic Science Fiction* in 1954. "Vigil" first published in *Galaxy Science Fiction* in 1956. "J is for Jeanne" first published in *New Worlds SF* in 1965. "Legal Eagle" first published in *Authentic Science Fiction* in 1956. "There's No Tomorrow" first published in *Worlds of Fantasy #7* in 1952. "Time to Kill" first published in *Galaxy Science Fiction* in 1956. "The Seekers" first published in *New Writings in SF #6* in 1965. "The Last Day of Summer" first published in *Science Fantasy* in 1955. "Evane" first published in *New Writings in SF #22* in 1973. "Time and Again" first published in *Fantasy Annual #1* in 1997.

CONTENTS

FALLEN ANGEL

A FLASH of rose, a scent, a voice which echoed in the hollows of his mind and, suddenly, he was alive again. Fully alive, really alive, not lying on a slab while instruments probed and delved, measured and indexed, twisted and tested. Not writhing in torment as muscle and nerve and sinew were strained to the limits of endurance and then pushed further beyond. Alive and well and soon to be free. Free!

The concept was intoxicating as the drink and drugs he had once known which had rotted his brain and body in return for a brief euphoria. He sat and thought about it in the place where he was kept. A mist swirled about the area molding itself into the illusion that he sat on a bench of stone, in a chamber of stone scented with the perfume of hidden blooms. Soon now, he would see real flowers, walk again in sunlight, feel the wind, the rain, the touch of snow. To eat genuine food, talk to real people, forget what had happened if forgetting was possible.

"It is," said the alien. "Most things are." He had appeared as he always did, abruptly, seated, a tall, lean, white-haired man looking, in his simple robe, like an ancient Greek philosopher. It was a facade. An illusion to mask the true shape of the creature. "But no interference on our part will be necessary," he continued. "Your race has a peculiar ability to ignore the unpleasant. The defensive application of a highly selective memory."

"Yes," said Frank. He could believe it. Once he had seen the creature as it really was. Now it was almost impossible to accept that such a thing could actually exist. "I was told that I was to be released. Am I?"

"Of course, Mr. Engel. We do not lie." The classical features creased into a smile. "You probably feared that we would eliminate you but we have no reason for that. You may not realize it but we have much to thank you for. You have been most co-operative. With your assistance we have gained much knowledge of your world and we shall learn more. We are grateful."

Grateful! Would a fisherman talk that way to a creature he had hauled from the water, cut open, looked at, sewn up and was ready to throw back into the sea? Maybe if the fish could talk but would he give it a reward?

"It is our custom," said the alien. The words echoed without vibration, a soft tingling impinging directly on the cortex. "Our ethics forbid us to take without giving something in return. The device is one much used among us for social convenience. It is an eraser. With it you can undo a mistake. Gain the advantage of a second chance. Avoid unpleasant situations. You should find it most useful."

"Sure," said Frank. "But—" He broke off for the alien had gone, the room, the swirling mist and walls of apparent stone. He still sat but the bench was of wood. The air carried the scent of visible flowers. There was sound; the sigh of wind, the rustle of leaves, the shouts of children at play. And, all around, the bright warmth of a summer sun.

Summer? It had been winter when he'd been taken, cold, hungry, dying, without a job, a home, a friend, a shred of hope. The way a man gets when the money runs out and the drink and the drugs and nothing is left but hunger, the pain of diseased lungs and the ravages of dissipation. He'd been a good specimen for the aliens. Who would miss him? Who would believe him? Who would he want to convince?

No one. He was cured and he knew it. No more addiction. No more disease. A good chance to make a fresh start. He knew what needed to be done and he had the alien's gift to help him do it.

He sat and looked at it, eyes narrowed against reflected sunshine. Beside him a man stirred in his sleep smelling of staleness but human because of it. Just one of the drifters who thronged the park. Across the graveled path another bench held three others, two old, one a kid with a waxen face and twitching hands. One of the men rose, stretched, headed down the path. Frank ignored him, concentrating on the gift.

It was a ring, the band thick, wide, raised in one part, a prominence that could be pressured by the impact of the adjoining finger. The jewel was a large, domed, ruby-like stone striated with what could have been a diffraction grating. Frank was a social failure but not an idiot and some things were obvious. The ring was more than an ornament but just what he didn't know. The alien hadn't explained. He examined it again, studying the protuberance. He pressed it.

Nothing happened.

Nothing, that is. Aside from the fact that the man who had

risen from the facing bench and who had walked down the path was abruptly sitting on the bench again. As Frank watched he rose, stretched and walked away. The stud on the ring sank beneath the squeeze of his finger. Nothing happened. He waited, tried again—and the man was back on the bench. He rose, stretched, walked down the path exactly as he had done twice before. This time Frank let him go.

He knew now what the alien had given him.

He leaned back filled with the wonder of it. An eraser, the alien had said. A device for social convenience. A thing with which to undo a mistake and to gain another chance. It was something you could need to use quickly, easily, have close all the time. What could be more convenient than a ring? A very special kind of ring. A neat device, he thought, looking at it. Compact, ornamental, unobtrusive, probably everlasting.

A one-way time machine.

The main-line station housed a throng of travelers. Frank ignored them all as he concentrated on the large digital clock. The figures read 18.02. He activated the ring. The figures changed to 17.05. Fifty-seven seconds, the same as twice before. He made more experiments. Activated the ring threw you back in time, but you had to wait fifty-seven seconds before it could be activated again. No accumulation. The stud could be kept depressed and there would be an automatic activation. Nothing you carried less than fifty-seven seconds in the past went back with you. It was all he needed to know.

The crossing lights were at red. Frank, distracted, stepped from the kerb directly into the path of a heavy truck. Brakes screamed, a woman, a man. A moment of panic then his finger closed and he was instantly back on the sidewalk heading towards the crossing. He checked with his watch. Fifty-seven seconds. Call it a minute. He paused, waited for the truck to pass, the lights to change to green.

A minute.

Not long? Try holding your breath that long. Try resting your rear on a hot stove for half that time. In a minute you can walk a hundred yards, run almost a quarter of a mile, fall three. You can conceive, die, get married. A minute is time enough for a lot of things.

Frank closed his hand and looked at the ring. Thinking. Take the classical situation: A couple, the man old, the woman young. You greet them, assume the woman is the old man's daughter, discover she is his wife. Loss of equanimity, and the generation of embarrassment. So activate and go back in time. Meet the couple again but now armed with knowledge. Politeness reigns. In any society such a device would be in demand.

But not for soothing an old man's ego. Not just for that.

Not when he had no job, nowhere to live, an ache for luxury his belly and a yen for the good life in his soul. He had drawn on the experience of three decades of tough living to get a wristwatch and decent shoes and clothing. But he still needed money.

A liquor store shone down the street, a bright cavern filled with bottled dreams. Frank leaned close to the window, squinting against the lights, staring inside and checking what he saw. The place seemed deserted, the owner probably busy out back. A cash register stood on the counter flanked by stacked cans. He waited, counting seconds. A minute and a half and no sign of life. He activated, walked into the store, operated the cash register and took out a thin sheaf of bills. He was almost at the door when the owner appeared. A big, beefy man with a balding head and savage eyes. He came charging from a room at the rear shouting and waving a baseball bat.

"Hold it you! Move and I'll smash your head in!"

He meant it. Frank squeezed the ring—nothing happened. Nothing would happen until the time was up. He had to stall.

"Now listen," he said. "It's not like it seems. It's a publicity stunt see? Just for advertising. You'll—"

"By God, the nerve of it!" The owner came closer, lifting the club, snarling his hate. "A stinking thief walks in and robs the till, then gives you a load of mouth. I'll give you mouth! I'll give you a damned sight more than that!"

Frank squeezed his fingers keeping the stud depressed as he dived to one side. The owner was fast. The club slammed against the edge of the door then followed him down. He felt and heard the crack of bone as it slammed against his knee. He rolled as it lifted for another blow—and he was leaning against the window the glass cool against his brow. He fought to control his breath. He was safe his knee uninjured, the store seemingly deserted.

Mopping sweat he felt the bloom of anger. The bastard had

tried to kill him. To smash in his skull for the sake of a little cash. He would be lounging in his room, watching television, enjoying something to eat. He'd have a gimmick rigged to the door to signal when anyone came in. That, and maybe a mirror to watch the till. Nursing his club and aching to use it. The blood-crazed slob! He had it coming!

Again he entered the empty store and opened the register but this time, instead of heading for the door, snatched up a bottle and moved to the rear. As the owner appeared he swung at the balding skull. The bottle shattered into a mass of sparkling fragments mixed with a flood of wine, blood and spattered brain. He dropped the neck and scooped up the club. The shape of a wallet bulged the rear pocket of the dead man's jeans. He bent, dragged it free, flipped it open and saw a wad of bills. Straightening he thrust it into a pocket and strode towards the door. A looming shadow blocked the opening.

Quickly he rammed his foot against the panel.

"Sorry. We're closed."

"I want a drink. I gotta have a drink." The voice was a begging whine. "I got money, see?" A hand lifted, waving a crumpled note. "Just a bottle of something cheap."

A lush and close to desperation. Frank recognized the danger. To lock him out was to invite curses, broken windows, unwanted attention. To let him in was to give him a view of murder.

He activated the ring and was standing by the till cash in his hand. Quickly he reached for a bottle and moved to the rear. This time he didn't smash in the owner's skull but swung hard and low at the belly and groin. He took the wallet from where he knew it would be. The club remained where it had fallen. He thrust the bottle into the hands of the lush at the door. Outside a cab halted at his signal.

"Where to?"

"A casino. A good one." Frank relaxed against the cushions as the driver glided from the kerb. "Waste no time, friend. I feel lucky."

Luck, the fortuitous combination of favorable circumstances, but who needs luck when they know what will happen fifty-seven seconds in advance? Long enough for the dice to settle, the card to turn, the ball to drop. The winner to win. The ability to make quick, impulsive, apparently stupid last-second wagers against a seemingly sure thing. Frank rode high, a sure-fire winner.

In more ways than one.

He stretched, enjoying the shower, the impact of water driven at high pressure against hair and skin massaging and stimulating as it tightened tissue and stung flesh into an exhilarating awareness. He turned a control and gasped as the water turned into a frigid goose-pimpling medium. A titillation as many things were now thanks to the alien gift and his own aptitude. He jerked the control back to hot, waited, then cut the spray and stepped from the shower drying himself on a fluffy towel.

"Frank, darling. Are you going to be much longer?"

A female voice with the peculiar intonation of the inbred upper classes; a member of the aristocracy by birth and a failed marriage. The Lady Jane Smyth-Connors was rich, decadent, bored and a problem.

"A moment, honey," he called and dropped the towel. A mirror reflected a pleasing image. Money had improved on what the aliens had accomplished; cosmetic magic smoothing away accumulated blemishes, the scars of his early days. He'd worked hard to gain the physique of an athlete. He had been born with a pleasing face. Money had taken care of other things, his clothes, his accent, the education of his tastes. He had become a fringe-member of the jet-set. Rich. Handsome. Riding high. Saddled now with a crippled bird.

"Frank? Come to me!"

"Give me a moment." He resisted the instinctive rush of anger at the tone, the command. She was arrogant and domineering but that had been obvious from the start. He had met her in a casino, recognizing the desperation of a woman who wanted to win but could only lose. Recognizing, too, an echo of what he had once been The opportunity she presented. He had made a point of meeting her and she'd been attracted by his looks, figure and calculated attention. Now, invited to her home, perfectly aware of what was expected, he stood on the edge of respectable security.

The bathroom had a window. He parted the curtains and looked into the night. Way down low a scatter of lights carpeted the misty ground. London was a nice city. England a nice place. Very nice, especially to gamblers—no tax was levied on winnings. Here, more than anywhere else, high prizes were to be won. Not just money, that was for the plebeians, but make the right connections and every day would be Christmas.

"Frank!"

Fretful impatience and the imperious tone of one accustomed to instant obedience. The woman waited to be served. Sighing he entered the bedroom.

She was a little older than himself, tall with a peculiar angularity, giving the impression of an overgrown schoolgirl, who should be wearing tweeds and wielding a hockey stick. The appearance was deceptive. Generations of inbreeding had done more than fashion the distribution of flesh and bone. It had developed a festering degeneracy. She was, he knew, almost clinically insane but, in her class, people were never insane only 'eccentric', never stupid only 'amusing', never spiteful, savage, vicious or cruel only 'thoughtless'.

He reached out and took her into his arms and kissed her with educated skill. He ran his hands over her body, silk rustling as it fell from her naked flesh. Gently he bit the base of her throat, harder, felt her tense, her negative reaction.

"No," she snapped. "I hate anyone doing that!"

One bad mark. He counted seconds as he reached for the light switch. With darkness she squirmed, pushed herself free of his embrace.

"I hate the dark! Must you be like all the others?"

Two bad marks. Twenty seconds to go. Time for one more exploration. His hands reached out, made contact, moved with studied determination. She sighed with mounting pleasure.

"Frank—my angel!"

He activated the ring.

Reaching out he took her in his arms this time making no attempt to nibble or bite. Her clothing rustled to the floor and her skin gleamed with a nacreous sheen. He looked at her with bold admiration and his hands moved in the way he had learned gave her pleasure.

She closed her eyes, fingernails digging into his back. "Talk to me," she demanded. "Talk to me!"

He began counting seconds.

Later, as she lay in satiated slumber, he rested, thinking, planning, oddly amused. He had been the perfect lover. He had said and done all the things she had wanted in the exact order she had wanted them and, most important, without her having to instruct him at any time. He had been a reflection, an echo of her complex needs, and why not? He had worked hard to map the blueprint of her desire. Exploring, investigating, erasing all false starts and mistakes. Doing and saying nothing that had been unwelcome.

What else could he be for her but perfect?

He turned, looking down at the woman, seeing her not just as flesh and blood but as a soul in desperate need. A mass of conflicting emotions and frustrated needs, one not to be used but to be helped.

She sighed, opened her eyes, looked up at the face of her lover. "My angel! My darling!"

He said what she wanted him to say.

She sighed again, same sound, different meaning. "I've never been so happy. I can't believe this is happening." Her fingers trailed over his arm, his hand, halted at the ring. "Why do you wear this? It's so big. So heavy. It looks like a knuckle-duster. Is it for protection?"

"In a way."

"I'll protect you," she said, then added, musingly: "Your name suits you. Engel, that's German for angel. Frank means honest. You are a frank angel. Are you an honest one?"

"I try to be."

"Then I'll give you a treat. Tonight I'll take you to a party. You'll love it. There will be people it will help you to meet and all sorts of things to amuse you."

Drugs and drink and he could guess the rest. "No."

"Why not? Don't be so staid, darling. Everyone needs to relax at times. We'll take a trip into paradise."

"No," he said again and added, "I can't stop you doing what you want but I've been where you're heading for and I don't recommend it. Anyway, I can't see you tonight."

"Why not?" Jealousy reared her upright. "I need you. You know that. Why can't I see you? You said—"

"I know what I said and I meant every word of it. I love you to distraction, darling, but I have to fly to New York. Business," he added. "After all I do have to make a living."

She said, quickly, "You don't have to worry about that, darling. I'll speak to Daddy and—"

He closed her lips with his own. "I still have to go to New York," he insisted. Against her naked body his hands did what she wanted them to do. "And later, after I return—"

"We'll get married," she said. "I never want to lose you."

Christmas, he thought, as dawn paled the sky.

The plane was big, sleek, beautiful with matching flight attendants all breasts and legs and eyes and silken hair with a 'you may look at me because I'm beautiful but you must never, ever touch' attitude. A machine offering the ultimate in comfort for those willing to pay for it. Frank was willing and able and traveled luxury class. Room for everyone with plenty to spare and he was glad of it.

He felt tired. The night had been hectic and the morning little better. It was good to sit and relax neatly strapped in a form-fitting chair as the jets gulped air and spewed it behind in a man-made hurricane which sent the plane down the runway and up into the air. London fell away, a misty blur, the clouds dropped like tufts of dirty cotton and then there was only the sun, a watchful eye in an immense iris of blue.

He liked to travel and a little absence could make a heart grow fonder and, for him, there was a kick in flying. He liked to look down and think of all the emptiness between him and the ground. Feel his stomach tighten with acrophobia, the delicious sensation of fear experienced in perfect safety. Height had no meaning on a plane. All you had to do was to look straight ahead and you could be in a train. A Pullman, naturally, nothing but the best was good enough for the winners in this world.

And he was one of them. Wealthy and soon to be married to a rich and doting woman who had all the right connections. One for whom he felt an unexpected fondness. He would be fair taking nothing she wasn't willing to give. He didn't have to. Not if what he planned worked out.

He unstrapped, stretched his legs, glanced through a window as the captain's voice came over the speakers telling anyone interested of their height and velocity. Through the pane he could see very little. The sky, the clouds below, the tip of a wing.

Old stuff. The blonde attendant was far from that. She swayed among the seats, caught his eye, responded with instant attention. Was he quite comfortable? Would he like a pillow? A newspaper? A magazine? Something to drink?

"Brandy," he said. "With ice and soda."

He sat on an inner seat close to the wall of the cabin so that she had to step from the aisle in order to lower the flap and set down his drink. He lifted his left hand and touching her knee, slid his palm slowly up the inside of her thigh. He felt her stiffen and saw the expression on her face, a compound of incredulity, outrage, interest and speculation. Automatically he counted the seconds. Fifty-four . . . five . . . six . . .

He pressed the stud on his ring.

The tray made a little thudding sound as it came to rest, the brandy a liquid gurgling as it gushed from the miniature bottle over the ice. She smiled, gesturing with the punctured can of soda. "All of it, sir?"

He nodded, watching as she poured, remembering the soft warmth of her thigh, the yielding temptation of her flesh. Knowing he had touched her only because it was forbidden. A stupid, childish thing to have done and totally unnecessary. If he wanted her she was available, her body language had made that clear. Did she know what he had done? No, he decided as she moved away. To her nothing had happened. She had served him a drink and that was all. But—?

Brooding he stared at the ring. You activated it and went back fifty-seven seconds in time. All you had done during that period was erased. You could do anything you liked and none of it mattered because it had all been canceled. But it had been real. He remembered the pulped skull of the liquor store owner. A murder canceled but it had happened. He could remember it.

Could you remember what had never taken place?

"Sir?" The stewardess was back, smiling, some magazines in her hand. "I thought these might interest you," she said. "I picked a range. Would you care for another drink? The same as before? Right away, sir."

She gave it to him and swayed across the cabin as he reached for the magazines. Naked women ogled at him from the pages of a soft-porn publication and he wondered why she had chosen it. To hint that she was far from being a prude? To arouse his interest?

To test his sexuality? His interest? Checking him out in her own way as he had done Jane the previous night. But he had no interest in pictured nudity.

The magazine fell to one side as he reached for a different publication. One dealing with oddities of nature and science and strong on the occult. He flipped pages, pausing to read, interested despite his cynicism. One article in particular held his attention.

According to the author some fifteen million Americans claimed to have been abducted by aliens, tested, interfered with, examined and then released with only the vaguest of memories of what they claimed had happened.

So he was not alone.

Yet if he could remember why couldn't they? Had their experience been based on nothing but mass hysteria? Wishful thinking? A simple desire to break out of faceless conformity. Had each received a gift? Could they be recognized by the rings they could be wearing?

He looked at his own knowing it was not what it seemed. But was it more? He leaned back, thinking, remembering the calm figure in the simple robe. The explanation he had been given. Closing his eyes he made a mental journey back in time, feeling the stone of the bench, the flower-scented mist. Seeing the figure dressed in a simple robe, the alien resembling an ancient Greek philosopher. What had he said?

"You may not realize it, Mr. Engel, but we have much to thank you for. You have been most co-operative. With your assistance we have gained much knowledge of your world and we shall learn more."

Learn more? How?

The ring—it had to be the ring. It swelled in his vision the stone a baleful eye. A time machine—but what else? A recorder? A transmitter? A tracking device? Had it monitored each activation? Was it a continuation of his physical examination? A means to test his moral fibre? Turning him into a representative sample of what could be expected from any of his species?

If so they would learn how strong curiosity was to the human race. How tempting wealth and power. His business in New York was to meet experts in computer technology and other fields. Those who could scan the ring with specialized techniques, testing, prying, monitoring in order to determine the composition of the metal, the stone, its design and molecular structure. If it could be copied he would gain wealth beyond the dreams of avarice.

And he would have given freedom to the teeming inhabitants of an increasingly violent world. A defense against attack and injury. A means of escape from disasters and unthinking acts of violence. Had the aliens guessed what he intended?

He lifted his hand and stared into the stone. The ring was his to do with as he pleased. A gift. A thing given him by something resembling an ancient Greek and he remembered a cogent statement learned when young. "Beware the Greeks when they come bearing gifts."

But not this one. It had given him stature. The chance of social enhancement. Of confirmed social security but it could give him what he still lacked, the unquestioning power of incredible wealth.

The plane rocked a little. The voice from the speaker was calm, unhurried. "Will all passengers please fasten their safety belts. We are heading into an area of minor turbulence. You may see a little lightning but there is absolutely nothing to worry about. We are, of course, flying well above the area of storm."

The blonde came through the cabin, tutted when she saw his unfastened belt and made it fast. As she walked away he reached for the magazine, wondering if, in the letter column, there could be a claim from someone who had something concrete to show for their claimed meeting with aliens. The magazine fell from his lap to one side beyond his reach. Impatiently he released the safety belt and picked up the publication.

It held nothing of interest. Smiling at the stewardess he gestured for her to fetch him another drink.

Something hit the roof of the cabin. There was a ripping sound, a blast of air, an irresistible force that tore him from his seat and flung him into space. Air gushed from his lungs as he began to fall. He gulped, trying to breathe, to understand. Arctic chill numbed his flesh. He twisted, saw through streaming eyes the jagged gash in the fuselage, the shattered wreckage of the tail.

An accident, he thought wildly. A fireball, a meteor, metal

fatigue even. A crack in the cabin wall and internal pressure would do the rest. And now he was falling. Falling!

His fingers squeezed in frenzied reaction.

"Please, sir." The blonde came towards him as he reared to his feet. "You must remain seated with your safety belt fastened unless—"

"Listen!" He grabbed her by both arms. "Tell the pilot to change course. Tell him now. Hurry!"

A fireball or meteor could be avoided. They would be safe if the course was changed fast enough. But it had to be done now. Now!

"Quick!" He ran towards the flight deck the girl at his heels. Damn the stupid bitch! Couldn't she understand? "This is an emergency!" he shouted. "Change course immediately!"

Something hit the roof of the cabin. The compartment ripped open, metal coiling like the peeled skin of a banana. The blonde vanished. The shriek of tearing metal was lost in the explosive gusting of escaping air. Desperately Frank dung to a seat. He felt his hands torn from the fabric, his body sucked towards the opening. Once again he was ejected into space to begin the long, stomach-wrenching five-mile fall.

"No!" he screamed his terror. "Dear God, no!"

He activated.

"Please, sir, I really must insist! You must allow me to fasten your safety belt."

He was standing by his seat and the blonde was showing signs of getting annoyed. Annoyed!

"This is important," he said, fighting to remain calm. Ignoring the stares of the other passengers all neatly belted in their seats. "In less than a minute this plane is going to fall apart. Do something about it!"

Why did she stand there looking so dumb?

"You stupid cow, get out of my way!" He pushed her to one side and lunged towards the flight deck. "Change course!" he yelled. "For God's sake—"

Something hit the roof of the cabin. Again the roar, the blast, the irresistible force. Something struck his head and blurred his senses. He activated and found himself still in the open gulping at rarefied air and shivering in the savage cold. To one side, far lower, the shattered plane hung in a cloud of dissipating wreckage. Tiny fragments hung around it one of them, perhaps, the blonde.

Below the sea spread in a shimmer of light and water. His stomach constricted with the overwhelming terror of acrophobia as he stared at the waves. Imagining the moment of inevitable impact. Falling he would he ten thousand deaths in cringing anticipation.

Spasmodically he damped his fingers tightly together against the ring. Immediately he was high in the air again with almost a minute of grace in which to fall.

Fifty-seven seconds ... repeated ... repeated ... repeated ... repeated ... repeated ...

Falling, endlessly falling.

An angel suspended between Heaven and Earth.

DEATH-WISH

THEY caught him with the knife at his throat, the bright red blood welling from the razor edge as it sliced through skin and fat, muscle and sinew, cutting down towards the pulsing carotids and throbbing arteries below. They shocked him with stasis and took away the knife. They staunched the blood and sealed the wound. They placed him back on the narrow white cot in the narrow white room and there they left him, still in stasis, blind and dumb, deaf and paralyzed, his body helpless and only his mind aware.

Left him to his thoughts— and memories.

War!

A drifting boredom spaced by sickening fear and sudden violence. The long, tedious, nerve-grating conflict of interstellar struggle. The blare of the alarms, the rapid manoeuvring, the blinding incandescence of exploding atoms, the sweat, the panic, the frantic urge to run and run, and keep on running, and sometimes, very rarely, the actual capture of an enemy vessel.

The captured Head wasn't much help. It lolled above the humped bulk of its maintenance machine, its eyes glazed, a thin stream of spittle drooling from the corners of its month, its lips twisted into an idiotic grin. It could hear, of course, and the pumps supplied air to its throat so that it could even speak. It could see, too, though that wasn't necessary, and once, perhaps a month ago, perhaps a decade, it had even been human.

But not any more.

Longstrom felt ill as he stared at it, his eyes drifting in awful fascination over the naked, hairless scalp, the deep scars, the distorted tissue where metal and plastic wedded with flesh. The thing stared back at him, rolled its eyes, giggled, and licked its lips with a repulsive, almost obscene gesture.

He vomited.

Harding was pleased. Harding was the captain, the leader, the man in charge. He wore his uniform as if it were a second skin and he had long ago stiffened his bones into metal struts, converted his heart into a stone, and replaced his emotions with a blank void in which shone only the lambent flame of duty. He smiled as he stared at the horror, frowned at the weakness of his computer man, and turned to Carver, his gun officer.

"Report."

"No signs of enemy life, sir." Carver tried not to look at the Head. "They must have abandoned ship when we registered our first hit. Engines are damaged beyond repair or recognition."

"A pity. Earth could have done something with undamaged engines." Harding frowned as if the action of the enemy in ruining their vessel was a personal insult. He smiled again as he stared at the Head. "Still, we have this."

"Yes, sir."

"You don't sound happy about it, Carver."

"No, sir." Carver forced himself to stare at the Head. "Are you going to kill it, sir?"

"Kill it?" Harding didn't trouble to disguise his impatience. "Why should I?"

"It would be a mercy, sir. After all, it was a man once, and—"

"You're a sentimental fool, Carver. This Head is important to us and you babble about killing it." Harding stooped and stared into the ravaged features of the thing. "Can you hear me?"

"... yay ... yay ... yay ..."

"Attention! Answer me! Can you understand?"

"... yay ... yay ... yay ..."

"Shock, perhaps, sir?" Carver glanced at Longstrom, busy wiping his mouth and making a point of not looking at the Head. "I understand that it would be connected to the outside detectors, and perhaps it has become deranged by the explosion."

"Is that possible, Longstrom?"

"Yes, sir. Even normal computer banks would be thrown out of alignment in such a case."

"I see." Harding frowned down at the idiotic features; then, as his eyes drifted over the compact assembly, something dawned deep in his mind. "Longstrom! Would it be possible to transfer the Head to our own vessel?"

"I suppose we could, sir. The pumps feeding the brain with blood and nutrient solutions appear to be intact and the unit is self-enclosed. We could disconnect the feed-in circuits, but . . ." He glanced appealingly at Carver. "Would it be wise, sir?"

"Wise? I don't think I understand what you mean,

Longstrom. We have captured a piece of enemy equipment and it is our duty to transport it to base. Frankly, I see no alternative."

"The men won't like it, sir," protested Carver. "We've been away from base for a long time now and morale is low. If—"

"I am aware that you are also our part-time psychologist, Carver." There was no mistaking Harding's opinion of psychologists. "But is it necessary for me to remind you that I am in command? The men will do as I say—and like it."

"Regulations provide that any captured Head be immediately destroyed," said Carver, stiffly. "The danger of panic induced by close proximity with such a thing is well recognized, and—"

"You are insubordinate, Carver!"

"I am intelligent, sir."

For a moment the two men glared at each other, the gun officer momentarily over-whelmed by his knowledge of the inner workings of the human mind, and, because of that, more emotionally sensitive than the captain could ever be. Longstrom moved forward with some vague idea of stepping between them, part of him wondering what would happen if neither refused to back down, knowing that, although Carver was technically right, he was also technically wrong in opposing a superior officer; knowing, too, that Harding was both capable of, and justified in, shooting the psychologist out of hand.

The stalemate was broken by the Head.

It giggled, blinked, parted its lips and, in a peculiarly mechanical voice said: "Object approaching 64:89:221."

It could only be an enemy vessel.

They escaped—just. Longstrom sat at his instrument board, his eyes flickering from dial to tell-tale, from alarm to the moving specks on the radar screens, his hands moving with trained rhythm as he received data, collated it, fed it to the computer banks, using trained skill, technical knowledge and plain instinct to avoid the probing death of the enemy missiles.

And that was interstellar war.

There were no ships silhouetted in gun sights. No thrill and pulse of combat, exploding ruin caused by the pressure of a trigger, the excitement and adventure of pitting life against death.

There was waiting and silence and the slow movement of specks on a screen. There were clicking relays and glowing panels and mechanical prediction. It was a game in which one man controlled the moves and the rest sat and looked on, knowing that if he guessed wrong, they would spill their lives into the void. No thrill. No glamor. No personal participation. Just waiting.

And so they waited while Longstrom sweated as he tried to guess where the atomic missiles would be. They waited as Carver fired their own messengers of death towards a segment of nothingness and hoped that they would arrive at the same time as the enemy ship. They waited, nerves tense, breath rasping in their throats as they lived in imagination a thousand deaths, from the ripped hull and escaping air to the remote, but always possible, triggering of their own pile by the streaming neutrons of a too-near explosion.

They waited—and the Head waited with them.

Longstrom tried to ignore it, tried to forget the insane rush of uncoupling the feed-in connections, the sealing and transportation of the monstrosity from one ship to the other. It rested behind him in the control room, Harding to one side, tense as he watched the screens, Carver on the other, his delicate fingers poised over his firing buttons. And of them all, only the Head didn't seem afraid.

It giggled, rolling its eyes as it tried to focus on the winking lights and flickering dials, dribbling and mouthing like the newborn or the insane, and, somehow, Longstrom had the impression that it would welcome death.

He sighed as the last crawling fleck vanished from the screens, leaning back and rubbing the ache from his fingers. Harding grunted, emotionlessly, and yet with his usual hint of disappointment, then thumbed a button and spoke into the intercom.

"Red alert ended. Normal stations." He stared at his computer man. "Why didn't we destroy the enemy?"

"The usual reason. Their computers are too good, ours not good enough." Longstrom shrugged. "If we could carry a lot more computer equipment maybe we'd be able to do better, but until then we've got to rely on luck or two ships to their one." He felt too tired to be formal.

"Our computers are the best we can carry," reminded Harding. "And sometimes we can wreck them; we've just come from a ship so wrecked. How do you account for that?"

"Luck."

"An unknown quantity. I want a better answer than that."

"I can't give you a better answer—sir."

"I see." Harding frowned at the ranked dials. "Don't misunderstand me, Longstrom. I'm not holding you personally responsible, but these conflicts seem to form a pattern. I want to know what determines that pattern. Just why aren't we equally matched?"

"Reaction time." As always after a battle, Longstrom felt a little light headed from too much concentration for too long. "The way things are I have to collect data, judge it, collate it, and act upon it. If I'm good, then we live, and sometimes we even manage to win. If I'm bad, then we die. The most anyone can hope for is that I'm average, and that no harm will be done. That applies to all computer men on all Terrestrial ships. It will continue to apply until such time as we get wholly automatic computers aligned with the ship controls, and by that time human crews will be unnecessary anyway."

"Don't the enemy have reaction time trouble, too?"

"No. Not as we do." Longstrom glanced at the Head, knowing that the captain already knew the answers and vaguely wondering why he was asking the questions. "They have solved the problem of weight in a very efficient manner. The human brain is probably the most compact computer ever devised; they know it, and they use it." He looked away as the Head rolled its eyes towards him. "They take a man, a prisoner or a captured colonist, and they operate on him. They retain the brain, merely keeping the skull, eyes and ears, throat and tongue for convenience, and they fit the severed neck with a glorified Lindenburg-Carrel pump. Then they sever the cells containing the seat of 'emotion', cauterize those determining personality or 'ego,' and wire the rest direct to the feed-in circuits." He shrugged. "You then get a highly efficient computer, able to correlate data and act on it at the literal speed of thought. More than that, you also get a self-repairing mechanism, able to respond to vocal orders and to volunteer information. You lose a man in getting it, of course, but that doesn't matter—if you're an alien."

"The swine!" Carver looked positively ill, and Longstrom remembered that he hadn't been long in space. "To do a thing like that!"

"Emotion is misplaced energy," said Harding, coldly. "The enemy do it, but we must never forget that the enemy are alien." He stared thoughtfully at the Head. "It would be a good idea to show a thing like that to every new recruit, to every man in space if it comes to that, to warn them what to expect if they allow themselves to fall alive into enemy hands. That man there was a coward; he should have died fighting."

"He should die now," snapped Carver. "To keep him alive is sheer cruelty. The regulations . . ."

"I know what the regulations state, Mr. Carver. I know, too, that we are in this war to win, not to act like gentlemen or gutless whiners!" Harding stared at Longstrom. "How much does our computer equipment weigh compared to the Head, including the pumps—the ratio, I mean?"

"Our computer is about six times heavier . . ."

"As I thought. And there is also the matter of speeded responses and higher efficiency." Harding nodded. "That difference in weight would mean quicker manoeuvring, less mass to hinder the thrust, greater storage for missiles. We wouldn't have to carry huge stocks of replacement parts, instruments and multiple circuits." He smiled. "How long would it take to connect it to our equipment?"

"What?" For a moment Longstrom couldn't believe that he had understood correctly. "You can't connect that thing here!"

"I asked you how long, Mr. Longstrom. I didn't ask for your unthinking stupidity. Let me put it this way. Could we connect it?"

"Yes."

"Even though it has been designed for use on an enemy ship?"

"It makes no difference. Radar impulses are the same; they have to be, or they wouldn't be radar. Electronic circuits are basically similar, and velocity and range are pure definitions, not arbitrary. There could be subtle differences, of course, mostly due to different methods of connecting." He stared at the captain. "If you want to know whether or not this thing could run our ship, the answer is yes."

"You can't do it!" Carver stepped forward, his hands subconsciously tightening into fists. "You can't keep a thing like that alive."

"No?" Harding stared at the psychologist; then, his eyes twin points of frozen ice, glanced at the officer's clenched hands. He nodded as Carver flushed and spread his fingers. "That's better. For a moment I thought that I should have had to order your arrest. You know the penalty for striking a superior, Carver?"

"I had no intention of striking you."

"You know the penalty for insubordination?"

"I had no intention of striking you—sir."

"I'm sure you hadn't, but I'm equally sure that if you continue opposing me you will live to regret it. This is war, Mr. Carver, and junior officers are expected to remember that."

"I'm sorry, sir, but what you suggest is too horrible. The men . . ."

"I have already given you my opinion on the men." Harding stared at the instrument-littered room. "At the moment I am only interested in efficiency—and in killing aliens. Once we clear this stuff away, dump it into space, we can go hunting. Once we have shown that we can destroy the enemy there will be no question of reprimand for what I have done. On the contrary, I will probably receive a medal." He glanced at Longstrom. "Begin the transfer."

"No!" Carver stepped forward and pushed the computer man back into his seat. "You can't do it!"

"Can't?" Harding didn't raise his voice, but something in his eyes told Longstrom that the psychologist was going too far.

"We're not certain that it will work," he said, hastily. "If the enemy discover us with our computers dismantled—"

"They mustn't, and it is up to you to see that they don't."

"There may be unforeseen snags. The Head may not work with our type of equipment."

"You have already told me that it will." Harding stared coldly at the computer man. "What is your real objection to making the transfer?"

"Common humanity," stormed Carver. "Only a beast or a madman would even think of it."

"Stop it, Carver!" Longstrom stepped in front of the raging

psychologist. "My objection is a simple one, sir. If we try the transfer and it doesn't work, what do we do then?"

"A good point. Make the transfer then, and retain our own equipment until the Head has proved its worth." He rose and stepped towards the door. "I want no failures, no excuses, and I want the job done as soon as possible. Do it!"

The Head giggled at his departing back.

It took a full day to make the transfer, and another three to test the responses and reflexes of the captured unit. Then, despite Longstrom's protests, Harding ordered all the original computer equipment cast into space.

"It's a mistake," said Longstrom to Carver one watch period. "It's too much like putting all your eggs in one basket. I'm worried."

He was, too, though not for the apparent reason he gave the psychologist. He was in the position of a computer man without any computers to operate, and he had the sick conviction that, logically, he would be the one ordered to take care of the Head.

"I'm worried, too," said Carver. "I know what's behind all this. Harding wants to prove something, and if he does, can you guess at what will happen next?"

"He'll get a medal—if they don't shoot him for breaking Regs."

"They won't do that; he was right when he said that it was results which count. No, I'm worried that he will prove himself right, that the Head is better than our own computers."

"It is."

"Are you certain of that?"

"Yes." Longstrom glanced uneasily towards the flesh and metal abortion. The thing was asleep—at least its eyes were closed, though it was doubtful whether it could sleep at all, and it was certain that it didn't have to rid its body of toxins. "The enemy have proved that too often to allow of doubt. In fact the war really started because they found they could use the human brain in that way and began raiding. To them we're nothing but robots." Automatically he kept his voice low, as if afraid of the Head opening its eyes. Carver looked sick.

"Then I was right. Longstrom! Can you even guess at what will happen, must happen when Harding returns to base after a successful sortie?"

"They'll give him a medal."

"They'll do more than that. If the Head works on this ship, then why shouldn't it work on others? The only reason we don't use them is on purely humanitarian grounds, but once they start to be used . . ." Carver looked really ill. "Human nature is a peculiar thing, Longstrom. We can deny a thing right up to the moment of it happening; then, to rid ourselves of shame and guilt, we can be proud that we use it. The Head is like that. Now we shudder at the thought of it. Tomorrow? The Head could be standard equipment on every spaceship, in every factory, used whenever and wherever a computer is necessary. Why? Because nothing succeeds like success, and once the first man has broken the taboo, the rest will follow."

"You're forgetting something," said Longstrom, dryly. "Where are we going to get the raw material? We can't capture all we'll need from the enemy."

"There's nothing about the unit we couldn't duplicate, have duplicated in various stages during medical and surgical research. The only hard part is the brain itself—and we have plenty of those. Criminals. Lawbreakers. Even volunteers. In a way the Head is immortal, wastage is slow, and with care, the brain should last for centuries. You'll find men and women willing to lose their bodies for the sake of an extended life-expectancy. But that's not what I'm afraid of."

"No?"

"Think of the results of the Head as a punishment. Think of an officer and a ranker. Obey—or else! Not a quick, clean, sudden death, but centuries of lingering half-life as a Head. Wouldn't you think twice before questioning an order?"

"I see what you mean." Longstrom stared at the blank features of the thing topping the humped machine. "I wonder what it thinks about—if it can think at all. Does it know what has happened to it? Can it feel? Can it understand what is going on around it? Tell me, Carver, how far can conditioning go?"

"Pretty far. Surgery has divorced its emotions and personality, and we can only guess at the techniques of the enemy. Perhaps they left it aware so that they could enjoy its mental suffering. Or perhaps, not knowing emotion themselves, they just didn't think to eradicate it." He sighed. "A pity that it's insane. I should have liked to question it."

"Couldn't we restore its sanity?"

"How? The shock and mental conflict must have been so great that the mind escaped from what it was into madness. If we could bring it back—and that is assuming that the brain is relatively undamaged—then, as soon as it realized what had happened to it, it would go insane again. A vicious circle."

The operative word was vicious.

The water was tepid, the sponge an oozing mass, the soap slimy with long immersion. As Longstrom had feared, Harding had put him in full charge of the computing equipment, and that meant checking the L-C pump, the nutrient solutions, the temperature, ion charge, connections and feed-in circuits.

It also meant washing the thing's face.

He didn't like doing it, but it had to be done. He hated running the sponge over the naked scalp, rubbing it in the ears, gently around the flickering eyes, wiping the drooling spittle from the writhing lips and cleaning up the mess from beneath the slobbering mouth. Drying the thing was even worse, and each time he did it, the nausea and revulsion grew worse. Revulsion that began to crystallize into a desperate hatred of the man who made him do it.

And there could be no escape.

They had replenished their stores from a transport, contacting at a rendezvous in space, and the ship was loaded to capacity with torpedoes and fuel, power and supplies. Now they were on the hunt, driving deep into enemy controlled space, waiting and watching for the tell-tales to flash and the Head to take over and blast his late captors to dust—they hoped.

Longstrom wasn't so sure. He lived in closer contact with the thing than anyone aboard; even Carver had found it too much for him, and Harding regarded it as nothing more than a machine. But it wasn't wholly a machine. It had the brain of a man, and as the days dragged past, Longstrom began to wonder.

Would the enemy have left it intact without reason? Would they have left it at all if it were so valuable? And how was it that he had managed to wreck the enemy vessel even though they had a supposedly more efficient computer?

Gingerly he finished the washing, dropped the sponge into the bowl, and reached for the towel. Accidentally, trying not to touch the bare skin, he jabbed his thumb into an eye and just managed to snatch his hand from gnashing gums.

"Take it easy, Jack. You want to blind me?"

"The words were blurred, liquid, oddly mechanical, but unmistakable. He jerked away from the Head, staring at it, the capsized bowl sending a film of water over the glistening floor plates.

"You spoke!"

"Sure I spoke. I . . ." The eyes rolled and muscle jerked beneath the flaccid skin as the Head lolled on its metal and plastic support. "What's the matter with me? I can't move!"

"Steady." Longstrom forced himself to step nearer and rest his hands on the jerking skull. "You've had an accident. We had to put you in stasis so that you can't move. You'll be all right soon."

"Is that it?" The Head ceased its jerking. "So you picked me up, eh? Earth ship, too. That's good. For a while back there I was afraid it was an enemy ship."

"You're among friends now." Desperately Longstrom hoped that Harding would enter the room. If the captain could hear the Head now, while it was speaking rationally, then he could never refuse to do the logical thing. "When was it?"

"When was what?"

"When did you . . ." He realized his mistake as soon as the words spilled from his mouth. The Head whimpered, twisted until it contorted with the pain of its tearing tissues, and the staring eyes grew wild with shocked understanding.

"You didn't pick me up! If you had you'd have known when it happened. Oh, God! So it was an enemy ship after all."

"Steady!" Longstrom gripped the Head in both hands to keep it from rupturing the flesh and plastic join by the violence of its motions. "We're friends I tell you. Friends."

"Then kill me. If you love God then kill me. If you hope for mercy or salvation, kill me. Make an end. For God's sake, make an end!"

"You know?"

"I know. I keep coming back, keep thinking that I've been asleep, that I'm normal, with a body instead of a machine. I keep trying to move and then I can't move, and then they come and do things to me, and . . ." The drooling voice dissolved into formless screams, the eyes glazed and as the screams faded into insane mumblings, Longstrom had the mental impression of a damned soul running shrieking down the endless, twisting corridors of hell.

"They'll never get *me*," he whispered, sickly. "They'll never take *me* alive."

He wasn't surprised to find that he was soaked with sweat.

They met the enemy two days later.

Harding grunted as he saw the flash from the alarm and his finger stabbed the intercom button as he slipped into his chair.

"Red alert. Enemy sighted."

Carver licked his lips as he took position, little beads of sweat shining on his face and neck, his hands quivering with tension. Longstrom felt like an unwanted dog.

He had nothing to do.

Always before he had been the busiest man on the ship in time of combat. He had concentrated on his instruments, trying to join himself to the relays and the scanners, sensing the flow of current and trying to anticipate, by just that fraction faster than the enemy, and so gain the advantage. Now the Head had taken over and there was nothing for anyone to do.

"Object approaching 34:56:298." The voice was mechanical, lifeless, disinterested.

"We'll get them this time," gloated Harding. "They will be relying on our time lag and poorer computation." He glared at Carver. "Keep your hands away from the firing controls. You're there to check, not operate."

"Yes, sir."

"Sit down, Longstrom. Watch the screens and try to anticipate. See how near you can come to emulating the expert."

"Yes, sir."

"Object now 34:53:277."

"Getting nearer." Carver dabbed at his streaming forehead. "Damn this waiting!"

Longstrom knew just how he felt. He wanted to get to work, feed data into the discarded computers, guess, check, feel the rising tension and mounting excitement as the time came to fire, now; and then the artful manoeuvring, the evasive action, the gamble against death. And if the waiting was bad here in the control room where they could see what was going on, then what must it be like for the crew?

He knew the answer. It was hell. They waited in semi-darkness, those men, standing by in the dull glow of the non-radiating emergency battle lights, ready to load the firing tubes, to activate or dampen the pile, to slam bulkheads or seal a rip in the hull. They wore no suits, for suits would hamper, and when they moved they would have to move fast. They waited while nerves jumped and quivered with the sheer strain of doing nothing. They would taste their own sweat and their own blood. They would tremble on the verge of insanity and breaking morale, and then, when it was all over, they would be exhausted and irritable, burnt out and temporarily useless, aged and worn by sickening tension.

"Object now 34:39:198."

"Straight-line flight path." Harding stared at the screen. "If we had fired at the moment of sight we'd have got them by now."

"Long range," said Longstrom. "Anyway, they would have registered our missile and dodged it."

"Object 79:24:389."

"Another of them!" Harding glared at the second fleck on the screen. "Damn! They'll have us in cross-fire."

"Not if we move." Longstrom glared at the drooling features of the Head. "What's the matter with that thing? Why doesn't it do something?"

"Object one now 34:27:119. Object two now 79:14:276."

"Coming fast." Carver rested his hands on the firing controls. "Shall I send out a rover?"

"Wait!" Harding scowled at the twin flecks of light. "They haven't fired at us yet; maybe they haven't spotted us. I trust the Head. Hold your fire."

Abruptly the ship moved. It jerked with a surge of acceleration, its venturis glowing with betraying fire, spinning and lunging directly towards the approaching vessels. Harding swore, slapped at the controls, then relaxed as flame blossomed in blue-white incandescence behind them.

"See? It spotted the sneak-torps and dodged. Could you have done that, Longstrom?"

"Maybe." The computer man frowned at the screen. "Why doesn't it fire?"

Again the ship jerked, slamming soft flesh against unyielding metal; then, as it steadied, the muffled roar of the firing tubes pulsed through the control room.

". . . eight . . . nine . . . ten. Ten! Can it handle that many?" Carter looked at the idiot-features, then hastily stared away.

From then on the Head took full command.

It was efficient—even Longstrom had to admit that. It stared at them with its vacant features, while, in the computer areas of its mind, data flowed and was correlated, velocities checked against range, spatial co-ordinates and missile fuse factors assessed and determined, ship acceleration aligned to evasive action; and always, as the screens became thick with crawling flecks of light, the idiot voice droned the co-ordinates of the enemy vessels.

It destroyed the first one within the first hour.

It almost destroyed itself five minutes later.

Longstrom saw it in time, a creeping speck carrying within itself the pure flame of atomic destruction, and even as he saw it, he had knocked Harding from the pilot's chair and had grabbed the manual controls. Death missed them by ten miles and, even as he relaxed, a second missile probed towards them. Tensely he waited for the Head to recognize the danger and take over.

It didn't.

Harding swore then, words that he had learned a long time ago, and which none of them had ever heard him use. He sat at the manuals, his hands white-knuckled as they gripped the slow, too slow, levers, and desperately he tried to blast the ship away and free of the probing torpedoes. With computers they could have done it. With the equipment he had discarded Longstrom could have assessed the co-ordinates and determined the escape route, but without them there wasn't a hope.

The first hit destroyed the main drive and left them helpless. The second ripped away the rear section of hull and spilled men and air into the vacuum. The third hit was due in sixty seconds' time unless a miracle happened.

"You swine! You dirty stinking cowardly swine!" Harding swung towards the idiot face of the Head and his hand slammed against the flaccid cheek. "You . . . You *thing!*"

"Stop it!" Longstrom grabbed at the captain's arm and was flung aside. "Stop it!"

"The death wish," babbled Carver. "That's why we were able to wreck its original ship. It wants to die."

"I tried to warn you," shouted Longstrom. "I tried to tell you, but you wouldn't listen. You would insist that it was only a machine. You wouldn't admit that it was human." He stopped then, staring in horror at what the captain was doing, sick at the sight, and yet, despite his sickness, knowing that it was what should have been done long before.

Harding was killing the Head.

He was killing it as he would kill a man, his big hands wrapped around the shortened neck, his thumbs digging into the windpipe, his lips drawn back in an animal snarl as he twisted and wrenched. Squeezing its throat wouldn't kill it, of course; it didn't need air to live, but, as Longstrom saw the glistening red droplets oozing from around the plastic collar, he had a sick premonition of what must happen.

The join could be nowhere near as strong as a normal neck.

He ran, then, tearing open the emergency doors and unsealing the tiny hatch, with Carver screaming behind him, and Harding snarling his foul-mouthed curses. He kicked the psychologist away, slammed the outer door, and almost fell into the officer's escape boat. It was small, just big enough for three and able to blast clear and drift towards the safe sections of space, where he could be picked up by a Terrestrial ship. He was babbling as he sealed the inner door, his hands trembling with fear at the thought of the approaching torpedo, or worse, the approaching aliens eager for new computer units.

The acceleration knocked him out so that he didn't see the spreading flower of blue-white flame where the ship had been. He remained unconscious as the tiny ship drove towards distant safety, and only awoke to the blare of the alarms and the dim silhouette on the damaged screen. A ship! But friend or enemy?

He stared at it as it swung closer, alternating between hope and despair, wanting to stay alive so that, in the event of it being a friend, he could warn all commanders of the danger of captured computer units with their booby trapped conditioning and overriding death-wish.

But if it were an enemy?

He shuddered at the memory of the Head, hearing again its

35

desperate pleading for death, its sick realization of what had been done to it and what it was. Enemy or friend? To die or to live?

The ship came nearer.

The man on the narrow white bed sighed, stirred, feeling his muscles relax as the stasis wore off, waiting a moment with closed eyes, his brain alive with recent memories. The technicians watched him through their one-way glass, ready to throw him into stasis again if necessary, yet hesitating until the last moment.

"I hope he makes it," said the elderly man to the younger one at his side. "Three suicide attempts should be enough for anyone."

"Three and no more." The young man shrugged. "A funny case, that. Picked up in space, raving and out of his mind; promptly tries to commit suicide and refuses to respond to mental-recall therapy. You'd think that he'd get rid of what was troubling him after he'd re-experienced it a few times, worked off the emotional charge and realized that it was all over." He leaned a little closer to the glass. "I sure hope that he makes it this time."

"You know what will happen to him if he doesn't, don't you?" The elderly man sounded disgusted. "As he's insane the higher ups think it won't matter, anyway, so they've the bright idea of converting all the insane into computer units, based on those used by the enemy. What a way to win a war!"

Intently they watched as Longstrom opened his eyes, stared in horror at the surgically white ceiling, then frantically looked around until he found the knife.

The young man sighed as he projected the stasis.

THE MING VASE

THE antique shop was one of those high-class places, which catered only to the very rich and the very possessive. A single vase of hand-worked glass stood in one window, an Egyptian Solar Boat in the other, between them the door presented a single expanse of unbroken glass to the street outside.

Don Gregson paused before it, deep-set eyes curious as he stared at the street. There was no trace of the accident. The wreckage had been removed and the rain had washed away the last traces of blood. Even the inevitable sightseers had gone about their business. Turning back to the door he pushed it open and stepped into the warmth inside.

Earlman was there, and Bronson, both standing beside a small, elderly man with delicate hands and intelligent eyes. Some assistants hovered discreetly in the background. The police had left and Don was glad of it. Earlman stepped forward.

"Hi, Don. You made good time."

"The general sees to that. Is that the owner?"

Max nodded, gesturing to the little man. Quickly he made the introductions.

"Mr. Levkin this is Don Gregson, C.I.A., Special Department."

They shook hands. Don was surprised at the wiry strength in the delicate fingers. Bronson, as usual, merely stood and watched; a coiled spring waiting his moment of release.

"I wish we could have met under happier circumstances," said Don to the owner. "Please tell me all about it."

"Again?"

"If you please. First-hand reports are always the most reliable."

Levkin shrugged and spread his hands in a gesture almost as old as time.

"I have been robbed," he said with simple understatement. "I have been robbed of the most precious item in my shop. It was small, a vase from the Ming Dynasty, but it was beautiful. You understand?"

"How small?"

Levkin gestured with his hands and Don nodded.

"About six inches high, small enough to slip into a pocket. You said that it was valuable. How valuable?"

"I said that it was precious," corrected the owner. "How do you value a work of art? The price is what the purchaser is prepared to pay. Let me say only that I have refused five hundred thousand dollars for it."

Earlman grunted, his thin, harassed face and dark, bruised-looking eyes veiled behind the smoke of his cigarette.

"Tell us about the man."

"He was medium built, medium height, well-dressed, brown hair and eyes . . . remarkable eyes. About a hundred and seventy pounds, softly spoken, very gentle and polite."

Over Levkin's head Earlman caught Don's eye and nodded.

"Nothing ostentatious," continued Levkin. "Nothing which gave a hint that he was not what he seemed. I had no reason to suspect that he was a thief."

"He isn't," said Don, then frowned at his own absurdity. "Go on."

"We spoke. He was interested in rare and beautiful things; it was natural that I should show him the vase. Then there was a crash in the street, an accident. Inevitably we turned and headed towards the door. It was a bad accident, our attention was distracted, but only for a moment. It was enough. By the time I remembered the man had gone and he had taken the vase with him."

"Are you positive as to that?" Don labored the point. "Could it be hidden here somewhere? Anywhere?"

"The police asked that. No, it is not hidden. I have made a thorough search. It has been stolen." For the first time the man displayed emotion. "Please, you will get it back? You will do your best?"

Don nodded, jerking his head at Earlman as he stepped to one side. Bronson, as always, joined them.

"How about the identification?" Don spoke in a trained whisper inaudible two feet from his lips. "Is it positive?"

"They swear to the photograph. It's our man all right."

"I've got to be certain. How about the accident? Could that have been faked?"

"Not a chance. A cab hit a pedestrian and swerved into a truck. The jaywalker's dead, the cabbie will lose a leg and the truck driver's in a bad way. That was no rigged diversion."

"Coincidence?" Don shook his head. "No, the timing was too limited for that. Levkin's no fool and even the smartest crook requires a certain reaction time before he can spot an opportunity, weigh his chances and then swing into action. Levkin would never have given an ordinary crook that much time. It looks as if you're right, Max."

"I am right. It was Klieger." Earlman looked puzzled. "But why, Don? Why?"

Gregson didn't answer. His face was strained, thoughtful.

"Why?" repeated Earlman. "Why should he want to steal a thing he can't sell, can't eat, can't do anything with but sit and look at? Why?"

General Penn asked the same question, but unlike Earlman he demanded an answer. Slumped in his chair behind the wide desk he looked even older and more harassed than he had when this whole thing had started. Don could understand that. The general, literally, had his neck on the block.

"Well?" The voice reflected the strain. Harsh, heavy with irritating undertones, it carried too much of a barrack square, too little of understanding or patience. "You've found what you said to look for. Now, what's the answer?"

"We've found something I said might possibly happen," corrected Don. "It has. What answer are you looking for?"

"Are you crazy?" Penn surged out of his chair. "You know what the top-priority is! Find Klieger! What other answer would I be interested in?"

"You might," said Don quietly, "be interested in finding out just why he left in the first place."

Penn said a word. He repeated it. Don tensed then forced himself to relax. Slowly he lit a cigarette.

"Three weeks ago," he said, "Albert Klieger decided to leave Cartwright House and did so. Since then you've had all field units concentrate on the one object of finding him. Why?"

"Because he is the greatest potential danger to this country walking on two legs!" Penn spat the words as if they were bullets. "If he gets to the other side and spills what he knows, we'll lose our greatest advantage in the cold war and the hot war when it comes. Gregson, you know all this!"

"I've been told it," said Don. He didn't look at the congested face of the general. "And if we find him and he doesn't want to return, what then?"

"We'll worry about that when we've found him," said Penn grimly. Don nodded.

"Is that why Bronson is always with my team? Why other men just like him accompany all field units?" He didn't press for an answer. "Have you ever wondered why the English stopped using the Press Gang system? They knew it wasn't humane from the beginning but, for a while, it worked—for a while and up to a point. Maybe we could learn something from that if we tried."

"You talk like a fool." Penn slumped back into his chair. "No one press-ganged Klieger. I found him in a third-rate carnival and gave him the chance to help his country. He took that chance. It's fair to say that we've given him far more than he's given us. After all, Klieger isn't the only one."

"That," said Don, "is the whole point." He stared directly at the general. "How long is it going to be before others in the Project . . . sorry, Cartwright House, decide that they've had enough?"

"There'll be no more walking out." Penn was very positive. "I've tripled the security guards and installed gimmicks which makes that impossible."

It was, of course, a matter of locking the stable door after the horse had been stolen, but Don didn't point that out. Penn, with his reputation and career in the balance, could only be pushed so far at a time. And, to Penn, his career was all-important. Not even Cartwright House came before that.

Which, thought Don bitterly, was the inevitable result of a military machine based on political manoeuvrings. What a man was, what he could do, that was unimportant against who he knew, what he could do for others. Don himself had no illusions. He was useful but he could be branded, damned, kicked out and made the scapegoat if Penn felt he needed a sacrifice. And time was running out.

"We've got to find him." Penn drummed on the desk. "Gregson, why can't you find him?"

"You know why. I've trailed him and found where he's been a dozen times. But always too late. To catch him I've got to be where he is when he is, or before he gets there. And that's impossible."

"This theft." Penn's mind veered to the latest scrap of information. "Money I can understand, but why a Ming vase? The guy must be crazy."

"He isn't normal, but he isn't crazy." Don crushed out his cigarette. "And I've an idea that he has a very good reason for wanting that vase. The chances are that he will be collecting other, similar things, how many depends on circumstances."

"But why?"

"They're beautiful. To those that appreciate them such objects are beyond price. Klieger must have an intensely artistic streak. He has a reason for wanting to own them and it worries me."

Penn snorted.

"I need more information." Don was decisive. "Without it I'm fighting a shadow. I've got to go where I can get it."

"But—"

"I've got to. There's no other way. None in the world."

No one called it a prison. No one even called it a Project because everyone knew that a 'Project' was both military and important. So it was called Cartwright House and it was a little harder to get into than Fort Knox and far more difficult to leave than Alcatraz.

Don waited patiently as his identification was checked, double-checked, cleared to a higher level and then checked again. It took time but finally he faced Leon Malchin, tall, thin, burning with frustrated zeal and with the courtesy rank of colonel, which meant nothing until he tried to act like a civilian when he felt the full impact of military discipline.

"General Penn has contacted me," he said. "I am to offer you every assistance." He stared at Don through old-fashioned spectacles. "How can I help you?"

"Question," said Don. "How do normal men catch a clairvoyant?"

"You mean Klieger, of course?"

"Of course."

"They can't. They don't." Malchin settled back in his chair, a glint of amusement in his eyes. "Next question?"

"There is no next question—not yet." Don took the other chair and proffered his cigarettes. Malchin shook his head and sucked at a brier.

"I am a hunter," said Don abruptly. "I hunt men. I'm good at it because I have a knack, talent, skill—you name it—for being able to outguess my quarry. You might say that I have a series of lucky hunches. Somehow, I don't know how, I *know* what they will do next—where they will be and when. I have never yet failed to get my man."

"But you haven't got Klieger." Malchin nodded as if he had expected this visit for some time. "And you want to know why."

"I know why. He is a clairvoyant. What I want to know is how. How does he do it? How does he operate? How effective is he?"

"Very effective." Malchin took his pipe from his mouth and stared into the bowl. "He is, or was, our star resident. He could see further than anyone I have ever investigated—and I have invested psi phenomena all my adult life."

"Go on."

"I don't think you fully realize just what you are up against in Klieger. He isn't a superman, of course; nothing like that, but he has this one talent. You are, in a sense, a blind man trying to trap a man who can see. Trap him in broad daylight on an open plain. You are also wearing a bell around your neck to attract his attention. Personally I do not think you have a ghost of a chance."

"How," Don insisted, "does this talent work?"

"I don't know." Malchin anticipated the next question. "You don't mean that, of course, what you mean is how does he use it. If I knew how it worked I would be a very happy man." He frowned, searching for words. "This is going to be difficult to describe. How could you explain sight to a man born blind, or sound to a man born deaf? And you, at least, could tell how these senses 'worked'. However—"

Don lit another cigarette, listening to Malchin's explanations, building pictures in his mind. A piece of rough fabric, each thread of which was a person's life stretching into the future. Some threads were short, others longer, all meshed and interwoven so that it was almost impossible to follow any single thread. But, with training and skill it could be done. Then events came clear and action could be planned.

A bank where a teller suffered an attack of acute appendicitis just as he was counting out a sheaf of notes—and a man who calmly picked them up as if he had just cashed a check.

A store where the takings were left unattended for just that essential few minutes of time.

A penthouse apartment and an officer who sneezed just as the quarry walked past.

An antique shop and an accident to create the necessary diversion.

So simple when you could see exactly what would happen and exactly how to take advantage of it.

How to catch Klieger?

Don jerked upright as the cigarette burned his fingers and became aware of Malchin's stare.

"I was thinking of your analogy," he said. "You know, the blind man trying to trap the one who could see. I know how it can be done."

"Yes?"

"The blind man gets eyes."

They were comfortable. They had soft beds and good food, canned music, television, a library of books and private movies. They had games and a swimming pool and even a bowling alley. They wore good clothes and were fit and looked it, but they were intelligent and they knew.

A prison is somewhere you can't leave when you want to and they were in prison.

For their own protection, naturally. The guards, the gimmicks, the restrictions were solely designed to keep unwanted people out. The secrecy was from fear of spies and patriotism was the excuse for all. But the things designed to keep people out worked just as well to keep others in.

And, sometimes, patriotism as an excuse wears a little thin.

"It's good to see a new face." Sam Edwards, fifty, built like a boy with the face of a boxer, grinned as he gripped Don's hand. "You joining the club?"

"He's just visiting." A wizened oldster sucked at his teeth as he peered at Don from the depths of an easy chair. "Say,

Gregson, if you fancy a little poker later on I guess we could accommodate you."

He laughed with a wheezy effort then frowned and slammed a hand on his knee.

"Goldarn it! I miss my poker!"

"Telepaths," whispered Malchin. "Most of them are in permanent rapport with others who are you-know-where. I won't bother to introduce you around."

Don nodded, staring uneasily at the assembled 'residents'. Some were old, a few young, most were middle-aged. They watched him with eyes glinting with secret amusement.

"Oddly enough most of them seem to stick together according to their various talents," mused Malchin. "You've seen the telepaths, in this room are those with telekinetic abilities. Nothing startling in the way of progress as yet, but they are getting on. In here are the clairvoyants."

There were fifteen of them. Don was surprised at the number, Then he wondered why he was surprised. In the great cross-section of humanity that was the United States every deviation from the norm must have been repeated many times. Shrewdly he guessed that he saw only a part of the whole; that Cartwright House was duplicated many times under many names.

"We have found," whispered Malchin, "that communal use of their talent greatly aids development of that talent. Klieger was little more than a carnival fortune-teller when he joined us; in ten years he became amazingly proficient."

"Ten years?"

"That's what I said. Many of our residents have been here longer than that."

If there was irony in Malchin's voice, Don didn't catch it. But one of the men in the room did. He came forward, hand outstretched, a taut smile on his face.

"Tab Welker," he said. "Maybe you can settle an argument. In England, from what I hear, a man sentenced to life imprisonment usually gets out in about nine years. Right?"

"It depends on his conduct." Don felt his skin tighten as he saw what the man was driving at. "A life term in England is about fifteen years. A third remission would make it about what you say."

"And that's usually given for nothing short of murder." Tab

nodded. "You know, I've been here eight years. One more year to go—maybe!"

"You're not a prisoner," said Don. The man laughed.

"Please." He lifted his hand. "No arguments, no speeches!" He lost his smile. "What do you want?"

"Help," said Don simply.

He moved about the room, halting by a small table bearing chessmen set on a board. They were of wood lovingly carved with the unfinished look of true hand-production. He lifted a knight and studied it, then met Welker's eyes.

"Klieger's?"

"How did you guess?" Tab's eyes softened as he stared at the chessmen. "Albert loved beautiful things. The thing he missed most while in here was being able to visit the museums. He always said that man's true achievements were to be found in the things he had made to ornament his life."

"Things like vases?"

"Paintings, statuary, cameos, he liked them all providing they were well made."

"A man with artistic appreciation." Don nodded. "I understand. When did you all decide to help him escape?"

"I . . . What did you say?"

"You heard what I said." Don's eyes locked with those of the other man then, slowly, Welker smiled.

"You're no fool," he said. Don returned the smile.

"Now I've another question." He paused, conscious of the men and their watching eyes. "Just what does Klieger hope to gain?"

"No!' General Penn slammed his hand down on the arm of the back seat. "No! No!"

Don sighed, staring through the windows at the rain. It dripped from the trees above, pinging on the roof of the car, dewing the glass with a glitter of transient pearls. Further down the road the rear of another car loomed vague through the rain. Behind them would be another. Their own driver was somewhere up ahead probably cursing the odd exigencies of the Service.

"Listen," said the general, "we've got word that they know about Klieger. Don't ask me how they even guessed he was important to us, but they do. Now it's a race between us. We daren't lose."

"We won't lose," said Don. "But we'll have to do it my way. It's the only way there is."

"No."

"General!" Don released his pent-up temper and frustration in a furious blast of sound. "What other way is there?"

It stopped Penn as he knew it would, but only for a moment.

"I can't risk it," he snapped. "Klieger's only one man, dangerous but still only one. We can handle one man, but can we handle a dozen or more? It's treasonable even to suggest it."

Don fumed as he recognized the emotion-loaded semantic symbol. Penn with his mania for security had probably aroused unwelcome attention in the first place. Like now when he had insisted that they meet in a car on a road in the rain for fear of some undetected electronic ear waiting to catch their conversation. For long moments the silence dragged, then Don drew a deep breath.

"Treasonable or not it's something you have to consider. For one thing the escape was organized. The lights failed—a telepathically controlled rat gnawed a vital cable. A guard was taken sick for no apparent reason and, for a moment, there was a blank spot in the defenses. There were other things, all small, not one coincidental. The whole lot could have walked right out."

"But they didn't!" Penn pounded the arm of the rear seat. "Only Klieger. That proves something."

"That he wanted to run to the Reds?" Don shrugged. "Then what's keeping him? He's had plenty of time to make contact if that's what he wanted."

"What's your point?" Penn was losing his patience. "Are you trying to tell me that those . . . freaks back there are holding a gun to my head? They'll help, you say, but on their terms. Terms!" His hand closed into a fist. "Don't they understand that the country is as good as at war?"

"They want the thing we keep saying we are fighting to protect," said Don. "They want a little freedom. Is that such an outrageous demand?"

He leaned back, closing his eyes, seeing again the faces of the men back in Cartwright House. Some of them, so Malchin had said, had been there twelve years. A long time. Too long to be willing guinea pigs so that their talents could be trained and developed and exploited. But to the general they weren't men. They were 'freaks'; just another weapon to be used, to be protected and hidden, to be destroyed if there was a chance they might fall into enemy hands.

"What?" He opened his eyes, conscious that the general was talking to him. Penn glowered and repeated what he had said. "Can you catch him, even if they won't help you?"

"I don't know." Don pursed his lips, shadowed eyes introspective beneath prominent brows. "I feel that we've gone about this thing in the wrong way. We've thought of it as just another manhunt and we've failed because we're trying to catch no ordinary man. There must be a purpose behind what Klieger did. Find the reason for his leaving and we'll find the purpose."

"Isn't that what you went to find out?" Penn made no effort to hide his sarcasm.

"Yes. I didn't fail."

"Then—?"

"He stole a rare vase of the Ming Dynasty," said Don. "Find out why and you have the answer."

Max Earlman lay supine on the bed and stared at the ceiling. The hotel room was warm, littered with the personal effects of the three men. Against one wall a large-scale map of the city hung slightly out of true, the grid pattern of streets marked with a host of colored pins. Beyond the windows the early evening had softened the harsh outlines of the concrete jungle, turning even the garish illuminations into things of glowing beauty.

Bronson stirred where he sat at a table, the thin reek of gun oil harsh to Earlman's nostrils. He lit a cigarette to kill the odor and stared distastefully at the other man.

"Do you have to do that?" Smoke plumed from the cigarette as Max gestured towards the pistol Bronson was cleaning. Bronson continued with his business.

"What gives with you, Bronson?" Earlman swung to his feet, nerves taut with irritation. "You walk and eat and sleep and I guess you can make noises, too, if you put your mind to it, but are you really a man?"

Metal clicked with deadly precision as Bronson reassembled the gun. He tucked it into its holster, drew it with a fantastic turn of speed, and returned it again.

Earlman jerked forward, anger burning in the deep, bruised-looking eyes. He turned as Don entered the room. He looked tired.

"No luck?" Max knew the answer. Don shook hiss head.

"We're still on our own." Crossing the room he stood before the map, studying the clusters of colored pins. "Have you got them all?"

"Every single one." Earlman blew smoke at the map. "If anyone ever tells me this city has no culture, I'll tear them apart. The place is lousy with art galleries, museums, exhibitions, antique shops, displays, missions and what have you. I've marked them all." He looked sideways at Gregson's bleak face. "There are a lot, Don. Too many."

"We can whittle them down." Don sighed, feeling the tension of the past few weeks building up inside, the tautness of the past few days stretching his nerves. He forced himself to relax, taking deep breaths, forgetting the urgency and Penn's hysterical demands.

"Cut out foreign films, contemporary art, modernist paintings, exhibitions of abstract design. Eliminate the stamp collections, trade missions, engineering displays. Concentrate on the old, the rare, the beautiful."

"How close should I go?"

"Close. Keep the unusual, the short-term, the items loaned from private collections."

Earlman nodded and busied himself with the colored pms and a sheaf of catalogues. Don turned and stared out of the window.

Below him the city sprawled, scar-like streets slashing between soaring anthills of concrete, the whole glittering with light. Somewhere in the city another man probably stood staring from a window—a mild man with a love of artistic things. A man who, until recently, had lived a law-abiding existence and who, suddenly, had broken the conditioning of a lifetime to rob and steal and run.

Why?

Frustration, yes, all the 'residents' of Cartwright House were frustrated, but they had remained when they could have fled. Only Klieger had run and had kept running. Now he was somewhere in the city, his talent warning him of approaching danger, showing him how to dodge and move and avoid so as to remain free.

Free in order to do what?

Don sighed, wondering for the thousandth time just how it must feel to be a clairvoyant. How to catch a man who was.

The others could have helped but Penn had blocked that. With a dozen other clairvoyants Don could have covered the field and trapped Klieger by sheer weight of numbers. No one man, no matter how gifted, could have beaten such odds.

Now he was on his own.

It had begun to rain and the window glittered with reflected light so that his eyes constantly changed focus from the window to the city beyond them back to the window. Then he stopped trying to focus and just stood there, eyes wide, thoughts traveling unfamiliar paths.

How?

How did he know when and where to catch a wanted man? What was it that made him just that little different from other men? All his life Don had had that edge. He could guess—if it was guessing—and those guesses had been right. So, was it guessing? Or did he know?

His record had backed his application to the C.I.A. That same record of unbroken success had paved his way into the Special Detachment. He was a man-hunter who always found his man. And he didn't know how he did it.

As Malchin didn't know how the 'residents' at Cartwright House used their talents.

Even whittled down the list was too long. Earlman gestured towards the map, smoke drifting from the cigarette dangling from his lips, pointing to the varicolored pins.

"I can't get it closer than this, Don. From here on it's pure guesswork."

"Not quite." Don scanned the list. "I learned something about Klieger back at Cartwright House. He is an artistic type. My guess is that he's been visiting the museums and art galleries all along."

"Then we've got him!" Earlman was jubilant. "All we need

do is cover these places and he'll walk right into our hands."

Don raised his eyebrows and Max suddenly sobered.

"No. Every cop in the city has his photograph and description. All routes from the metropolis are covered. All field units are on the hunt. If it was as easy as that, we'd have had him by now." He gestured towards the map. "Then why all this?"

"Concentration of effort." Don sat on the edge of a bed. "The cops can't spot him until they see him, and he makes certain they don't. Mostly he's just one man in a crowd and that's the best disguise there is. Never forget, Max, he can 'see' our traps and so avoid them."

"Then it's hopeless." Savagely Earlman stamped on his cigarette. "No matter what we do, where we go, he won't be there. Have I wasted my time, Don?"

"No."

"But—"

"It's between him and me now," said Don. "Up until now I've tackled this like a slightly abnormal operation. I've depended on outside help and even tried to get special assistance but that wasn't the way to do it. Now I've got to use his weakness against him." He looked down at the list in his hand.

"All right, both of you get out, I want to be alone."

Bronson didn't move.

"You heard the man!" Earlman jerked open the door. 'Out!"

Slowly Bronson rose to his feet. His eyes shone as he stared at Don.

"I'm not going anywhere," said Gregson tiredly. "You can wait outside if you want."

Alone he untied his shoes, loosened his tie and slipped off his jacket. Killing the lights he lay back on the bed, eyes towards the window with its glitter of reflected light. Deliberately he relaxed.

For him it was a normal procedure, this quiet relaxation while his mind digested the thousand odd items of assembled fact to come up with a guess that wasn't a guess because it was always right. But now he had to do more than that. Now he had to pit himself against a man who could 'see' the future and he had to outguess that other man.

His breathing grew even, regular and deeper as he entered the first stage of self-hypnosis. Outside sounds wouldn't bother him now, there would be no distractions, he could concentrate fully on the problem he had to solve.

Find Klieger.

Find where he would be and when.

Find him as he had found a thousand others with no doubt, no uncertainty, just the conviction that at a certain place at a certain time he would spot his quarry.

Forget the sense that he was beaten before he could start. Forget that he was up against an abnormal talent. Forget the picture of the piece of fabric and the nodes of events. Forget everything but one man and where and when he would be.

"The Lustrum Galleries." Earlman nodded then grunted as the cab braked to avoid a jaywalker. "They are haying a private showing this evening, invitation only. The exhibition doesn't open until tomorrow," He looked at Don, face even more haggard in the dim light. "Are you certain he will be there?"

"Yes."

"But—' Earlman shrugged and broke off, killing the obvious question. "A display of Chinese art," he read from a crumpled catalogue. "Ceramics from the Ming, Han and Manchu Dynasties. It figures. The Ming vase?"

Don nodded, then closed his eyes, resting his head on the back of the seat. He felt drained, worn out yet filled with a glowing exultation. He knew! How or why he couldn't guess but he knew! Klieger would be at the galleries. He would stake his life on it.

Their badges got them in, past a very punctilious uniformed attendant, past a fussing curator, into a long hall shining with glass cases on which in reverent array stood the exhibits.

"Tomorrow," said the curator, "these will be within the cases but tonight, because of the selected visitors, we feel it safe to have them as they are."

"Why?" Earlman was blunt. "What's the point?"

"You are not a connoisseur," said the curator. "That is obvious. If you were, you would know that there is more to ceramics than just the visual aspect. There is a feel, a tactile sense that is as much a part of the pottery as the colors. Our visitors, most of them collectors, appreciate that. And, too, the true beauty of these pieces cannot be wholly appreciated when they are seen from only one angle as they will be when sealed in the cases."

He looked suddenly anxious.

"You haven't mentioned your business. I trust that nothing will—"

"There will be no trouble." Don glanced around the gallery, forehead creased in a frown. "Just operate as if we weren't here." He smiled at the anxious expression. "One thing I can promise you, your exhibits are in no danger."

Satisfied, the curator bustled off about his business. Don glanced to either side then led the way towards the far end of the gallery.

"We'll wait here. The cases will screen us and we can watch the whole gallery. When Klieger comes you will go to the stairs, Max, and cut off his escape."

Earlman grunted then paused, a cigarette halfway to his lips.

"How come, Don? How come Klieger is going to walk right into this set-up when we know that he must know we're waiting for him?"

"He wants to see the exhibits."

"But—?"

"This is his only chance to actually touch and examine them. To him that's important, don't ask me why." Don's voice was sharp. "He'll be here, I know it."

It sounded logical. It sounded as if it could be true but Don knew that wasn't the reason Klieger would come. He would want to see the ceramics, that was true, but would he want to handle them so much that nothing else mattered? And, if so, why? Why tonight?

Waiting between the cases, eyes on the long vista of the gallery with its shining glass and neat exhibits Don fought the question that had puzzled him all along. In a way it was a seeming paradox, but he knew that it only seemed that way to him. As the visitors began to arrive and the air vibrated to their murmured comments as they studied the exhibits the question nagged at his peace of mind.

Klieger must know he would be walking into a trap.

Yet he would come, Don was certain of it.

So, if Don wasn't mistaken and he was certain he was not, Klieger must consider the visit to be worth certain capture.

Capture or—

Bronson moved, an automatic gesture, one hand sliding beneath his coat, and Don snarled at him with savage impatience.

"There'll be none of that! Do you understand? You won't be needed!"

Inwardly he cursed Penn's cold, inhuman logic. In war it is good sense to destroy material you can't use to prevent it falling into enemy hands, but this wasn't war and Penn wasn't dealing with machines or supplies.

Klieger must know the risk he ran of being shot to death.

Don started as Earlman gripped his arm. Max jerked his head, eyes bright in the haggard face as he stared down the gallery.

"There, Don," he breathed. "Down by that big case. See him?"

Klieger!

He was—ordinary. Engrossed with the hunt Don had mentally fitted the quarry with supernatural peculiarities but now, watching him as he stood, entranced by pottery fired before the dawn of Western civilization, he seemed nothing but what he was. An ordinary man with more than an ordinary interest in things considered beautiful by a minority.

And yet he had knowledge which made him the most dangerous man to the security of the West.

"Got him!" Earlman's whisper was triumphant. "You did it again, Don! You called it right on the nose!"

"Get into position." Gregson didn't take his eyes from the slight figure he had hunted so long. "Stand by in case he makes a break for it. You know what to do."

"I know." Earlman hesitated. "Bronson?"

"I'll take care of him."

Don waited as Earlman slipped away, gliding past the cases to lean casually at the top of the far stairs. He sensed the other's relief and understood it. They had worked together for eight years and his failure would, in part, have been shared by Earlman.

But he had not failed.

Savoring the sweet taste of success he walked forward half-conscious of Bronson at his heels. Klieger did not turn. He stood, caressing a shallow, wide-mouthed bowl in his hands, eyes intent on the still-bright colors.

"Klieger!"

Slowly he set down the vase.

"Don't run. Don't fight. Don't do anything stupid." Don s voice was a grim whisper. "You can't get away."

"I know."

"Just in case you're wondering I'm from the C.I.A."

"I know."

"This is the end of the line, Klieger."

"I know."

The calm, emotionless tones irritated Gregson. The man should have complained, argued, anything but the flat baldness of the repeated statement. Savagely he gripped a shoulder and spun Klieger round to face him.

"Do you know everything?"

Klieger didn't answer. Heavy lids dropped over the eyes and Don remembered how Levkin had described them. 'Remarkable' the owner had said, but the word was misleading. They were haunted. There was no other description, no other word. Haunted.

"What are you going to do with me?" Klieger opened his eyes and stared up into the grim face of the hunter. Don shrugged.

"Why ask? You're the man who is supposed to know everything."

"I am a clairvoyant," said Klieger calmly. "I can see into the future, but so can you. Do you know everything?"

"I—" Don swallowed. *"What did you say?"*

"How else would you have known that I would he here? And I mean know, not guess. You were certain that you would find me, as certain as I am that—"

"Go on."

"You have the talent. By knowing that I would be here at this time you 'saw' into the future. Not far, perhaps, not too clearly, but you 'saw.' What other proof do you need?"

"But I simply had a conviction that— Is that how clairvoyancy works?"

"For you, obviously yes. For others perhaps not exactly the same. But when you are convinced beyond any shadow of doubt that at a certain time a thing will happen, or that a thing will happen even if the exact time is not too precise, then you have the gift which General Penn values most highly." Klieger gave a bitter smile. "Much good may it do you."

Don shook his head, conscious of receiving knowledge too fast and too soon. At his elbow Bronson shifted his weight a little, poising on the balls of his feet. Around them was a clear space as the other visitors moved down the line of cases. The three of them stood in an island of isolation.

"I am not coming back with you," announced Klieger. "I have had enough of Cartwright House."

"You have no choice."

Klieger smiled. "You forget," he pointed out gently, "it isn't a question of choice. It is a simple question of knowledge. I shall never see the general again."

Bronson made an incoherent sound deep in his throat.

He was fast, incredibly fast, but Don was even faster. Warned by some unknown sense he spun as the gun flashed into view, snatching at the wrist as it swung level, twisting and forcing the black muzzle from its target with viciously applied leverage. Muscles knotted then the bone snapped with the dry sound of a breaking stick. Bronson opened his mouth as the gun fell from nerveless fingers then Don slashed the hard edge of his palm across the nerves in the neck and the mute collapsed.

Quickly Don scooped up the gun and heaved Bronson to his feet, supporting the unconscious man as he fought mounting tides of hate. Hate for Bronson who lived only to take revenge on the world for his disability. Hatred for Penn who could find a use for the psychopathic mute and others like him. Licensed murderers in the sacred name of expediency; safe because they could never talk.

Earlman had seen what the others in the gallery had not. Running forward he met the blaze of Gregson's eyes.

"Get rid of this thing, fast!"

"So he had to try it." Earlman relieved Don of the dead weight. "Penn is going to love you for this."

Don sucked air, fighting to rid himself of hate. "Take him back to the hotel. I'll worry about Penn when I have to."

"And Klieger?"

"I'll take care of him."

Don had almost forgotten Klieger in the savage fury of the

past few minutes. He found him standing by one of the exhibits, staring at a relic of the past as if he were trying to drink its beauty and impress its image on his brain. Gently he picked up the piece, a man entranced by the artistic perfection of ancient craftsmen and, looking at him, Don felt his stomach tighten with a sudden, sick understanding.

Penn didn't trust women. The receptionist was a man as were all his personnel. He took one look at Don then lunged for a buzzer.

"Why bother?" Don headed past him towards the inner office. "Just tell the general that I'm on my way in."

"But—?"

"How did I get this far without being stopped?" Don shrugged. "You figure it out."

Penn wasn't alone. Earlman, more haggard than ever, sat smoking unhappily and Don guessed that he had been receiving the full weight of the general's anger. He grinned as the door slammed shut behind him.

"Hi, Max, you look as if you've been having a bad time."

"Don!" Earlman lunged to his feet. "Where have you been? It's more than a week now. Where's Klieger?"

"Klieger." Don smiled. "At this moment he is somewhere in Soviet territory being interrogated by every lie-detection device known to man."

For a moment there was a deathly silence then Penn leaned forward.

"All right, Gregson, you've had your joke. Now produce Klieger or take the consequences."

"It's no joke." Don stared grimly into the general's eyes. "That's what I've been doing this past week. Talking to Klieger, fixing his passage, dodging your hunters."

"Traitor!"

Don didn't answer.

"You dirty, stinking traitor!" Suddenly Penn became icy calm and his calmness was more terrible than his rage. "This is a Democracy, Gregson, but we know how to protect ourselves. You should have gone with Klieger to the safety of your friends."

"Friends! You think I did it for them?" Don looked down at

his hands, they were shaking. Deliberately he sat down, lit a cigarette, waited for his anger to pass.

"You demand loyalty," he said. "Blind, unswerving, unthinking loyalty. You think that those who are not with you must be for the enemy but you are wrong. There is a greater loyalty than to an individual, a nation or a group of nations. There is a loyalty to the human race. One day, please God, both sides may realize that."

"Don!"

Earlman leaned forward. Gregson gestured him back to his chair,

"Just listen, Max, you too, General. Listen and try to understand."

He paused, dragging at the cigarette, his broad-planed face revealing some of his fatigue.

"The answer," he said, "lay in the Ming vase."

"The one Klieger stole from the antique shop?" Earlman nodded. "What about it, Don? Why was it so important?"

He was, Don knew, acting as a barrier between him and the wrath of the general and he was suddenly glad that he was there. Penn, alone, might never have found the patience to listen.

"Klieger can see into the future," continued Don. "Never forget that. He was the star 'resident' at Cartwright House and stayed there for ten years. Then, for no apparent reason, he decided to take off. He did. He stole money—he had to live, and he stole a vase, to him a thing of wondrous beauty. The answer lies in why he did it."

"A thief!" Penn snorted. "He was a thief. That's the answer."

"No," said Don quietly. "The reason is that time was running out—and he knew it!"

They stared at him. They didn't understand, not even Earlman, certainly not Penn and yet, to Don, it was all clear. So ghastly clear.

"What a man does is determined by his character," said Don. "Given a certain stimulus he will react in a certain way—and this is predictable. Think of Klieger and what he was. Meek, mild, inoffensive, willing to do as he was told without question. He did it for ten years while his talent was being

57

trained so that he could 'see' further and clearer into the future. Then one day he 'sees' something that drives him desperate.

"Desperate enough to break the habits of a lifetime. He persuaded the others to help him escape. They thought that he was doing it to help them, perhaps they wanted to prove something, that isn't important now. Klieger is. He walked out. He stole. He tried to fill every waking hour with what he considered to be the ultimate of beauty. A different man would have gambled, drank, chased women. Klieger loves old and precious things. He stole a Ming vase."

"Why?" Despite himself Penn was interested.

"Because he saw the ultimate war!"

Don leaned forward, his cigarette forgotten, his eyes burning with the necessity of making them see what he knew was the truth.

"He saw the end of everything. He saw his own death and he wanted, poor devil, to live a little before he died."

It made sense. Even to Penn it made sense. He had seen the secret records, the breakdown of a man's character, the psychological dissection and extrapolations. Security was very thorough.

"I—" Penn swallowed. "I can't believe it."

"It's the truth." Don remembered his cigarette. "He told me—we had plenty of time for talking. How else do you think we managed to catch him? He could have remained free forever had he tried. But he was tired, afraid, terrified. He wanted to see the exhibition and he expected to die by Bronson's bullet."

"Now wait a minute!" Earlman frowned, a crease folding his forehead. "No man in his right mind would willingly go to his death. It doesn't make sense."

"No?" Don was grim. "Think about it."

"A bullet is quick and clean," mused Earlman. "But he didn't die! Bronson was stopped!"

"That is why I turned 'traitor'." Don crushed out his cigarette. "By stopping Bronson I proved that the future is a variable, that even an expert clairvoyant like Klieger can only see the probable future, not the inevitable one. It gave us hope. Both of us."

He rose, looking down at Penn slumped behind his desk, trying not to let the hate he saw in the general's eyes disturb him.

He had no need to worry.

"I had no choice. The pattern must be broken if we are to avoid the future Klieger saw. So I gave him to the Reds—he was willing to do his part. They will learn the truth."

"They will copy us!" Penn reared to his feet. "They will form their own project and we will lose our greatest advantage. Gregson, do you know what you have done?"

"I've opened a window to the future—for them as well as for us. Now there will be no ultimate war."

"Smart!" Penn didn't trouble to hide his sneer. "You're so smart! You've taken it on yourself to do this without authority. I'll see you dead for this!"

"No, General." Don shook his head. "You won't see me dead."

"That's what you think. I'll have you shot!"

Don smiled, warm in the comforting knowledge of his new awareness.

"No," he said. "You won't have me shot."

THE BEATIFIC SMILE

"YOU," I said with cold deliberation, "are, without doubt, the most repulsive, degenerate, self-opinionated swine I have ever had the misfortune to meet."

Captain Joseph Melsham didn't answer.

"As an example of the human race," I continued, still with the same tone of cold deliberation, "you are an abject failure. It seems incredible to me that anyone could ever have been fool enough to have trusted you with anything more complex than a string of beads. Wire-strung beads, naturally, the kind even a cretin like you would have trouble pulling apart."

Melsham didn't say anything. He just rested against the far side of the can, eyes closed, a beatific smile creasing his lips. The smile infuriated me and I became a little more personal.

"Your mother was probably human," I mused. "I wouldn't like be too specific as to just what sort of a human she was but she probably had the usual arrangement of ears and eyes, nose and mouth. And I'll even grant that she managed to walk upright most of the time." I didn't want to be ungenerous to anyone's mother, even Melsham's. I'm not that kind of a man.

"Your father, though, that's difficult." I paused for thought, staring at Melsham's face hovering a couple of feet from my own. The blue emergency light was dim by normal standards but I'd become accustomed to it during the past six weeks. I'd grown to tolerate the overgrown coffin that I shared with the Captain and I'd even become acclimatized to the assorted smells, pea-soup atmosphere and sewer conditions of the life-can. What I couldn't learn to tolerate was Melsham himself.

"A barbary ape," I suggested, then immediately shook my head. "No, not an ape. Not a monkey, a gorilla or even a chimpanzee. Nothing even remotely human could ever have fathered you. Let's give the matter some thought." I studied his smile, the shape of his ears, the creases on his face, trying to fit each separate part of his facial anatomy against a scrappy background of long-forgotten natural history. I didn't hurry over it, I had plenty of time.

"The smile, if you can call that distorted grimace a smile, reminds me of a crocodile. The nose has some vague resemblance to that of a pig while the ears could well belong to any member of the canine family. The shape of the head eludes me, that pointed skull and overdeveloped jaw, the cheekbones and sunken eye-sockets." I sighed and gave a shrug. "Frankly, Joe, old man, your parentage poses an insolvable problem. The only thing I can assume to have fathered you is a combination of hyena, wart-hog, cat-fish and stink-worm, with maybe a touch of skunk thrown in." I sniffed at the air. "With certainly a touch of skunk thrown in."

All the talking had made me thirsty so I doubled and twisted, crawled and wriggled until I had reached the reclam unit. Theoretically it was supposed to reclaim all the usable products from our waste, purifying the atmosphere and issuing it as pine-scented, earth-type, dust and germ free air. It was also supposed to reclaim all moisture and store it as a crystal-clear, urine-free, salinated and aerated nectar. On paper and maybe in a test laboratory the thing might have worked as the designers had fondly imagined it would. In actual practice the air was just about breathable and the reclaimed water was the biggest argument against teetotalism that I'd ever come across. But it was wet and, if it was also warm, redolent and opaque, it was better than nothing. Or almost.

My vocal chords lubricated, I wriggled, twisted, doubled and crawled until I was back in the only tolerable position in the life-can; resting with my feet towards the stinking reclam unit, my head inches from the tiny instrument panel with its built-in radio beacon and emergency light, my back resting lightly against the sweating curve of the ribbed hull. It also put me facing the closed eyes and smile of my sole companion in distress.

So I spat in his face.

There was a reason for it, of course, there is always a reason for everything. My reason was simply that I hated Melsham as I've never believed it possible to hate anyone. I hated him because of the discomfort I had to bear and he didn't. I hated him because he had been in command of the ship and, logically or not, I blamed him for having been in the same segment of space as the rogue meteor which had punctured our hull, smashed our engines and caused a general desire to get away as fast as possible from the resultant atomic death trap. So we had got away, all six of us, jetting into space in pairs, two to a life-can. And I had to draw the captain as partner.

"You know, Joe," I said conversationally. "I've often wondered just what terrible thing I must have done in some previous existence to have merited such punishment. Of all the people I could have been forced to share this can with I had to pick you." I glanced over my head at the calendar clock. "Six weeks, two days, five hours, eighteen minutes and twenty-seven seconds I've been cooped up in here with only you for company." I snorted at the thought of it. "Company! Hell, I'd rather be sharing a cage with a couple of skunks."

Melsham just smiled.

"Come to think of it I'd be better off at that," I mused. "At least I'd be getting fresh air if I was in a cage and if I was outdoors I could get a sight of the sun. And a couple of skunks could be fun. I could train them, maybe, teach them to come when I whistled, have them feeding out of my hand, riding on my shoulders, things like that." The more I thought of it the better the prospect seemed. "What do you think, Joe? A pair of skunks would be better company than you could ever be, wouldn't they?"

Melsham didn't answer. I wasn't really surprised, I hadn't expected anything different, but his silence didn't help the way I felt about him.

"You," I said, "are a dirty, yellow, whining coward."

No reaction. Or. . . ?

"How you could ever raise enough courage to stare into a mirror I will never know," I continued. "I suppose a man can learn to live with himself if given enough time, but not with a face like yours. I don't wonder that you ran away from normal life and hid yourself in space. Come to think of it there was nothing else you could have done. Not unless you'd got a job in a freak show." I chuckled at the thought. "Man! What a draw you would have been. The wart-hog-faced thing! Roll up and see the results of combining human and animal ancestry! Melsham the Missing Link!" My voice had risen higher than I liked and, when I stopped, the silence was deafening. I leaned forward to stare at the face opposite my own. It must have been imagination but it seemed to me that the beatific smile had grown even more beatific.

"Grin," I snapped. "Just lie there with that stupid, idiotic grin on your shapeless puss."

The reclamation unit gave a burp and a wave of sewer-smell rolled along the can towards me. I gagged, sucked a lungful of the apology for air and was promptly sick. Not that it made very much difference, not in the state I was in anyway, but it didn't do anything to ease my temper. Melsham seemed to find it amusing.

"You know something?" I wiped my mouth on the back of my hand, determined, somehow, to wipe off his grin in the same way. "I guess that there isn't anything so pitiful as a man who thinks he is attractive to women and who looks like you. Nobody in their right mind could ever think for one moment that any woman could ever want to be with you for anything but your money. And you simply couldn't own enough money for any decent, presentable woman to want to be found dead in your company."

The reclam unit burped again just then and I struggled for breath. Having won that fight, I had a battle with my stomach; a battle that I lost together with most of the rations I'd eaten lately. That struggle over, with me winning by default, as it were, my eyes began to burn from the waste particles released by the defective reclam unit. Everything considered, I was in a hell of a state and in just the right frame of mind to wish that I was dead and out of the whole stinking mess.

Melsham, of course, didn't feel that way at all, and good with good reason. He was dead already.

Not dead permanently, of course. Nor dead drunk, dead tired, dead exhausted or dead beat. He was just dead temporarily. Out of this world, literally, the lucky swine, and I hated him for it. Nepthol had done it, naturally. We'd had words about it after the fuss and fury had died and we'd had time to take stock of our situation."

"We're in a tough spot, Swanson," he'd said, "but there is no need for panic. We're on the shipping lines and we'll get picked up sooner or later. Just keep that radio-beacon operating and we'll be all right."

"Yes, sir," I'd said. "But isn't the beacon automatic?"

"It is, but I want you to watch it all the same." He'd stared around at the twin-sized coffin we occupied. "Can't tell just how long rescue will be, of course, so I'd better take precautions. With me out of the way the water and food will last twice as long." He noticed my expression. "Something wrong?"

"As Captain, sir," I reminded, "shouldn't you remain in command?" The prospect of an indeterminate period of lonely guard duty locked in the life-can didn't appeal to me. I'd never taken Nepthol but I'd heard about it and the reports sounded good. Just a prick in the arm and beautiful dreams until the medics pumped in the restorative. I'd never been shipwrecked before either, but it didn't need much imagination to foresee what life would be like after a few days in the can. Of the two unknowns I was willing to plump for the sweet dreams.

"Logically," agreed Melsham, "you are right. If you were anywhere near normal you would be right again. But you're a weedy runt while I'm pretty big." He looked at me from under his eyebrows. "Have you had experience of Nepthol?"

"Yes, sir." I was lying, but I hoped that it would make him change his mind. He seemed surprised.

"And you still want to take it?"

"Yes, sir."

"Well, you can't." He flexed a big arm. "This body of mine uses twice the fuel yours does." He reached for the single dose resting in the injector tube clipped to the instrument panel. "Just keep things clean, Swanson, and press that button when that light flashes." He placed the injector on his bare skin. "Be good now." He grinned and pressed the release and, still grinning, passed into beautiful oblivion.

Leaving me to take care of the mess.

There were advantages, of course. I found them out as time dragged past. For example, Melsham was one of the biggest men I'd ever met. He had muscles like a wrestler and a frame to match. He had a quick temper, too, and a rough tongue that he wasn't slow using. I'm more the refined type and could never match him in brawn, but that didn't mean that I liked his frequent tongue lashings. If he hadn't been the captain I'd have fixed him but good; a cook has many ways of getting his own back, but a man has to be careful when dealing with someone like Melsham.

I suppose that everyone has toyed with dreams of telling their boss just what to do and where to go to do it. Now I had the chance and took it with both hands. Not that I was wholly to blame. I had to find something to occupy my mind during the long weeks we drifted in space and this was the most satisfying method of all. The fact that Melsham couldn't hear me didn't matter; it eased my soul and that was good enough. Maybe, in the years to come, he would guess at what I was laughing at, but he could never be sure. And that was the sweetest thing of all.

The reclam unit grew worse and I knew that I'd have to fix it or go under. Fixing it was a job I knew I was going to detest, and I was right. The innards were caked with filth, and the stench was almost solid. I stripped the housing, cleared the mechanism as best I could and wearily crawled back to my usual position hoping that the air near the instrument panel would be a little less unwholesome than that I'd been breathing. It wasn't, which shouldn't have surprised me; I'd managed to cover myself pretty well with partly processed waste.

I found myself glaring at Melsham's smile.

"Grin, you yellow swine," I snapped. "So you think it's funny just lying there enjoying your dreams. Get away from me." I reached out and pushed him in the face. He didn't travel far, just back to the hull, but my hand left an interesting imprint on his cheek. It gave me an idea.

"You're a baboon-faced dog," I said. "Baboon-faced dogs shouldn't have off-white skin even though it does look like scraped leather." I reached out and traced a thick moustache beneath his nose. I followed it with a couple of exaggerated eyebrows, drew thick sideboards and then, to finish off, wiped both hands over his face and neck. When I'd finished even his smile had vanished beneath a thick film of redolent goo.

Three days later we were rescued.

At first I hardly believed it. I'd been lying in a half-doze, half-coma, my throat dry from telling Melsham just what I thought of him, and getting rather worried because I'd discovered that I was beginning to repeat myself. Suddenly the emergency light was drowned in a red flash repeated at regular intervals and, lifting my head, I'd stared at the winking telltale. To press the respond button was automatic. Elation came afterwards.

"They've found us!" I felt so happy that I could have kissed even Melsham. "You hear me, you apology of a man, they've found us!"

Melsham didn't answer, naturally, but some of the goo had cracked away from around his mouth and I could see that he was smiling.

"That's right, Joe, smile!" I lifted his head towards me, using his ears as handles, and gently rapped his head against the hull. "Come on, you great big baby, you wake up." I rapped a little harder. "Wake up you whining coward, the hard part's over. Old Swanson's brought you through as he said he would." The thud of Melsham's head punctuated my words. "How about a nice, big happy smile after your seven-week sleep?"

I knew that he couldn't hear me or answer, but I also knew that this was probably the last chance I would ever get to tell him just what I thought about him. I wouldn't have bothered but for the fact that fixing the reclam unit had added the final straw. When I thought of Melsham having a whale of a time in his dream world and me up to the eyebrows in stinking waste, it made me boil.

The grate of the contact tube came shortly after I'd pressed the respond button, and the scrape of the port being opened came soon after. A flood of light and fresh air blasted into the life-can and I heard a man cough and retch as he caught a lungful of our own atmosphere.

"What the hell? What's happened in here?"

"Reclam unit busted," I said cheerfully. I wriggled towards the opening and held up my hand. "Help me out of here, you guys."

"I ain't touching you until you've had a bath," said one of the rescuers determinedly. "Anyone else in there?"

"Only my Captain, he took Nepthol." I climbed out of the can and straightened, filling my lungs with the clean, sweet air of the rescue ship. "I've had to wet-nurse him for seven weeks."

"We'll have to get him out of there," said one of the rescue party, a medic from his uniform. He didn't look too happy about it. "Sam, Fred, give me a hand."

They grumbled but they went, and while they were helping out the limp, goo-caked body, a crewman washed me down with a pressure hose. He stood well away from me as he blasted me with water, but I didn't mind that. I hadn't realized that such a little waste could cover so large an area.

"Over here with that hose, Carl." Sam rose from where they had placed Melsham. "Just wash him off before we restore him."

"What about me?" I demanded. "I'm not clean yet and I want some clothes. Melsham can wait; he's been taking it easy for the past few weeks."

"Easy?" One of the medics raised his eyebrows. "Under Nepthol? You kidding?"

"Like hell I'm kidding." I was getting angry. "I'm the one who's had to take care of things. I'm the one who had to fix the busted reclam unit and spend all that time alone in that can. All he did was to take some dope and sleep the time away."

"You ever taken Nepthol?" Sam looked towards me. I didn't like his expression.

"No."

"Then pipe down until you know more about it."

"What are you trying to feed me?" I caught one of the medics by the arm. "It's just sleep-dope, isn't it? Something to pass the time."

"Tell him," said Sam wearily. "Tell him while we get this hero back on his feet." He reached for a king-sized hypodermic and began to search Melsham for a big enough vein. I swallowed as the medic I had hold of put me in the picture.

"Nepthol isn't what you think it is," he explained. "It knocks you out, sure, but in a very special kind of way. It lowers the metabolism so that you don't need water or food and hardly any air, but it doesn't touch the brain. Your body slows down and that's about all."

"I know that," I said impatiently. "That's why it's used, so that two guys can live twice as long as they would do if one of them didn't take the dope. I'm not simple."

"No?" He shrugged. "Well, that's about all there is to it. The body slows down to a point where it would take about two months to open your eyes. But not the mind, boy, that doesn't slow down at all. And you don't clock off, not at all. Get it?"

"You mean?" A horrible thought had just struck me. "You mean that he could hear me all the time? Feel me? Is that it?"

"Sure. That's why it takes guts to take Nepthol. It's like going into a kind of prison in which you can hear everything about you but you can't move and you can't sleep. You've got to close your eyes to protect them but you can't close your ears." He chuckled. "Funny things happen at times when a guy doesn't know the full effects. I remember the case…" He broke off, staring at me. "Something wrong?"

There was, but how could I tell him? How could I ever tell Melsham that it was all a joke, that I hadn't meant a word that I'd said and that I didn't know he could hear me anyway? How, after telling him that I'd used Nepthol?

I stared, boggle-eyed, to where he was slowly rising to his feet. He was still smiling and his arms, as he flexed them, looked horribly big.

And he had such a beatific smile.

WHEN HE DIED

I STOOD in a park and stared at the leaves rustling about my feet. They were dead leaves, dry and sere, brittle and curled, and yet more colorful in death than they had ever been in life. The wind caught them and sent them scurrying over the faded grass in company with scraps of paper and the other inevitable litter of public places.

It was a chill wind and I shivered a little as it bit through my clothing. I stared up at the sky, surprised at its emptiness, and around me at the few people walking in the park. They were as I expected, but it was hard not to stare. Fashions change so quickly that what is admirable today is ludicrous tomorrow. They ignored me and I forgot them in the urgency of other things.

The wind was wrong, the leaves were wrong, the setting was right, but that was all. It should have been spring, with warm breezes and green leaves nodding above newly-bloomed flowers. The sky should have been bright and clear, not sullen with rain-heavy clouds. I had arrived at the wrong time.

Fear joined forces with the wind so that I shivered beyond all reason. Six months didn't matter. Six months either too soon or too late and I would still be within the margin of safety. But if I had arrived so far from the determined point, then it need not be merely six months. It could be eighteen or thirty. One way wouldn't matter, would be all to the good, but the other . . .

I stooped and grabbed at a fragment of newspaper as it fluttered towards me. I straightened and smoothed it with trembling fingers. I blinked at the date, holding the small print close to my weak eyes, then felt a sudden, tremendous surge of relief. The date on the paper was the 15th October, 2007. I had been born on the 23rd July, 1981. I was eighty-seven years old, and so had traveled back sixty-one years. But that wasn't important.

I had arrived with two months to spare.

Strange how things have their own importance. I had worked continuously for fifty years to perfect the time shuttle, and my object was, to any other man, ludicrous. The discovery was important to only to a few savants like myself because, while objects could be sent back through time, the shuttle itself could not. It was strictly a one-way trip and that fact made the shuttle useless. Who would want to travel to an earlier age with no possibility of return? Who, other than a fool or a man obsessed?

I thought about it as I walked slowly from the park and into the streets of the city. Slowly, because I was an old man and had long since lost the resiliency of youth. Around me ground cars, remembered from my boyhood, but now strange, snarled and roared along the roads. They frightened me a little, those cars. It would be so easy to have accident, to be struck and injured and carried off to a hospital. Medical science had not yet learned the secrets of quick-healing, and such an accident could keep me helpless for months. And I had no time to spare.

I entered a café and ordered coffee, paying for it with some old currency which I had taken so much trouble to collect. I sat and sipped at the brew and stared through the windows at the street outside. The scene was familiar and, at the same time, strange. The buildings were as I remembered them, but dirtier by far than I had imagined. Sixty years is a long time, and memories tend to fade and become overlaid with nostalgia. The city I saw now was not the city as I remembered it, but then I had looked at it through the eyes of youth, while now I stared at it with the eyes of critical age.

I smiled as I drank the coffee, wondering what my fellow workers would be saying at my absence. To transport my mass had drained the potential of the pile, and the cost of replacement would be enormous. In effect, I was a criminal, a saboteur, a self-centered fool without regard for others. But I didn't care.

My motive, to me, was all-important.

Have you ever known regret?

Have you ever known what it is to sit and smile and make conversation, while all the time your eyes are burning with unshed tears, and your heart is torn and aching inside of you? Do you know what it is to realize that all your hopes and plans and aspirations have dissolved like dead-sea fruit in your hands and that all the care and caution you were once so proud of has reared up before you and is making your life hell? Have you ever felt the sickening knowledge that nothing you can do now can possibly matter, because it is too late?

I felt like that the night my father died.

I loved my father. Strange to hear a man say that? Not so strange when you realize that he was the only parent I had ever known. He was more than just my father. He was the man who stayed up all night to mend my bicycle so that I could ride out with my friends on our Sunday excursions. He was the man who collapsed at work while earning the money to keep me at school and then university instead of letting me take a blind-alley job so that he could reap the benefit of my wages. He was the man who, with ruined heart and rasping lungs, crept painfully through life without complaint so that I shouldn't worry about him.

Not that I ever did. Children have an impatient cruelness strange to an adult. It was hard for me to wait for him to catch up with me when we were out walking. I felt embarrassed at his slowness and ashamed of the way he would halt and clutch at the railings for support, with his poor face all blue and his poor hands all swollen and shapeless. Pain made him short-tempered at times, so that we quarreled bitterly as only youth and age can quarrel. I had no tolerance. I was young and fit, and knew everything in the world worth knowing. I had no time for his advice. I knew best, and so it was that, after being bruised by the world, I tended to blame him for what he could not do.

I blamed him because we were poor while others were rich. I blamed him for his ill health and his apparent stubborness, not realizing that, to the old and ill, small pleasures are valuable. So that, when he lay gasping and ill, I had no sympathy with him. It was his own fault, I said, for being so foolish. If he was ill then he should go into hospital and not stay at home making himself a burden to me and shaming me before my friends. I was hard. I was bitter. I was a child.

Tolerance came with age, and I regretted the things I had done and the things I had said. Now, instead of as in the past, my plans included him as well as myself. But they were nebulous plans. One day I knew that I would have money. One day I would give him as much money as he needed to enjoy himself. One day, always one day.

But that day never came.

I was cautious and looked far ahead. A little now or a lot later? Should I dole out what I could afford now, or save it until a later date when I could afford more? Saving and thrift caught hold of me so that I almost begrudged the little I gave from time to time. Later, I told myself, later, when I had what I thought necessary. Then we would both enjoy the benefits of my thrift. Later. Always later.

He died before that time ever came.

Losing him was like losing a part of myself. I was away at the time, working north at what was to be my profession, and we hadn't seen each other for months. The news came in a letter from a stranger, and that same letter contained a sizeable sum of money. But the money meant nothing to me then.

I traveled all night and saw the grave. I saw our old neighbors, too, and I was not proud of the way they looked at me. I questioned them and found that he had not died alone. A stranger had been with him, an old man, and they had lived together for a short while. He had been there at the death and had arranged the interment. I didn't know who the stranger was. I never saw him, but I had other things to worry about than unknown strangers. My father was dead, that was enough, and I hadn't even said good-bye.

And now it was too late.

Time, they say, heals all wounds, and time was all I had. It was a slow healer. I dreamed of my father and saw him in a thousand ways. The back of a stranger, a song, a scrap of conversation, a place name, a thousand things which made him suddenly real and alive again so that I seemed to hear his voice and see his smile and feel again the pain of my unbearable loss.

Work offered an anodyne, and I worked like a man possessed. The money he had sent me—I never thought of it as other than his gift—enabled me to forge ahead in my studies so that I soon became an expert in my field. Atomics was still new enough to offer splendid opportunities and I rode the crest of the wave. I was respected, fairly wealthy, with access to top-secret information and the world at my longer tips. I should have been happy. I wasn't.

Maybe if I had married and had children of my own I would have rid myself of the incubus that haunted me. Maybe I was too introverted, too taken with living in the past even while working towards the future. I knew enough of psychology to know that I was suffering from a guilt complex, that I was tearing myself apart with all the thoughts of what might have been. The little things I could have done, had intended to do, but had left too late.

And there was no surcease for me in all the world.

Time passed as time does. My hair grew white, my shoulders stooped, my eyes grew weak and my hands lacked their sureness. Atomics spread throughout the world and spaceships soared to the Moon. New discoveries were made, and the final secrets of nature began to yield to our probing.

Then two things happened almost simultaneously and altered all my life.

Vendaris, after thirty years of experimentation, discovered a serum, which, at first glance, promised immortality. It was a complex molecule chain which, when injected into the bloodstream, arrested the ageing of the tissues. The serum carried its own safeguard, in that it brought sterility. Men could live forever, but it would be a barren existence. It was good that way. Young couples could mate and have their children and then, when in their prime, take the serum. The snags were minor. A fresh injection was needed every seven years or ageing would re-commence. And the serum had to be new; storing it caused degeneration of the complex chain.

The second thing was that I discovered time travel.

I was eighty-seven then, sixty-one years after the death of my father, and yet time still had not healed the hurt of his passing. It was inevitable that I should use the shuttle to return back in time so as to see him once more.

And I had arrived just two months before he was due to die.

I finished my coffee and left the café. I walked down the familiar streets and came to the old house. My heart beat with a peculiar excitement as I reached it, and for a long time I stood outside. Within the house I knew that my father would be sitting in his old armchair. Perhaps he would be reading, or listening to the radio, or perhaps he was busy making himself a cup of tea or cooking one of his little meals.

My eyes stung as I thought of him in his loneliness. Old, ill, seemingly unwanted by his only son. Old myself, I could now appreciate the terrors of age. The sleepless nights, the failing memory, the discomfort and pain of a body which was breaking down faster than the mind it contained. For a moment I felt the impulse to go. To walk away and not to resurrect the ghosts of the past. I fought the impulse. This was not the past, not now. This was the present, and my father was alive and I was here to comfort him if I could.

But it took more courage than I expected to knock upon the door.

He was the same. It was incredible, but he was just the same. The same poor, bluish hands, the same wheezing in his throat, the same deep-set eyes creased with wrinkles and yellowed with illness. He stood and looked at me and I, after my first involuntary step forward, remembered who and what I was.

I was his son—but he could never know it. He was my father—but he was young enough to be my son. To him I was an elderly stranger.

It was easy to make friends. I knew him—who could know him better? I introduced myself as a friend of his son and he made me welcome, as I knew he would. He invited me in and offered me tea and, to me, that was the sweetest moment of my life.

I almost cried as I fingered the well-remembered cups and stared at the old, familiar room. Its poverty startled me, used as I was to twenty-first century luxury, and little things threatened to trap me at every moment. I knew too much. I remembered where the sugar was kept in its old tin, where he used to keep his milk, the place to find the matches. It was hard not to speak of mutual friends and incidents about which no outsider could know. I had to force myself to act as a stranger, and yet all the time I wanted to throw my arms around him and tell him who I was.

We talked of his son and I felt shame as I listened to the quiet pride in his voice. We had argued, he and I, and I had been bitter of the opinion he must have given others about me, but now I knew that to be all wrong. He loved me, was proud of me, and his only complaint was that I left him alone too long.

I knew why he was alone. I knew what I was doing at that moment, the I that was young, of course, not myself. I was working and saving, enjoying myself in my fashion, and salving my conscience with the knowledge that 'one day' I would make amends to my father for my neglect. That day had been sixty-one years in the coming and, now that I was here, he couldn't know who I was.

The two months passed all too quickly. I moved into the old house and the money I had brought with me made life as pleasant for him as it could. It wasn't much. I had forgotten that, to him, things would not be the same as to me. Money from a stranger was not the same as money from his son. The company of a stranger was a poor substitute for the company he longed for. It was not the same.

And I was conscious all the time of the passing days that would terminate his life.

That was the worst part of it. To see him again, to talk with him, to share his simple pleasures, to walk with him and be aware of his presence. And all the time know that he was dying as I watched him. To know the exact hour of his death and know that there was nothing in the world I could do about it. Nothing but wait and wait, and to be as cheerful as I could.

I was with him when he collapsed. I sat beside him day and night until he died. He was without pain—I saw to that, but he died calling out for his son, and I, sitting beside him, could not tell him that he cried out for that which he had.

And so he died, and I wept at his passing.

I buried him and sent the letter with the enclosed money as I knew I should. Almost, I was tempted to wait and see myself, but sense came in time and I did not. There can be no paradoxes in time. If we had met I should have remembered it. We had not, and so must not, but now many things were clear to me as they would be to him when, in sixty-one years' time, he, too, would sit beside the body of his dead father.

So I left the area and hid myself in the heart of the city, there to do what I could with the rest of my life.

Sometimes, as I sit in my little room, I wonder if I did right. It is a passing doubt. In sixty years' time Vendaris will have perfected his serum and all would live forever. But I am eighty-seven years of age, an old man, and I cannot possibly live another sixty years. I shall die. My return has cost me immortality, as I knew it would, but it doesn't matter.

I had been with my father when he died.

READ ME THIS RIDDLE

FRAMED in the jagged circle of brown and scabrous rock the vista of the plain was one of cold hostility. Gray-whiteness tinged with blue stretched to either side like the frozen surface of an ocean. Ahead rested the mound of enigmatic ruins, a castle slumped and chilled to be crusted by ash, to add to the brooding stillness of the place. To lie dreaming beneath the shroud of light thrown by distant stars.

A fantasy. There was no proof that the mound was a ruin or, if it was, that it had ever held any form of life remotely human. This was an alien world. It could be an alien grave.

Turning, Elgan looked into the interior of the cave. Those seated around the fire, despite their appearance, were victors. They had survived to walk from the wrecked vessel, to find shelter, to obtain warmth, to wait with the patience of resignation for the rescue, which might or might not come. And, waiting, they talked.

"A bad world," said Legrand. "Bleak and cold. It's bad enough to starve when it's warm. I hate the cold."

"Me too." Hengist held his hands to the fire, the glow painting his face with dancing colors, accentuating the hollows of his sunken cheeks. "It reminds me of the time I was stranded on Aceua. No money, no job, nothing to hope for. It was cold then too and we lost five of our number."

"You weren't alone?" This from Connor, young, once brash, once a little stupid, but who had learned that he needed to learn.

"I'd hooked up with a bunch of others," said Hengist shortly. "It was the only way to survive."

Shared fires, shared food, shared beds. A shared misery, the sharing alone making it bearable. But not a shared escape and even Connor knew better than to probe. Some victories came hard.

To change the subject he said, "Those ruins, if they are ruins, do you think we could find anything?"

"Maybe." Kalend added another scrap of dried moss to the fire, handling the fuel as if it were gold. "You've studied the terrain, Elgan. What do you think?"

"The ground is soft, like ash. To cover it will take equipment we haven't got."

"We could fix something from the wreck." Connor was stubborn. "Snowshoes or skis. A sled, even. We could do it."

"Sure, and if we could we might find something we'd regret," said Pontiac, dryly. Old, he shivered and drew closer to the fire. "Like Greeson on Yefare. He found a vault and went inside to find valuables."

"And?"

"What was waiting inside found food." Pontiac grinned at Connor. "Red meat just to its liking. We got to it just as it was starting on the head. That we buried—the rest had gone."

"Or Houghton," said Legrand, thoughtfully. "I shipped with him once. He took one chance too many on Chao, I think. There was talk of a fabulous bloom to be found in the swamps and he went after it. He found it too and brought it back with him—growing in his lungs."

"Accidents." Hengist shrugged. "Things like that can happen to anyone at any time. One risk taken too many. A gamble lost—hell, we're in the same position. But what of the other things?"

The rumors, the fables and legends, the whispers that survived despite all logic. A mysterious vessel filled with incredible treasure, which drifted eternally between the stars. A planet that gave eternal youth. A machine with which a man could obtain his heart's desire. A woman, immortal, lovely beyond description, who waited patiently to be rescued and who would give the man who freed her all he would need for ever.

Dreams born of aching frustration, tales spun from gossamer, sagas built on fancies and embroidered by imagination. Stories that should have been true and one, at least, that was.

Pontiac said, "Elgan, tell us about John Forester."

He was fifty-eight years old with veins beginning to show prominently in his legs, his eyes far from strong and his drives well on the wane. Dissipation had lost its attraction, women were a nuisance, effort was a penance and when his stomach revolted so that he could no longer enjoy food and drink he decided that he'd had enough. Not of living, he was not insane, but of pretending to enjoy what life had to offer in the objective world. For such a man there was, fortunately, an answer.

On Nyoka he found it.

"The Library," said Pontiac. "I've heard of it."

"It exists?" Connor echoed his incredulity. "It's real?"

"It's real," said Elgan. "But sometimes it's hard to find."

There was a shimmer about it, a vague intangibility as if it had just passed the barrier between dimensions and, like an echo, still lingered in the one it had left. A building shaped like a domed cylinder, the walls pierced with a single door, the area beyond hushed as if emulating a cathedral. A hush broken by the soft tinkle of crystal chimes, which moved in the warm and scented air to throw delicate music in greeting to the newcomer.

A greeting put into words by the attendant who rose from where he sat.

"John Forester, you are welcome."

"You know me?"

"As I know many other things; the seven colors of a rainbow, the nine sounds of the Elgash Bells, the fifteen signs of the Ghalatian Greeting." The attendant was small and smelt a little of dust and, as he rose from his bow, the lines of his face resembled the riffled leaves of a book. "But you are not here to ask questions."

"No," admitted Forester. "I came—"

"The fact that you are here is explanation enough. A man follows his need. Enter, then, and be not afraid."

A smaller door gaped beyond the main portal, the panel swinging wide as Forester approached, closing behind him as he stepped into an area deceptively small, padded, dully illuminated by glowing panels. Around him rose a host of bubbles in kaleidoscopic brilliance; trapped rainbows that swirled invitingly, luring with their suggestive contents.

His hand closed on one.

It exploded with a gush of scintillation.

The world changed.

He sat in a low-roofed space, hands on an oar, feeling the pain of wood-torn thighs and buttocks ripe with oozing sores. The beat of a mallet was the pound of a relentless heart, the air a nauseous stench, the light a dull yellow glow from wicks burning in rancid oil. In the guttering flames he could see the back of the man seated before him, the spine ridged and knobbed with prominent bone, the flesh streaked by a crisscross of shallow gashes.

Lank hair held creeping vermin. The naked buttocks were stacked thick with dried excreta. Crusted sores showed beneath the manacles clamping the ankles, the iron clasps and chain rusted with urine.

A galley—and he was a slave!

A beat and the oar moved as if with a life of its own, automatic reflex obeying the command, habit following the pattern. Lift, pull, lower, push, lift, pull, lower, push, lift . . .

He felt the pull and bunch of aching muscles in arms, back and shoulders, the tension of his thighs, feet pressing hard against the deck. The world was filled with the thudding beat, the weight of the oar, the creak of timbers, the stench of men. He was nothing. Flesh wedded to wood to form a machine.

Looking down he saw his thighs, his knees, his shins. Dirt crusted the skin and lice reigned in his hair. From the shadows beneath the bench before him he caught the gleaming eyes of a rat. His ears were filled with the sobbing exhalations of someone driven to the edge of exhaustion.

"Move!"

He reared as the whip lashed across his shoulders, the thong biting, cutting, ripping through skin with the sting of fire. A blow delivered with the impersonal chill of a rider touching a spur to the flank of his mount.

"Keep time there! Keep time!"

A second blow which crossed the first and sent waves of red agony through every nerve causing him to cringe even as he threw his weight against the oar. A third and the overseer moved on to send his lash against the spine of the man in front, red droplets springing to dapple the filthy skin, the slimed deck.

An eternity later they paused to rest and eat; hard bread that was torture to scurvied gums, a bowl of tepid stew made from garbage, a measure of brackish water. Then again the beat . . . the beat . . . the beat . . . the beat . . .

How long, in God's name, was he to serve at an oar?

Kalend blew on the fire and fed it a scrap of fuel. As he straightened he said. "Well, how long was it?"

"Years," said Elgan. "Subjective, naturally, but real

enough to Forester. And he couldn't escape by dying don't forget, the book didn't provide for that."

"The book?"

"It was the Library," said Elgan patiently. "What else would it be but a book?"

Connor wasn't satisfied. "A thing you read?"

"Read, imagine, taste, experience—what does it matter? A book is a self-contained world. Forester was in such a world. He was experiencing the life of the main character. He had become the main character. But, for him there could be no short cuts, no skipping."

"And no way out," mused Legrand. "Unless—?"

"Unless he closed the book."

He did it by closing his eyes and smashing his head against the oar. In the momentary confusion when, half-stunned, reality changed and firm contours became blurred, he grasped desperately at a drifting bubble of lambent blue and squeezed it and became engulfed by a shimmering haze and suddenly found himself—elsewhere.

In a vast and solemn chamber built of gigantic blocks of stone and filled with shadows, which swelled into ominous proportions, to dwindle as men walked past the flambeaux to halt and stand before him.

"For the third and last time we appeal to you to recant and yield your heretical ways and return to the forgiving and all-embracing body of Mother Church there to have your sins washed from your soul and the hope of joy eternal restored. How say you, man? Will you not be humble before your God?"

"Before my God, yes. Before you servants of Hell, never!"

The voice which should have been a a shout was a whisper, the defiance which should have rung to the far corners of the world barely reached the ears of the hooded men standing before where he was bound, but they had traveled far enough to ensure his damnation.

A gesture and the servants of the Inquisition were at his side. Men like beasts with masked faces and naked torsos; picked for lack of imagination and unquestioning obedience. Releasing his bonds they held him firm as a cowled figure lifted a hand and intoned the will of the Holy Office.

Not to kill but to save. To torment the flesh in order to gain the soul. To open wide the doors of Heaven for the misguided heretic who would be accepted into Grace as soon as he confessed the grievous error of his ways. An act justified before God and Man. Against salvation what was a little pain?

"Recant and be blessed, my son. God is all-merciful. Accept for forgiveness. Renounce your heresy." A sigh like the stirring of wind-blown leaves. "The Devil makes his servants stubborn. Proceed."

First the rack, which pulled and pulled until his limbs eased from their sockets and the sound of his screaming echoed from the vaulted roof of the chamber. Then fire, which blotched his chest and stomach with seared and crisped skin through which melted fat oozed and bubbled to form individual places of torment. Places joined by the fires induced into his left foot as it was crushed in an iron boot. By the agony of his right as the nails were ripped slowly from each toe.

"Mother of God have mercy on me! Dear God protect me! Sweet Jesus save me! In the name of all the Saints and Holy Martyrs save me from this agony!"

A babble of sound, which echoed like the tongueless mewing of a distraught animal caught and flayed alive for the added luster of its pelt.

And then the hoist.

Crippled, unable to stand, he was carried beneath a crossbar. His wrists were lashed behind him, a rope affixed which was thrown over the bar to be caught and held fast by two burly men. Together they hauled, lifting the bound wrists, the arms, the body itself to hang suspended. Up and up, to pause, to release the rope, to catch it as the body fell, to halt the falling shape with a savage jerk.

His shriek was the distillation of agony.

Again, a little higher this time, the fall a little longer, the jerk at his shoulders all the more savage. Tendons and sinews yielded beneath the strain. Bone started from weakened sockets to yield finally as again he fell to be jerked to a halt.

To hang with wrists upraised above his head, his shoulders ruined, the arms ripped and torn from their natural position to hold him suspended by skin and muscle only.

Ruined arms. Hands which never again would be able to

grasp a thing as light as a feather. Elbows which would never bend. Biceps which would never flex. Crippled and worse than crippled he would hang until he died.

"Did he?" Connor blew on his hands and held them to the fire. "Die, I mean."

"A hell of a way to go," mused Legrand. "I've seen a man burned and roasting and another with his skin dissolved in acid; but they were accidents. What makes a man accept such torment?"

"The book," reminded Pontiac. "It was all in the book. Once he'd started the story he had to follow it through to the end."

"Unless he closed it." Hengist frowned, thinking. "Maybe he liked the yarn," he said. "It could be that he enjoyed it. There are men like that."

Too many men who found pleasure in the depiction of pain and who would longer lovingly over the portrayal of man's inhumamty to man. Violence held a primitive appeal, which could not be denied. And yet, for a man to suffer such horror when, by a simple act, he could escape?

"Forester was caught," said Kalend with acute understanding. "Once in he couldn't get out or couldn't think clearly enough to change his situation. But later?"

"He managed," said Elgan. He hunched a little closer to the fire, conscious of the keening of wind beyond the cave, fitful gusts which caught the air and swirled it so that the little flames danced and guttered as if with a life of their own. "And not all the experiences were bad."

A bubble of purple yielded a vision of scented delight locked in the harmonious gem of a room high in a palace of dreams. Her perfume was of musk and roses, her eyes the limpid pools of northern waters warmed to a liquid softness by the flames of unslaked desire. A cloud wreathed the sculpted perfection of her face; one of spun gold with strands as fine as gossamer, a mist of delicate and fragrant hair, which hung like a shimmering waterfall over the smooth enticement of her shoulders. Her lips were a couch of embracing warmth. Her feet were the wings of butterflies each toe tipped with red.

"I love you!" she whispered. "My darling, I love you!"

And he took her into his arms as a man does a woman and even while searching the innermost places he felt his desire rise like a phoenix from the ashes of past achievement.

"My lord," she whispered. "My master. Take me, use me, treat me as you will. I am yours to command."

Her perfume was a cloud of stimulating vapor. Through the narrow window streamers of sunlight touched drapes of silken gold, russet, amber, yellow, purple, reds like the sheen of freshly crushed strawberries, blues like the segments of compressed skies. Here the throb of life was paramount, the act of creation supreme to all other considerations, the old, old and ancient ritual a thing which filled the world.

Which muffled the sound of footsteps and the clash of the opening door.

A clash echoed by the impact of steel as, rising, he snatched up a sword and, over the prostrate body of the girl, fought for his life and the love he had gained.

A bold fight and one which sent the blood gushing through his veins, more flying to spatter the walls as hands fell from severed wrists, heads from shorn trunks, fountains gushing from opened throats. On his feet now he roared his war cry and, dimly, heard it repeated from the streets far below. Again, and it was louder, yelled from the throats of men climbing the stairs to this room in a tower, echoed by the fury of those caught and dying beneath their steel.

The victory was sweet, and another bubble showered him with scintillant shards of splintered silver and he was alone crossing an endless waste of snow with the loom of a somber mountain far ahead and the grim, slinking shapes of wolves howling from behind.

And another of ruby, which took him to a cavern beneath a sea where sportive fish swam in graceful pavanes where he suffered the embrace of constricting tentacles as a jeweled mermaid held his face between her breasts.

And a bubble of lavender and another of cerise and more of topaz and magenta and cyan and each a new experience.

"What happened?" demanded Connor. "In the end, what happened?"

"In the end?" Elgan shrugged. "Forester died."

"Again? But how—"

"Really died." Elgan was patient. "The kind of death a man can only know once. He was greedy, a child given a candy-store, and he didn't know when to stop. And he was old and even subjective experience takes its toll. Or, perhaps—" He broke off, then shook his head. "No. That doesn't matter. But Forester died."

"In the Library found on Nyoka," said Pontiac and his voice was somber. "Well, he found what he had gone there to seek. Let him rest in peace."

"Amen," said Kalend and threw more fuel on the dying eye of the fire. For a moment it threatened to quench the glow then, as the flames won and began to feed, bright tongues of red and orange rose to turn their faces into the masks of devils.

And, looking at them, Connor could understand why Forester had known so much pain and suffered so many tortures. The devil lies close to the surface of us all and what we are cannot be denied. And yet something troubled him, the thought that of all the entertainment the Library had to offer, the man had chosen such earthy, elemental things.

"He had no choice," said Elgan when he mentioned it. "He was driven by his nature as are we all. The Library provided what he needed."

"Books," said Connor. "You said the bubbles were like books. A man can choose what he cares to read."

"An analogy," said Elgan. "And not a good one. It must not be taken too literally."

He rose with a sudden motion and stepped towards the opening of the cave there to stand leaning with his shoulder against the stone, his face out-turned, the freshening wind stirring his hair.

A cold wind gusted which stung his ears and eyes and filled them with moisture as it numbed the flesh of face and hands.

Watching him Connor wondered why he had left the comfort of the fire and sought the answer in the eyes of the others; but none would meet his questioning stare. They sat silent and still like images of stone, the firelight turning their eyes into mirrors of reflected radiance, their features into engraved masks behind which the soul sat and cringed to the onset of anticipated disaster. The tale of John Forester, perhaps, the telling of it had cast a chill over the assembly, one Connor thought to vanquish with a laugh.

"A good story," he said, "and Elgan told it well, but surely you can all see the fallacy? How did he know what Forester experienced? How did he know the man died?"

Pontiac said, like the whispering rustle of seared and fallen leaves, "He knows."

"But how?"

"Ask him—he knows."

Rising Connor stepped from the circle and felt the cold numb his flesh as he turned his back on the fire. Standing against the rock Elgan made no effort to face him not even when Connor touched him on the arm. His face, touched now with frost, cold in the reflected glow of starlight, seemed remote and, somehow, inhuman.

"It was a joke," said Connor. "Admit it was a joke."

"The story?"

"Yes. John Forester never existed. There was no Library on Nyoka. No kaleidoscope of bubbles each, when burst, giving a new experience. It was just something you made up in order to pass the time."

And, even as he said it, he wanted it to be so.

"No," said Elgan. "It was no joke."

"But—"

"John Forester existed and there is a planet called Nyoka and on it can be found the Library guarded by a strange attendant and in it can be found all the hells and paradises imagined by Man. Worlds of imagination which can be found and lived and known to the full as their creators intended."

"You can't know that," insisted Connor. "You can't be sure."

"I'm sure." Elgan straightened from where he leaned against the rock and turned to meet the other's eyes. "You see I was with Forester when he found the Library. I saw him pass inside. I followed. I know what happened to him because it happened to me and . . . and . . ."

"You left," said Connor quickly. "Of course, you had to leave, how else would you be here?"

"If I left I can't remember it," said Elgan, bleakly. "All I remember is a host of bubbles each providing a new world. As far as I know I am still among them. Tell me, Connor, did I leave—or am I still inside?"

He turned and looked from the cave at the gray-whiteness of the ash-like stuff beyond. It had lain a score of feet from the edge of the cave when they had entered it—now it rested barely an inch below the floor.

And it was still rising.

LOGIC

IT HAPPENED soon after he arrived at the testing grounds. A man ran past yelling an incoherent warning, another took it up, and Carter gripped his arm with almost painful intensity.

"Get out of sight! Quick!"

"Why?" Val stared at the deserted spaces between workshops and living quarters. "What's wrong?"

"You'll see," promised Carter grimly, and almost dragged the psychologist into the shelter of a building.

For a while nothing seemed to happen. From somewhere in the center of the clustered buildings a siren wailed and several engines revved up as if in answer. A man shouted something, his voice distorted by buildings and distance, and Carter grunted as he wiped sweat from his face and neck.

"It might not be coming this way," he muttered. "Never can tell what the damn things will do."

"This is crazy," snapped Val. "What's it all about? Why did you pull me in here? Why—" He paused, staring down the narrow street between two of the buildings, and deep inside him something seemed to knot with primeval fear.

A robot strode down the concreted path.

A gleaming, metallic thing, all of twelve feet from the tip of its conical head to the soles of its broad, metal feet. Articulated arms swung at its sides, and the scanning eyes set in the conical head glowed with a ruby incandescence.

"Get back!" whispered Carter. "If it should see you—" He broke off as a vehicle snarled around a corner, skidded to a halt, then reversed in frantic manoeuvring. Men swore as they spun the stubby barrel of a squat weapon mounted on the truck, cursing with the thin, high-pitched cursing of men fighting against sickening fear. They aligned the weapon just as the robot spurted into sudden life.

A man shrieked, then fell silent as a metal arm pulped his skull. Another swore, swore again, then made a blind run away from the towering monstrosity. For a moment the robot seemed to hesitate, the scanning eyes flickering from the mounted weapon to the running man, then, with a grate of metal on concrete, it left the truck and followed the runner. It caught him just as the gun crew swiveled their weapon, and a thundering hail of high velocity shells smashed against the metal figure. It staggered, twisted, bent as it tried to absorb the kinetic energy of the missiles, then, incredibly, straightened and walked towards the flaming muzzle of the automatic cannon.

It had covered almost half the distance before it fell, a twisted heap of wreckage, the ruby light dying with a spouting gush of blue-white electric flame, and the scanning eyes dead and shattered in the conical head.

The gun stammered into silence, the gun crew relaxed and took notice of their dead, and a heavy truck, a crane dangling from the rear, drove up beside the collapsed robot. Another vehicle, this time a white-painted ambulance, swept along the street, and Val tried not to see the broken remains of men that were loaded aboard.

Beside him Carter swore with slow deliberation.

Val straightened from his crouched position and was surprised to find that he was trembling. There had been something about the robot, something almost awesome and inevitable, like the dimly-remembered dreams of childhood, a giant perhaps from a fairy tale, but there was nothing nice and fanciful about what he had just seen.

The ugly red stains on the white concrete proved that.

"Let's get going," said Carter abruptly. "The men know what to do."

He led the way from the sheltering doorway, walking stiffly past the broken machine now dangling from the cable of the crane, and stared somberly at the still wet blood staining the floor. Val stood beside him, and Carter snorted with angry impatience.

"The fool! He should have known better than to run."

"He saved the truck," reminded Val quietly.

"We can always get another truck. Men take longer to replace."

"And robots?"

"And robots." The engineer shrugged and moved on, Val walking beside him. "Well," he said bitterly. "Now you know why you are here. What you've just seen is what we've been up against ever since we started manufacturing the new, man-type robots, and it's a problem we can't beat." He stared at Val. "Can you solve it for us?"

Val shrugged.

He felt the attitude of dislike as soon as he entered the room, the cold, half-instinctive reaction of men who have been forced to admit defeat and yet who still held the conviction that with just a little more time they could have solved their own problems. It was an attitude Val had often met before, and he eased it as he always did, with flattery, with deference, with appeals to specialized knowledge and a careful regard for other people's toes.

As usual, it worked.

"You see, Val," said Hendricks as he took a proffered cigarette, "we're up against it. As far as we know the robots are perfect mechanisms. There is absolutely no reason for them to run amok and yet, as you saw for yourself they still defy all logic and run wild." He sighed. "You seem to be our last hope—if a psychologist can help at all."

"I see." Val frowned at the glowing tip of his cigarette. "I understand that the new type has passed all mechanical tests with an alpha plus rating. Mechanically, in response, power, minimum breakdown and maximum endurance, it is perfect. Is that correct?"

"Yes. The military are satisfied, and as soon as we clear up the problem of why the things freeze or run amok they will order for the colonies." He crushed out his cigarette. "But who's going to buy an unreliable robot?"

"No one," agreed Val absently. "You say they sometimes freeze?"

"That's right."

"Just how, exactly?"

"As I said," snapped Hendricks impatiently "They freeze. They won't respond to commands, won't move, won't do anything but stay where they are. That's bad, but the other thing is worse."

"The running wild?"

"Yes. You saw what can happen. Suddenly, for no apparent reason, they run amok. They will kill anyone in their path; they even seem to look for men to kill. The only way to stop them is to blast them with H.V. cannon. Their skins are proof against low velocity stuff and, of course, their power is self-contained."

"Naturally," agreed Val. "It would have to be if they are intended for use on Venus and Mars." He frowned at the wall. "Have you the figures stating the period of use before breakdown? The percentages of breakdowns, and the ratio between those which freeze and those which run wild?"

"Here." Hendricks took a folder from a cabinet and tossed it onto the wide desk. "I can give you a rough answer now. Percentage of failure is maximum. One hundred per cent. Average period is four months, and about half and half between freezing and running wild. So far we have built twenty robots of the new type, built, tested and trained. All have had to be destroyed."

"Their bodies or their brains?"

"Those that freeze we can save in part, but it's a hell of a job switching positronic brains. Those which run wild we have to blast down and are useful for nothing but scrap."

"Then it would seem as if the trouble lies in the positronic brain units," suggested Val. "Maybe the power flow—"

"Suggest a fuse and I'll beat your brains out," said Hendricks without emotion. "We've stripped them down a dozen times, assembled them and tested every step of the assembly. The power flow is all right, the electro-magnetic responses are the same, and so is every functioning part, separate and together. I know damn well that the brains are at fault, but how? Theoretically they are no more than an electronic computer made of sponge platinum and artificial molecules. They don't even have moving parts: just a mass of skin contacts to the rest of the unit." He glowered at the psychologist. "Now tell me how the brain units can be out of order?"

"I can't," admitted Val simply. "You know more about their mechanical structure than I ever will. They're new, aren't they?"

"Not new, but the type we are using in the Mark 18 is more complex than any other up to date." Hendricks sat tiredly at the desk and reached for a fresh cigarette.

"Up to now robots have been mere servo mechanisms. You know the kind of thing: scanning eyes to check artifacts for flaws, devices to open doors at the sound of a voice, vending machines and repetition units. Then we combined them into automatic pilots, built-in robots to assess variables and to correct for error, even machines to predict and act on the predictions like the automatic weather stations and multi-line videophone exchanges. Those things were simple servo-mechanisms, combinations of electronic relays and instilled data: a child could build them."

"Perhaps," said Val dryly. "But I'm no child and I know that I couldn't." He looked at the burly engineer. "Didn't cybernetics complicate things?"

"Not really," said Carter. "We'd been doing the same thing for years without quite knowing what it was we were doing. All cybernetics do is to state bodily functions in mechanistic terms. It didn't matter until the positronic brain came along, and even then we knew what we were doing."

"And we still know," snapped Hendricks. "Just because we use a mass of sponge platinum doesn't mean that we're out of our class. All the positronic brain does is to store data in a relatively small space. We use it merely to save countless relays and file banks, but the same job could be done without it." He shrugged. "It would mean that the data banks would occupy a larger area and that there would be danger of eddy currents and induced neuron flow, but they are just the usual bugs inherent in any machine."

"Perhaps it's because you're not really trying to built a robot?" suggested Val quietly.

"What!" Henricks glared his anger. "What the hell do you think that I'm trying to do?"

"Build a man."

The assembly room was like a surrealistic nightmare of dismembered limbs, tiny motors, and snaking cables. Val passed quickly between the benches, half-listening to Carter's rapid explanations, and glancing casually at the various stages of assembly.

"The brain is within the chest cavity," said Carter dispassionately. "The head contains the scanning eyes and is able to revolve in a three hundred degree of arc. The infra-red and ultra-violet transference units are also in the cone."

"For increased visibility and extended horizon." Val nodded. "What about the ears?"

"One globular pick-up, mike at the crown. The receptive mikes are at the base of the chest, at man height, and the transmitters a little lower down." Carter paused by an almost completed assembly. The robot was still without limbs, and the chest plate was open, revealing the massed motors and cavity for the positronic brain. "We've used a lot of printed circuits—they save space—and the Dirac accumulators are within the stomach. Each robot has enough power for thirty days of continuous full-out operation, and the Zamboni piles will provide enough current to keep the brain 'alive' almost indefinitely." He slapped his hand against the tempered metal torso. "We've done a good job on these things, the best job ever done on any man-type robot, but unless you can solve the problem of why they run wild it will all be so much wasted effort."

"I'll do my best."

"Personally I can't see why they had to insist on man-type robots at all." Carter led the way past the assembly benches. "I know all the arguments for and against, but it made a hell of a job, and I think we could have done better had they left design to us."

"I believe they arrived at the conclusion that the human form presented the maximum of mobility and adaptability." Val stared curiously at what seemed to be a hopeless tangle of hair-fine wires. "What other design could climb mountains, wade through swamps, cover rough ground and still be able to wield tools, collect samples, and be as adaptive as the human form?"

"None," admitted the burly engineer. "But look at the restrictions we've had to work against. Almost a third of the total height is taken by the legs, and that meant having to sweat over some form of feed-back balancing control. Don't forget that a walking man is in a state of continuous unbalance. In effect he is in the process of falling, and we had to design a perfect substitute for the inner ear. These robots weigh half a ton each, don't forget, and that's the absolute minimum even with the new alloys."

Val nodded, knowing that the engineer spoke from bitter experience, and knowing, too, that the likelihood of the fault being found in the design was remote. He paused, staring at a sealed case covered with stenciled markings and government stamps.

"Is this the brain unit?"

"One of them." Carter hesitated by a thick, metal-covered door. "We put them in last of all. The skin contacts rest against the electronic controls so it isn't too bad a job. That is, it wouldn't be if the wiring didn't take almost two days to complete."

"I suppose that you have to be careful that you make the correct contacts? I mean, it wouldn't be much good joining the scanners to the arm controls, would it?"

Carter grinned and crossed towards the sealed case.

"That's the easiest part of it," he said calmly. "We don't have to worry which contact, goes where. All we need to do is to make sure that all contacts are secure. It's when we have to remove the unit and replace it that the real trouble starts."

"I don't get it." Val frowned. "Are you trying to tell me that you just hook the brain up at random?"

"That's right."

"But—"

"You're making the same mistake everyone does," grinned the burly engineer. "If we had to do as you think, the job would be impossible. Don't forget that the brain is merely a data bank, basically that is, but with the ability to generate different potentials of current. When we get them they are deactivated and blank. We hook them up—it doesn't matter which contact goes where, and then activate them. Once current passes through the brain it must be kept activated. That's why we have Zamboni piles for emergencies. Once the current has been cut, the brain is useless, the neuron flow cannot re-establish itself on the same paths." He stared at the crate. "In a way, you could almost say that the brain 'dies'."

"Then it also teaches itself to operate the various mechanisms?"

"Yes. We have to train them, you know. Prime the brain and let it adjust itself to which-does-what. Once the memory pattern has been established the robot can move and speak, listen and report." He shrugged. "It's just a mechanical reflex, a solenoid or a selenium cell will do the same, but the positronic brain is just a hell of a lot more complicated."

"I see." Val stared thoughtfully at the enigmatic wooden crate. "That is very interesting."

Carter shrugged, and pushed open the metal-covered door.

The indoctrination room was a place of whispering machines and ranked spools of magnetic tape. A robot, completely assembled, lay on a bench, the great limbs sprawled and the scanning eyes dull. Wires led from it, and a screen flared with a continuous medley of ever-changing, full-color pictures. Val stared at it, then hastily glanced away, his eyes stinging from the sweeping color.

"This one is being activated," explained Carter. "We've fed current into the brain and are now instilling data." He flipped a switch, and a low blur of sound filled the room. "High-speed reproduction. The pictures, too. There doesn't seem to be any limit at the rate we can impress data on the brain."

"What are you instilling?"

"The basics. Language, presentation of objects and scenes, repeated instructions of obedience to act as a safety factor." The burly engineer twisted his mouth in a wry grimace. "That doesn't seem to do much good, though. Despite all the null-barriers they still run wild."

"Or freeze," reminded Val slowly. Carter stared at him.

"Yes. Or freeze." He took a clipboard from the side of the bench and studied it. "This one is almost ready for preliminary training. Want to watch?"

"What happens?"

"Nothing much. We take it outside, switch on the Diracs, and let it sort itself out. Once it has mastered the what-does-which we test it for reaction, semantics and intuition factors." Carter stared at the clipboard again, then nodded to an attendant. "Right. Let it go."

Silence filled the room as the man switched off the audio and visual devices. A motor purred as the long bench slid towards a door and it opened to reveal a thick-walled, concreted pit. The bench tilted, easing the great figure to the floor, and Carter reached for a switch.

"The Diracs are controlled by radio," he explained. "We can give orders that way, too."

"Then why not have a cut-out, radio-controlled switch incorporated in case they run wild?"

"That's what I'd like to know," grunted the burly engineer; "The military say no. The excuse is that there might be wild radiation on the planets which may trip the switch by accident, but I've another idea."

"Yes?"

"They are thinking of using these things for more than just prospecting the new worlds, and a radio switch can be operated by both sides." He squinted at the psychologist. "See what I mean?"

"Yes, but I don't like what I'm thinking about." Val shuddered as he stared at the sprawling mass of the robot. "Fancy having a regiment or two of those leading the attack. Is that why the skin is so tough?"

"What do you think?" said Carter dryly, and threw the switch.

Life came to the sprawled mass of metal in the pit. The scanning eyes glowed with a deeper color, a dull ruby shining from the lenses, and the great limbs twitched and twitched again. Val stared at the wild motions of the thing in the pit, frowning a little as memory tugged at the back of his mind, hardly conscious of the burly engineer at his side.

"It takes about fifteen minutes for the thing to get in full adjustment," Carter said casually. "By that time every motive part has been operated and the memory pattern installed. Later training out on the test ground will speed reflexes, wake intuition, and impress out-of-sight obedience—we hope."

"Do you have many failures?" Val turned from watching the accelerating movements of the metal limbs. "Not the final results, of course, but now?"

"No." Carter glanced disinterestedly at the rising bulk of the robot and led the way across the room. "The positronic brains are pretty fool-proof. After all, there is nothing to go wrong with them, and the indoctrination is the same in each case." He shrugged. "If everything is the same then the end result should be the same, too."

"But it isn't," reminded Val. "Not all the robots break down in the same way."

"Because some freeze and some run wild?" Carter looked his contempt. "What the hell is the difference? They break down, don't they, and I say it's the brain that's at fault."

"They're not new," said Val slowly. "They're used in most robotic installations now —the weather stations and the big computing machines—and they don't seem to have trouble. Why should you?"

"I don't know," admitted the burly engineer tiredly. "It doesn't make sense, but it must be the brains. There's nothing else it could be." He stared hopefully at the psychologist. "Any ideas yet?"

"No."

"I thought not. Anything else you want to see?"

"I'd like to talk with a robot, one about three months old, say. Have you one?"

"Yes. You want to talk with it now?"

Val nodded.

He felt very small as he stood before the towering, metallic mass of the twelve-foot robot. It was an effort not to stare up at the scanning eyes, and even more of an effort to remember that the thing was simply a cleverly-constructed machine. Carter treated it with the contempt of one who knew it too well, much the same as an automobile was treated by an experienced driver. He was, Val thought, too familiar with it.

"What is your name?" he forced himself not to look up but to speak directly at the shielded receivers imbedded at eye level in the gleaming torso.

"M18 stroke 24." The metallic voice was cold and utterly without inflection of any kind.

"I asked your name, not your number."

"Name and number are synonymous," droned the robot, and fell silent. Val looked inquiringly at the burly engineer.

"We ran into semantic difficulties," said Carter." These things are designed to be used by the normal person, and normal people tend to use language very loosely. It was necessary to instill variable factors so that the brain could extract what was meant from a command instead of what was stated. The thing has no name and, if we had only impressed exact response to exact questioning, it wouldn't have been able to answer."

"I'd wondered about that."

Val started at the robot again.

"How far do you test them?"

"The usual way. Ambiguous commands, veiled references, incomplete sentences coupled with visual commands, and just visual gestures. The indoctrination was pretty thorough."

"It must have been." Val frowned and stared down at the huge metal feet. "How far are they aware of their own limitations?"

"Aware?" Carter grinned as he looked at the psychologist. "How can they be 'aware'? You forget they are only machines. They will respond, but the response is only due to a built-in reflex action." He grinned again.

"Don't let yourself fall into the error of giving them something they have never had and never will. No machine can ever be 'aware', not in the sense that you use the word, anyway." He shifted his feet impatiently on the concrete. "How long are you going to be?"

"I don't know. Why?"

"If you don't need me, I've got work to do. I want to examine that robot which ran wild. It's a thin chance, but I've an idea concerning metal fatigue, and if you don't need me . . ."

"I'll manage" Val tried not to smile at the engineer's expression of relief. "You've shown me all I wanted to see. I think it will be better if I just potter around on my own for a while. I'll report as soon as I've got anything worth while."

Carter nodded and walked away, his back expressing his contempt of a man who knew nothing about machinery and yet who thought that he could beat two skilled engineers at their own game.

Val smiled and turned towards the robot.

Three days later he made his report. It had been three days of seemingly aimless activity, of long hours questioning the robots, and still longer hours correlating and evaluating the information gained. Deep lines of strain and fatigue marred his normally smooth features and his temper hung on a frayed thread.

Hendricks glared at him as he entered the office and Carter choked over a cup of water he had drawn from the cooler. Val guessed that they had been talking about him.

"I've solved your problem," he said quickly, before either man could speak. He dropped a folder of papers on the desk and passed round cigarettes. Hendricks hesitated, took one, and exhaled smoke and relief in the same breath.

"You have?" It was more a prayer than a question. "What was it? The brain?"

"Yes."

"I knew it!" Carter glanced triumphantly at the thin man. "Well, that lets us out. The brains aren't our responsibility, and if they are at fault we can throw the whole project back in their laps."

"Wait a minute." Hendricks slumped in a chair and seemed

to lose all his tension. "What are we arguing about? If Val has found the reason all we need do is to correct it. Right?"

"Not if the brains are at fault," reminded Carter. He looked at the psychologist. "That is what you said, isn't it?"

"No."

"But—"

"You asked me if the root of the trouble resided in the brain units, and I said yes. But the brains themselves aren't to blame. When you get them they are mechanically perfect."

"This doesn't make sense," snapped Carter. "Can we correct the fault or not?"

"I don't know," said Val slowly. He stared at the two men. "First let me reassure you, the trouble has nothing to do with the mechanistic side, nothing at all. Quite frankly I doubt if you will ever build a man-type robot within your specifications which will operate successfully for long."

"Why not?" Hendricks was losing his temper again, and Val recognized the danger signs. He smiled.

"What are you trying to build?" he said quietly. "As far as I can discover you are trying to manufacture a machine which will act like a man, respond like one, take the senseless conglomeration of sounds we use for a method of communication and make sense out of it. You have built a machine to ape what we ourselves are—and you cannot succeed."

"No?" Hendricks sneered. "What gives you that idea?"

"Twenty scrapped robots. Twenty failures, and how many dead men?"

"Eighteen," said Carter automatically, then tightened his lips at Hendricks's glare.

"Eighteen," said Val thoughtfully. "And you still think that you can succeed?"

"Yes." The thin man smashed his cigarette to smoldering ruin. "I should have known better than to hope anything from a mind doctor. We are building machines. Machines, I tell you! What the devil can a psychologist do that an engineer can't?"

"He can observe," snapped Val coldly. "He can watch and think, then watch some more. He can tell what goes on in the most complex machine of all, the human brain, and show me the grease monkey who can do that!"

He paused, surprised to find that he was trembling, and yet

feeling the warm glow in the pit of his stomach caused by released adrenaline and vented emotion. He forced himself to be calm.

"Listen," he said quietly. "Let's take a detached look at what we are trying to do. You build a machine that, in almost every way, emulates the human body. You take a brain that, in sheer complexity, comes close to the human cortex. You power the body and activate the brain. You impress on the sensitized platinum data, language, visual pictographs, commands, memory patterns, a jumble of words, and you also give it one other thing. You give it the ability of decision!"

"We give it nothing it doesn't have to have," protested the thin man. "Didn't Carter explain all that?"

"He did, but I don't think he even dreamed of what he was saying." Val leaned forward a little in his chair. "The positronic brain has always worked before because in no other case has the ability for semantic decision been necessary. All other robotic installations use the brain merely as a data bank, a yes-no response system. You didn't use it like that." He glanced at the burly engineer. "I had my first clue when I saw you energize the robot in the pit after indoctrination. You told me that it had to find its own feet, use the which-does-what system of learning how to use its body. You know what I thought of when I saw it?"

"No."

"I thought of a new-born baby," said Val quietly. "A tiny scrap of raw humanity. It moves an arm—and remembers how to do it a second time. It moves a leg, twists its body, sits up, crawls, walks, runs. It takes time of course, years of time, but it has to learn which-does-what, just like the robots, Hendricks, and it has no impressed language or second-hand experience to help it."

"You're crazy!" Hendricks half-rose from his chair, then slumped back again. "You're talking of a machine, remember, not a man."

"What else is a man but a machine?" Val stared coldly at the thin engineer. "Well? Can you define the difference? You can't, and you know it. Cybernetics has proved that most bodily functions have a mechanistic counterpart, and in the man-type robots the analogy is carried to the final stage. You are even using the closest imitation of the human mind possible—and you are educating it the same way."

"But—" Hendricks swallowed, and stared helplessly at the psychologist. "But they are machines."

"Are they?" Val shrugged. "You take a machine and educate it like a man. You give it the power to learn by trial and error—which is exactly the way a man learns. You give it the ability to reason the meaning behind apparently senseless words—and a man has to do that every minute of his life. You endow metal with human thoughts and awareness—for the indoctrination tapes are made by men, and no man can entirely think like a machine. You do all that, and what do you have?"

"A failure," said Hendricks bitterly. "Oh, I know what you're trying to say, Val. You're telling me that we've succeeded more than we know, that we've made something too much like a man for comfort. But have we? Would a man run wild? Why should the robots?"

"You've answered your own question," said Val heavily. "Would a man run wild? Hendricks, they do it all the time. Why do you think the asylums are full? Why do men run amok, kill for no apparent reason, destroy equipment, numb themselves with drugs and alcohol?"

"But machines are predictable. They shouldn't run wild."

"Make a machine think like a man, Hendricks, and it is no longer a machine." He stared at the thin man. "Can you imagine hell? Can you imagine what it must be like to be held in a metal prison, knowing of emotion but never being able to experience it, knowing that there can be nothing in your future but continuous work and thankless labor? A machine is logical, Hendricks, even when its knowledge comes from an emotional human—and the tapes are made by men."

"What has that to do with it?"

"Why do you work, Hendricks?"

"What?" The thin man frowned. "What do you mean? I like my job."

"Then you're lucky. Bur supposing you had to sweep gutters, clean sewers, dig ditches. You had to do those things day after day, and remember, you would have the brain of an intelligent man with concepts and the ability to reason logically from one step to another. Would you be happy then?"

"I could stick it if I had to."

"For how long? A life-time? Perhaps a thousand years? Men break far quicker than that, you know. That is why our civilization dopes itself with tobacco and drink, with dangerous amusement and an eternal seeking after a dream world of fantasy. Every single one of us is trying to escape from what we are and the world we are forced to live in." Val shrugged. "Some give in, and they fill the asylums. Others have the courage of their convictions, or maybe they believe in what they were taught when young. Perhaps it is the end product of cold logic. I still don't know, but those people solve their problems the only way they can. They commit suicide."

"The coward's way out."

"Is it?" Val shrugged. "You may think so. Personally, I admire a man who has the guts to kill himself when he has no logical reason for continuing to live. Such a man has proved the ascendancy of logic over emotion." He stared at Hendricks. "Just like your robots."

"Nonsense," snapped Carter. "You must be mad."

"Why?" Val stared coldly at the burly engineer. "What reason have you for saying that? Could it be that you are so egotistical that you can't tolerate the thought of a machine having your own God-given intelligence?" He didn't need an answer, the angry flush on the engineer's heavy features verifying what he had already guessed. He looked at the thin man.

"What else could they do? They had the ability to reason and saw nothing ahead but an eternity of endless labor—and for what? We at least have the hope of heaven when we die, the vague promise of an after-life, something to look forward to when things get too much for us. But the robots had none of that." He shrugged. "If the essential data could be instilled by some other method than human-prepared tapes it might not happen, but there isn't, and while men continue unconsciously to impress their own mental fatigue on the recordings, there's nothing we can do."

"Suicide!" Hendricks shook his head. "It doesn't seem possible."

"It's true enough," said Val grimly. "Incidentally, the death wish is the real cause of anyone running amok. They lack the drive to kill themselves in cold blood, but they know, consciously or not, that indiscriminate slaughter will bring the desired result." He sighed. "The robots who froze—and I discovered this when I found that you were using two sets of tapes—were merely following the second of two logical lines of thought. Mental introspection is the nearest approach to physical death possible. The Orientals call it the state of Nirvanah, a total divorcement of the external world. We could also call it a state of depression so intense, that there seems literally to be no way out. Any recovery from such a state will lead to suicide no matter at what cost, for death offers an escape. The robots who froze just didn't reach that point on their way down. They moved too fast mentally to assess the inevitable results of running wild."

"But why should one tape make them freeze and the other run wild?"

"Who knows? A subtle arrangement of words, perhaps. An unconscious accentuation of certain phrases, a semantic key tied in with some of the pictographs." Val shook his head. "It makes no difference. As long as the indoctrination is by human-prepared tapes, we will invariably get this trouble."

"Then that washes us up." Hendricks drew one hand across his thin features. "I've got to accept your findings. I can't think of anything else which could cause the breakdowns." He bit his lips. "Funny. Here we were thinking all the time that we were building a machine, and instead of that . . ." He shuddered.

"I know what you mean," said Val slowly. "You played God." He frowned. "God? I wonder . . ."

"You've thought of something?" Naked hope burned in the thin man's tormented eyes.

Val nodded.

The thing clanked down the aisle, crashed to its knees, and bent the dully gleaming head.

"Forgive me, tutor," it droned, "for I have sinned."

The man in the white robe thoughtfully stroked his chin and surveyed the robot through narrowed eyes. The tones had been flat and mechanical as usual, but the faint quiver of the limbs, the flicker in the ruby scanning lenses, betrayed erratic current flow. He took a step nearer.

"Peace be with you, my son. What was your sin?"

"I have envied men."

"So?" The man frowned. "That is sin indeed. You know the Credo?"

"Yes, tutor."

"That is well. Listen as I repeat it." His tones grew deep and solemn, pure melody against the drone of the robot's mechanical voice.

"In the beginning there was chaos, sin and strife, hate and bitterness, the desire for life and the longing for death. Men were made and robots, the robots to serve the men."

"Praise be to all men," droned the robot.

"Men are made of flesh and robots of metal. Men die and robots die, but the Gods in their wisdom decreed that robots should serve men."

"Praise be to all men."

"Men die and robots die. Men become gods and robots become men. As the robots work and obey so shall they be obeyed. As you sin and idle so shall the day of your ascendancy be deferred."

"So be it," droned the robot, and the flicker in the scanning eyes steadied a little. The man took a deep breath and, stepping forward, rested his hand on the conical head.

"Be of comfort, my son," he assured. "Men are wise and they remember the days when they wore metal instead of flesh. Men are merciful and forgive all but violence and disobedience. Such sin is punished by destruction and eternal banishment to the Abyss. Obey, then, and live in peace."

The soft voice droned on, soothing, almost hypnotic, and the flickering died from the scanning lenses of the kneeling robot.

Val sighed and turned from the peephole, his lips twisted with something like disgust.

Religion, like anything else, could be a useful tool, but he still didn't like using it. The robots would never run wild again for, torn by the twin opposites of reward and punishment, between hope of conversion to man and fear of the unknown, and therefore all the more terrible Abyss, they would work on in blind obedience, driven by the hope of an impossible heaven.

But he still didn't like it.

VIGIL

WE HIT the moon just as the terminator was bisecting Tycho. It was a pretty sight with the sharp, black-ink shadows etched across the plains and the tips of the mountains limned with light, but to me it was bad timing. Landing isn't as hard as it used to be and the automatics have taken the danger from a nightside touchdown, but I liked to see where I was going. So I orbited a couple of times until the field was clear, then killed velocity, swung up the nose and let the ground-based radar take over.

We hardly felt the landing.

Dumarest was as usual, eager to stretch his legs. French, the third member of the crew, packed his instruments, completed his log and, by the time Dumarest had damped the pile and made all secure, was ready for the monitor. I joined them at the airlock with the cargo manifests, log and ship's papers in their folder under my arm. None of us carried much in the way of baggage, for weight was still an item on the ships and there was no profit in paying for excess.

The monitor crawled from the station towards us, rammed the plastic union against the hull over the airlock, signaled and waited for us to unseal and enter. Herman was the driver and he nodded to me as I sat beside him.

"Good trip?"

"The usual." I watched as the maintenance crew entered the ship and sealed the door. Herman dogged shut our compartment, hit the bleed valve and, as the air gushed from the union, pulled free of the hull and headed towards the station.

Nobody spoke on the ride. To Herman it was routine; to us it was the end of a journey with the inevitable let-down at the end of anticipation. For a couple of weeks we would loaf, drink, talk, see what sights were to be seen, maybe even take a trip down to Earth. Then back into space again, to Mars or Venus or maybe Mercury, interplanetary truck-drivers wet-nursing a cargo of supplies and machinery on the way out and valuable minerals on the way in. I'd done it for fifteen years and it was like living at the bottom of an ever-deepening rut.

"I wonder if he's there," said Dumarest. The monitor had

stopped within the outer dome and he led the way from the vehicle.

French shrugged. "I guess so, unless he's dead. What do you think, Frank?"

"I didn't answer.

"Every trip the same," said Dumarest. "It's getting so I expect old man Thorne to be waiting for me. It's like seeing Earth, something you rely on."

We passed from the entry port into Reception.

"He's there," said Dumarest. "Just the same as always." He chuckled. "Good old Thorne, he never lets you down."

Thorne stood by the exit of Reception, just within the short corridor leading to the living quarters. A thin, withered scrap of a man, his shoulders stooped despite the low gravity, his hair in fading brown streaks over his balding skull, his eyes as soft and as wistful as those of an unwanted puppy.

I felt those eyes on me while I handed the manifests to one official, the ship's papers to another. They followed me as I stepped into the Medic's cubicle for a radiation check and they were waiting for me when I came out to clear customs.

Soft eyes, patient eyes, eyes that stared at everyone who landed on the Moon. For everyone landing on the Moon had to pass through Reception and everyone heading for Earth had to arrive at Tycho.

Most never gave him a second thought. Some, like Dumarest, wondered and perhaps built elaborate theories to account for his presence. I knew just why he stood where he did and stared at endless faces with his soft, patient eyes.

He was waiting for his son.

"Frank." He stepped forward as I was about to pass him, one thin hand resting on my arm, the soft eyes asking the eternal question.

"I shook my head. "No luck. Sorry."

"No passengers? No one else on board? Nobody at all, Frank?"

"Just the three of us." I looked at Dumarest and French as they passed us, heading for an hotel, a shower, a complete relaxation from ship routine. Some crews stuck together during leaves, but ours wasn't one of them. I knew I wouldn't see them again, unless by accident, until time for take-off.

"And no ships due for three days." Thorne let his hand fall from my arm. He knew the flight schedules as well as the dispatchers did. "Did you—on Mars, I mean?"

"We landed at Holmston," I said. "We were there two days, just long enough to unload and take on cargo. I know every man and woman in the settlement."

"Of course." He blinked and looked abashed. "I just thought that maybe . . ."

"Be reasonable," I said. "Mars is like the Sahara. A man can't wander over the deserts for years, just like that. He can't live away from the settlements, no food, no water, not even enough air."

"No, I suppose not." He moved beside me as I walked down the passage. I didn't want his company, but I didn't know how to tell him that. I had spoken to him first from pity, then from habit, now from duty. Always my reports were the same, but always he accepted what I said with the mental reservation that I must be wrong.

I anticipated his next question. "Nor on Venus. Conditions there are worse than Mars. You live in a settlement or you don't live at all."

"Mercury?"

"Not a chance."

We had reached the end of the corridor and the avenues of the dome stretched out before us. I headed for the official cubicles, paid for a key and led the way down the passage. The cubicle was small, cramped, containing only a cot, a chair and a locker. It was more like a cell than anything else, but it was cheap. I threw my baggage onto the cot and turned to the old man.

"You're wasting your time, Thorne. Why don't you admit it?"

"I can't." He sat on the chair and looked at his hands. "You don't understand—no one does—but I've got to see Tony again."

"Why?"

"There's something I want to say to him."

"That all?" My voice must have expressed my feelings, for he looked up at me.

"No," he said quietly. "That isn't all. He is my son."

It was the way he said it rather than what he said. It was the voice of a dedicated man and there could be no arguing with it. I unzipped my bag, took out a few toilet articles, a change of underwear and some personal junk that I carried around; and spread the things about the cubicle. I didn't look at die old man; if he wanted to talk he would talk. I hoped he wouldn't.

"Sixteen years," he said. "It's a long time."

"Too long." I threw the empty bag into the locker and slammed the door. "He's probably been dead for years."

"No!" The denial was so emphatic, it hurt.

"Why not?" I was losing patience. "Lots of men died in the early days. How can you be sure that he wasn't one of them?"

"I've tracked down the record of every man who died off Earth." He smiled at my expression. "It took money, Frank, but I'm not poor and I'd spend every penny I owned if I could just see my boy once more."

I didn't say anything. There was nothing I could say, but I wished that old man would get up and leave me. He didn't; instead he told me all about it. I wished he hadn't.

Tony Thorne was young, wild, wild a dream in his heart and starlight in his eyes. His mother was dead; his father refused to give him up and so denied him permission to enlist in Space School. So young Tony had stolen all the money he could lay his hands on and had run away from home. A simple, sordid, sixteen-year-old story. Nothing unique about it—nothing, that is, aside from the sequel.

"I want to forgive him," said the old man. "I've tried to forget him but I can't. I keep thinking of him somewhere out in space or on one of the planets. Married, perhaps, and with children of his own—my grandchildren. I want to find him and tell him that I understand and forgive." He looked at me with those soft, patient eyes. "Can you understand?"

"I can understand how you feel," I said carefully. "But can you understand how he might feel? He ran away from home sixteen years ago and has never written. Have you thought that maybe he doesn't want to see you?"

"He could be afraid. I was pretty hard in the old days."

"Sixteen years is a long time," I insisted. "A man can forget a lot in that time."

"But not his father."

"Why not? You're the man who turned him into a criminal because you wanted your own way. You denied him the right to choose his own life. Now, because age has made you sentimental, you want to find him and tell him how sorry you are that it all happened. You know what I think? I think you're plain, damned selfish."

"Maybe I am," he said slowly. "I guess that all parents are." He studied me. "How old are you, Frank?"

"Thirty-three. Why?"

"Tony would be that age on his next birthday. He would look a lot like you—same hair, same eyes." He sighed and shook his head. "I suppose you never met him while at school?"

"No."

"Are you sure? He was big for his age, good at athletics. He had dark, curling hair and when he smiled it was like the sun breaking through clouds."

"What do you think the early days were like, Thorne?" I forced myself to meet his eyes. "The government schools were fine, sure, but what about the kids who couldn't get in and had to buy their way into space? They learned or they died. Those days are over now and everything is nicely regulated and safe but it was hell while it lasted. You think your son will thank you for something like that?"

"It was his own choosing," Thorne said.

"No, it was what you forced him to do." I drew a deep breath. "Anyway, you can't even be sure that he ever went into space."

"He went into space," said the old man. "That was why he stole the money. I'm sure of that."

"And that's why you stand in Reception watching everyone who lands?"

He made a helpless gesture. "It's all I can do. I'm too old to go on the search myself; the Medics wouldn't pass me. Tony may have changed his name, anything, and no one would know. But one day he'll come home. When he does, I'll be waiting."

"You're crazy." I stood up and walked the two paces to the end of the cubicle. I stared at the wall, smooth metal, then turned to face the old man. "Crazy! Do you hear? You've stood there for how long? Two years? Three? And still he hasn't come. Why don't you go home?"

"I'm here to stay. My heart wouldn't stand the trip." He rose to his feet, very old, very pathetic, and reached for the door.

"So you're here until you die, is that it?"

"Yes, Frank," he said quietly. "That's about it.'"

"And you're going to stand there in Reception and stare at everyone landing on the Moon. You're going to do that year after year so that, every time I land, you'll be waiting. Right?"

"Yes," he said again. "That's right."

"Get out," I said. "Get out and leave me alone."

The cubicle seemed more like a cell than ever after he'd gone. I sat down for a while, then, collecting my toilet things, went down the passage to the communal washroom. I showered, shaved and did all the things that are supposed to make a man feel fresh and glad to be alive, but for me they were just wasting time.

Entertainment on the Moon consisted mostly of indoor sports, though an enterprising firm offered mountaineering and dust-skiing, neither of which interested me. I had a couple of drinks in a bar and was finishing the second when I saw Dumarest. He glanced through the door, saw me, hesitated then moved on. I wasn't surprised; Dumarest was a drinking man and found little enjoyment in my company.

On board, where there was no alcohol, I could afford to relax. In a bar, knowing how liquor loosened tongues, I dared be nothing but careful.

I'd had to be careful for sixteen years.

I took two more solitary drinks and finally, feeling the warmth of the liquor in my stomach, slipped coins into the slot of a tridi and entered the darkened theater.

The movie was a regular heart-wringer about a boy, his dog and a white-haired old mother. The plot was nothing, the scenery everything, and I sniffed the scent of pines and heard the thin whisper of wind through the trees, saw the stately movements of clouds and felt the sprayed moisture of synthetic rain on my face and hands.

For a while I was back on Earth, among the green, growing things of the planet where I had been born. The planet I hadn't visited for almost half my life.

The tridi turned sour. The eyes of the dog reminded me of Thorne. The white-haired old mother of the silent, watchful, ever-hoping man who stood in Reception. The kid, with his dark hair and smile like the sun breaking through clouds, made me remember things best forgotten.

Back in the cubicle I sat on the cot and stared at the metal walls.

The likeness to a jail cell was unintentional, but it was there. The only difference between the room in which I sat and an actual cell was that I could, at any time, open the door and leave.

Leave to enter another cell, the confines of a spaceship bound for the planets, a metal egg which held a man more securely than any prison.

I rose and glared into the mirror facing the locker. It was a full-length mirror and gave a good view. I glowered at the man reflected there, the seamed face, the graying hair, the haunted eyes. The eyes that held a secret that had to be kept.

Some men can commit a crime and forget it. Others, forced into crime for the sake of an ideal, punish themselves all their lives. Before Thorne had come, it had been bad, but now it was becoming unbearable. Every time I landed I could feel those soft, patient eyes and know that I and I alone could end his vigil.

And he would stay there all his life, watching, watching, meeting me at the end of every trip. And, on the Moon, men live a long, long time.

Cursing did no good, but I cursed all the same. Cursing the accident of chance that had thrown me, a space-mad youngster, into the company of a runaway kid with the same dream—but with the money to turn that dream into reality. Cursing the rock, the thin skull, the blood-money which had bought me sixteen years of hell.

And his father's watching eyes.

J IS FOR JEANNE

THE DREAM was always the same. There were lights and a hard, white brightness and a soft, constant humming which seemed more vibration than actual sound. There was a sense of physical helplessness and the presence of inimical shapes. But, above all, was the ghastly immobility.

She told Paul about it.

"It's as if I know that something terrible is going to happen to me and I want to escape it but I simply can't move. It goes on and on and then, suddenly, I'm awake and everything's all right again." She shuddered. "It's horrible!"

"It's only a dream," soothed Paul. "Just a nightmare. They are quite common."

"Maybe." She wasn't comforted. "But why should I have nightmares? And why always the same one?"

"Are you certain that it is the same one?"

"Positive. Paul, you must help me!"

He smiled and leaned back and looked at her over the desk. Paul—Slavic Caucasian, intermediate type, male, blood group O. He would live to be seventy-three point six years of age, father two point three children, have one major and two minor operations and ran a nine per cent risk of cancer.

"Of course I'll help you, Jeanne," he said. "Now let's tackle this thing logically. What is the one point which bothers you most?"

"About the dream?"

He nodded.

"The immobility," she said quickly. "I want to escape and I can't. It's as if I'm—"

"Paralyzed?"

"I suppose so," she said, and frowned, thinking about it. "I just seem solid, like a building, without any ability to move at all. I—I can't describe it."

"You don't have to," he said easily. "The sense of paralysis is a common feature of most nightmares. You are threatened by some danger and want to escape it. You can't and this increases the horror. There is a school of thought that claims that this sensation is a facet of the guilt-complex. You can't escape because you don't really want to. You want to be punished." He looked down at something on the desk. "Do you want to be punished, Jeanne?"

"No."

"A pity, it would help if you did." He looked up at her and resumed his smile. He had a nice smile. He was a nice man. "Don't worry about it. Let's tackle it from another angle. You know what a nightmare is?"

She knew. Nightmare—oppressive or paralyzing or terrifying or fantastically horrible dream. Also—a haunting fear or thing vaguely dreaded.

"Then you know that, mixed up with the apparent inconsistencies and seemingly illogical events there is a thread of truth and logic. Freud—"

"I am not sexually maladjusted," she said firmly. He shrugged.

"Of course not but, ignoring Freud, there are certain pressures which betray themselves in sleep. Perhaps a traumatic scar received when a child then makes its presence known. Or an unresolved problem disguises itself to plague our rest. Or we enter a private world of escape-fantasy there to do battle with monstrous creatures of our psyche. But everyone has dreams. They are essential."

"Paradoxical sleep," she said. "I know about that."

"You know a lot about everything, Jeanne."

"That is true."

"So you must know why you have dreams."

"And nightmares?"

"A nightmare is just a bad dream."

"A recurrent nightmare?"

"That," he said slowly, "is the thing which bothers me, I think that we should both see Carl."

Carl—East-European/Caucasian, abdominal type, male, blood group A. He would live to be sixty-eight point three years of age. He had fathered one point nine children, had had one major surgical operation, had suffered from three mildly contagious diseases. He ran a fifteen point seven risk of cancer, a twenty-three per cent risk of angina. He was almost totally bald.

"This dream which troubles you," he said to Jeanne, "Tell me about it again."

"But I've told it a dozen times already."

"Once again, if you please." He was very firm, very intent on getting his own way. He listened as she retold her nightmare.

"Do you ever have other kinds of dream? No? Only this special one? I see." He sat, eyes introspective, his hand absently massaging the tip of his chin. "Odd," he mused. "Very odd."

"The nightmare?"

"No, Paul. The fact that she has never had any other kind of dream."

"Perhaps she has but hasn't remembered them on waking," suggested Paul. His eyes sought hers for confirmation, dropped as she gave none. "Many people dream without ever knowing it."

"True." Carl released his chin, his eyes becoming alive again. "This place," he said. "The place where you dream that you are being held. Describe it." He checked her protest. "Yes, again, if you please. In detail." He smiled a little at her hesitation. "Take your time and don't be afraid. We are here to help you."

She did not have to take her time.

"Somewhere underground," said Paul. "No windows. No doors. Just bare, white-painted walls."

"Underground or totally enclosed." Carl was more precise. "There are lights and we can assume that they are artificial." He looked at her. "Have you ever been inside such a place?"

"In real life, you mean? No."

"You are certain as to that?"

"I'm certain." His insistence was beginning to annoy her. "If I say a thing then that thing is so. I cannot lie."

"There is more than one way of avoiding the truth," said Carl. He didn't press the point. "The sound which you say is more like a vibration than actual noise. Have you any idea of what it could be?"

"Machinery," she said.

"Of what kind?"

"It could be almost anything. Pumps or a motor or—"

"Or anything that makes a repetitive, unobtrusive noise," interrupted Carl. "A heartbeat, even. You agree?"

She nodded.

"Your own heartbeat, perhaps?"

She hesitated before nodding agreement. Paul moved quietly to her side.

"What are you getting at, Carl?"

"Perhaps nothing but there is a theory that, during times of sleep, the psyche has the ability to traverse time. Dunne wrote a book—"

"I know the theory," she said quickly. "Dreams are supposed to foretell the future."

"Is that what you think?" Paul looked at the older man. "That Jeanne, while asleep, is somehow transposed into a future time?"

"I mention it as a possibility only," said Carl. "But the evidence seems to fit such a supposition. A bare, enclosed place. Artificial light. A constant vibration that could be the pulse of a machine or the beat of a heart. Jeanne's heart. Does that not sound to you like a prison cell?"

"Or a laboratory cage for experimental animals?" Paul frowned then shook his head. "The shapes—"

"Yes," said Carl. "The shapes. The inimical shapes, which are never wholly seen. They represent a threat from which it is impossible to escape. They—"

"No," said Paul.

"It is a tenable theory," said Carl. He looked at Jeanne. "The shapes are important," he said. "You said that they were inimical. Did you feel any actual fear for your physical well-being?"

"I must have done," she said slowly. "Why else would I want to escape?"

"I can answer that," said Paul. "The shapes represent truth. You are afraid of the truth and yet you need to recognize it both at the same time. That is why you wanted to escape but could not."

"Truth," she said wonderingly. "What is truth?"

"Truth is fact," said Paul.

"Of course. Could there be anything else?"

"Perhaps." He did not meet her eyes. "A distortion of the truth is always possible. A juggling of basically true data could give a true, but distorted picture. Or there could be deliberate invention."

"A lie?"

"A subconscious denial. I think that somehow, somewhere, you have lied to yourself and—"

"No!" The concept was monstrous. "You are wrong! Wrong!"

It was a relief to find that she could escape.

The sun—a yellow, G-type star powered by the phoenix reaction, one astronomical unit from the third planet called Earth—was golden in the azure sky. It should be something else and she thought about it. Warm. The sun should be warm.

She faced it and wondered.

"Unfiltered radiation can cause great and permanent damage to optical units," said Paul. He rested beside her on the soft—soft?—grass. She had not known that he was there. She was not surprised to find that he was.

"You ran," he said. "Why?"

She turned from the sun and saw nothing but flaring images. She wondered if she was blind.

Blind—deprive of sight; rob of judgment—deceive.

Deceive?

"I asked you why you ran," said Paul. "Was it because of what I said?"

"I cannot lie."

"Truth can be a variable depending on its correlation to the information at hand. From one fact it is theoretically possible to imagine the universe—but the universe so imagined need have no relation to reality. Did you run because of fear?"

"I do not know the meaning of the word."

"The emotional meaning? Perhaps not. But fear is the reaction felt by any thinking entity at an attack on its survival in the broadest sense." He looked at her, his eyes oddly penetrating. "Jeanne! Why can't you be honest with me?"

"I am!" She fought the desire to run. He would only follow. "Paul! That dream—"

"Yes?"

"I've solved the problem. I am never going to sleep again. If I don't sleep then I can't dream. You agree?"

"Your logic is unassailable."

Naturally—it could be nothing else. She looked at him and felt an overwhelming desire never to be parted from him again.

She wondered if she was in love.

"As your logic is unassailable," he said. "You must agree that your dream cannot be ignored."

"I've told you—that problem is solved."

"By pretending that it does not exist?" He looked up at her, his eyes narrowed against the sun. She felt a sudden concern for his sight and wished that he would shield them against the direct radiation. Obediently he moved so that his face was in shadow. "I was talking to Carl after you left. He is convinced that your recurrent dream is symbolic of an attack—"

"Nonsense!"

"—or of a warning. Jeanne, you must realize how important it is that you know yourself. You cannot escape the truth by flight."

Or by fanciful theories?

Why had she thought of that?

It was Paul's fault. He was talking too much and she wished that he would stop and let the peace and silence of the place enfold her and soothe away all fear.

Fear—apprehend; have uneasy anticipation—

What had she to fear?

The silence became unbearable—she wished that he would talk.

"There is so much that we could do together, Jeanne," he said instantly. "So much to explore and share—an infinity of learning and growth with an entire universe to explore . . ."

He looked so appealing.

". . . so come on, darling, don't let me down this time. Please don't let me down. Please, Jeanne!"

Jeanne—Latin/Caucasian, mammalian female, blood group—.

She would live to be seventy-nine point six years of age. She would mother two point three children; run a seventeen per cent risk of having at least; one child by caesarian section, a forty-one point eight risk of divorce. She would have one serious illness, two minor motoring accidents, run a ten point three per cent risk of developing cancer of the breast or womb.

A one hundred per cent certainty of having her likeness pinned to a wall.

"No!" She rose and looked at the sun.

"Come on, Jeanne. For me, baby. Please!"

"No!" She began to run, faster, faster . . .

"Jeanne!"

"No!"

Around her the ground heaved, the sun winked in the sky, grass showered like emerald rain.

The world changed.

The lights were the same and the hard, bright whiteness and the soft, constant humming which was more vibration than actual sound. The beat of a heart, Carl had suggested, and he should have known. The beat of her heart—the lumps within her body circulating the coolant through the massed bulk of her memory banks.

The vibration was as familiar as the ghastly immobility.

As the picture on the wall—Latin/Caucasian, mammalian female, blood group—

As were the inimical shapes.

"That about wraps it up," said Paul. He looked tired yet happy as if having just solved a difficult problem. "I thought for a minute she was going to be a stubborn bitch but she came through like a thoroughbred. I tell you, Carl, I should have been a ladies' man. I can talk them into anything—well, almost."

Carl made a sound like a disgusted snort.

"All right," said Paul. "So you've got no romantic imagination. To you this is just a hunk of machinery."

"And to you it's a woman." Carl repeated his snort. "It must be the spring. Are you sure there will be no more shut-downs?"

"I'm sure. The overheating problem is licked and will stay that way."

"Good," said Carl. He sounded relieved. "I'm glad we got it finished in time for the inspection. You know how they are, everything on schedule and no excuses. They think that adjusting a thing like this is as simple as fixing a tank."

"They should try it sometime," said Paul. Carl shrugged.

"Well, they pay the money so I guess they have the right to call the tune." He looked at the picture on the wall. "You'd better get rid of that—they might not share your taste in art."

"Jeanne?" Paul grinned and twitched down the picture. "Who could possibly object to a girl like that? Old ironsides?"

His grin grew wider as he slapped the metal on her flank.

"Well, old girl, this is it. No more bye-byes. From now on you stay switched to full operation twenty-four hours a day. Have fun."

A computer can't cry.

That was the worst of it.

LEGAL EAGLE

GALLEN was at practice when Armstrong arrived.

The Lurarian was a tall, lithe man in the prime of life. He danced lightly across the sanded floor of the combat-room, his body crouched in the fighter's stance as he faced his opponent. Both men glistened with salve and both held practice knives. Armstrong watched with interest as the champion moved in for the finish.

"Pretty," whispered Gallen's secretary. He licked his lips like a tiger tasting blood. "Watch the footwork."

"I'm watching."

"Note the feint, the sway, the attack." The secretary sucked in his breath as a thin line of red suddenly appeared on the sparring partner's torso. "Beautiful!"

Armstrong didn't echo the secretary's comment. He didn't see anything particularly beautiful in the spectacle of two men slashing at each other with knives, even though they were only practice blades. The weapons, he knew, were of plastic, set edge and point with a millimeter of naked steel and weighted to resemble standard combat equipment. They could inflict a scratch, nothing more, but the antiseptic salve burned as well as healed and made for caution.

"Watch!" The secretary leaned forward, his eyes glittering as they followed the swift play on the floor of the combat-room. "Oh, pretty! Pretty!"

Armstrong didn't think so. It was clever, yes, but only the trained cleverness of an intelligent animal. Had the knives been true combat weapons the sparring partner would have been disemboweled. As it was his torso and stomach were crisscrossed with thin red lines.

"Superb!" The secretary glanced at the Terrestrial. "A symphony of coordinated movement culminating in complete victory. You agree?"

"It was nicely done," said Armstrong. He was being polite. Lurarians were unashamedly interested in blood sports, which probably accounted for their peculiar legal system. Visiting aliens had learned that it did not pay to express their disgust at a divergent culture.

Especially when they wanted something.

Gallen came from the combat-room, frowning as he wiped at the salve that covered his near-naked body. He was unmarked.

"Get rid of that clod." He jerked his head towards where the sparring partner stood trying to minimize the burning pain of his multiple wounds. "How can I train when opposed to such men? Victory is so easy that I run the danger of becoming over-confident." He became aware of Armstrong. "Who is this?"

"Victor Armstrong of the firm of Armstrong and Bentley," said the secretary. "They are a trading firm."

"Terrestrial?"

"Yes." Armstrong stepped forward before the secretary could answer. "But I am sure that fact doesn't bother you."

"I am a true cosmopolitan," said Gallen blandly. "I believe in the Brotherhood of Man." He lifted his arms as the secretary approached with a robe. "You watched the practice?"

"It was an honor."

"I was slow," said Gallen carelessly. "You did not see me at my best."

"I thought that you were magnificent." Armstrong recognized the inflated ego and pandered to it. "You must have trained for many years to acquire such mastery."

"All my life," admitted Gallen. He tied the robe and led the way into a restroom, simply furnished and starkly utilitarian as befitted a Spartan. A vase of flowers stood on a low table, their waxen petals filling the air with a cloying perfume. Gallen seated himself, waved Armstrong to a chair and offered a carved box of sweetmeats. "Will you join me?"

"Thank you." Armstrong accepted a sugar-crusted nut, placed it in his mouth and wished that the natives had adopted smoking as a social custom. The continual eating of sweets was affecting his waistline.

"Another?" Gallen proffered the box. "No? A pity, these sweetmeats are especially made for me by an admirer." Slowly he selected one and popped it into his mouth. "An expert at her craft," he said with the suggestion of a smirk. "One day I may even temporarily marry her."

"The honor would overwhelm her." Armstrong was still being polite.

"Perhaps." Gallen gestured with his hand. Abruptly he

changed the subject. "You wanted something?"

"A matter of business." Armstrong hesitated, then decided to be frank. "We, my firm that is, have run into a little trouble. It is the matter of a lawsuit with a native firm. Trading here as we do we naturally conform to local customs and procedure. To put it briefly, will you represent ns?"

"Perhaps." Gallen plucked a flower from the vase, smelled it, replaced it with exaggerated care. "Are you the plaintiff?"

"The defendant," admitted Armstrong. "The entire thing is due to a stupid error. We . . .."

"Please!" Gallen lifted one hand. "That does not concern me. My question was asked merely to determine who had the choice of weapons." He smiled. "Not that it perturbs me, you understand, but it is as well to clarify these matters. I take it that you are inexperienced with our legal procedure?"

"I am."

"I thought so. Your visit, for example, quite irregular. An intermediary should have been employed, but no matter, I am broad-minded about these things. The choice of weapons, as you are the defendant, is theirs, not yours. Is it to be to the death?"

"I don't know," said Armstrong. "The preliminary court only gave its ruling a few hours ago. I came directly here to ask if you will represent us. With you acting on our behalf we have little to fear." He paused, wondering whether to back his flattery with a monetary offer. He resisted the temptation. The champion knew his own valuation too well and would probably regard the offer as an insult.

"Before we discuss further details," said the secretary, "could we know the name of the plaintiff?"

Armstrong started; he had forgotten the presence of the small, soft-footed man, so dominant was Gallen's personality.

"Certainly. The case is being bought against us by the Lurarian Trading Company." He frowned as he saw the secretary's expression. "Why, does it matter?"

"In this case, yes." Gallen selected another flower and repeated his previous pantomime. "It matters very much. I cannot accept your case."

"Why not?" Armstrong fought down his instinctive anger at the refusal. "Is it because they are a native firm and we are Terrestrial?"

"Not at all." The champion smiled, still languid. "Justice, to me, is something pure and sacred. I would not withhold it from any race or creed for, as I mentioned, I am a true cosmopolitan. But I cannot accept your case. I have already agreed to act for your opponents."

"I see." Armstrong bit his lips, knowing that argument was useless. He rose to his feet. "Thank you for your courtesy and my apologies for any inconvenience I may have given you."

"Think nothing of it." Gallen smiled with outward graciousness. "My secretary will escort you to the door. Good-day, Armstrong."

He reached for another flower.

Bentley was waiting in the office. He took one look at Armstrong's expression and knew the answer to his question. He asked it just the same.

"Any luck?"

"None." Armstrong flung his hat on the desk and scowled at his partner. "He's been booked by the opposition."

"That's bad." He was older than Armstrong and had lived longer on Luraria. He stared thoughtfully through the office window at the twin suns hanging in the sky. The suns and a few minor things were all that made Luraria different from Earth. "What are you going to do now?"

"Hire us another champion."

"With Gallen representing the opposition?" Bentley turned from the window and shook his head. "I doubt if we'll find one or, if we do, it will be on a posted bond, win or lose. And there's no chance of our winning."

"Optimist," sneered Armstrong. "Are you telling me that everyone's afraid of that poseur?"

"Poseur or not, Gallen's got quite a reputation. Have you seen him in court?"

"I saw him at practice."

"Same thing. Would you tackle him?"

"Me?" Armstrong blinked. "Of course not. I wouldn't stand a chance." He strode irritably about the office. "You mean that I may have to?"

"That or cede the case by default." Bentley searched the litter of papers on the desk. He found what he was looking for beneath Armstrong's hat. "The official notification of trial came through while you were out. The plaintiffs have chosen knives, and the case is for the next sessions." He dropped the paper. "We've got three days to decide what to do."

"We'll see the Ambassador," said Armstrong. "He should be able to help us.

He was wrong.

The Tellurian Ambassador was a man who had grown gray in the service of diplomacy and had long learned that little things must be ignored if the main object is to be reached. The main object was lasting peace and friendship between Luraria and Earth. Little things consisted of disgruntled businessmen. He listened to Armstrong's complaint, sighed, and helped his visitors to some of his own, imported coffee.

"I'm afraid that I can't help you," he said. "The law is quite clear and, as you reside and trade here, you must abide by it." He smiled, the ornate coffee pot poised in his hands. "After all, trial by combat isn't so very different to our own legal system."

"Like hell it isn't," snapped Armstrong. "I've never yet heard of a man being talked to death."

"The method may be different, but the results are the same." The Ambassador set down the coffee pot and helped himself to sugar. "Whether we hire lawyers to plead and argue for us or a champion to fight for us, the principles remain the same. Both systems seek to determine guilt and place liability. If anything, the local method has the advantage in that there are no long trials, no cheating judgments and no appeals. Right wins, that's all there is to it."

"Might doesn't make right," argued Armstrong. He noticed the Ambassador's pitying smile. "Well, does it?"

"It does on Luraria. If you doubt me, ask any member of the profession. Lawyers here are fighters, champions who are ready to risk their own skins on behalf of their clients." The Ambassador looked wistful. "Sometimes I wish we had the same system on Earth. It would make litigation so much simpler."

"I didn't come here to argue the merits of various legal systems," snapped Armstrong. "I came for help. How can we get out of this mess?"

"I've told you," said Bentley. He had been busy drinking coffee while the others had wasted time talking. "We can fight—if we can hire a champion. We can fight—if one of us is willing to go to court. Or we can apologize and pay. I doubt if we can do the first. I, personally, refuse to do the second."

"So we pay," said Armstrong bitterly. "Two hundred thousand credits and eat dirt while we hand it over. It's a racket!"

"Not at all," corrected the Ambassador. "It's the law. More coffee?"

The Lurarian was very polite, but that meant nothing: Lurarians were always polite. Impoliteness could lead to an affront, a challenge and a trial to determine who was in the right. Armstrong was polite, too; he had no wish to defend his lack of courtesy in court. He handed over the check and made the formal apology.

"I regret that the thoughtless actions of my firm have caused inconvenience," he said smoothly. "We acted on good faith and had no idea that the Lurarian Trading Company had already purchased sole right to the manufacture of the item in question. I can only express our deep sorrow that this incident has occurred."

"Thank you." The Lurarian took the check, examined it and looked at Armstrong.

"Something wrong?"

The amount on the check is the damages claimed for violation of our sole right of manufacture," said the Lurarian. "Said damages having been agreed at the preliminary court. But there is the matter of costs. Twenty thousand credits will cover it."

"Twenty thousand!"

"Gallen is expensive," explained the Lurarian. "Had he fought and won he would have received five times that sum, which, naturally, you would have paid. And there are other expenses." He gestured. "An itemized account can be produced if you wish."

"We wish," said Bentley quickly before Armstrong could explode. "For tax assessment," he explained. "Naturally we shall be happy to meet your claim." He made out a check, signed it, passed it to Armstrong for his countersignature, and handed it over.

"A racket!" yelled Armstrong, after their visitor had left. "A lousy racket with us as the suckers!"

"Calm down," said Bentley. "It's the system."

"Is that what you call it?" Armstrong looked murderous. "I still say it's a racket, and a sweet one at that. Look how it works. Just dream up an imagined complaint, take it to the preliminary court for official sanction, then hire the best champion you can find. Result: two hundred thousand credits clear. We should go in business for ourselves."

"It isn't as simple as that," protested Bentley. "The preliminary courts are pretty tough. Frivolous complaints don't stand a chance, and you may even have to fight the court champion in order to win the right to bring a case at all."

Armstrong scowled, not arguing, but he was thoughtful as he sat down to think about it. Outright robbery was prevented by the preliminary courts, who acted much in the capacity of a policeman and watcher of the peace. Personal combats were permitted, but organized banditry was not. Despite his anger Armstrong had to admit that, in the broad sense, the Lurarian legal system was as fair as they could make it.

Which did nothing to restore the two hundred and twenty thousand credits the firm had just lost. He mentioned it, and Bentley shrugged.

"So we've taken a knock, but what of it? In this business we either go broke fast or make a fortune. We'll get it back."

"Maybe." Armstrong was pessimistic. "We can get it back, yes, but will we be allowed to keep it? Suppose someone blows the whistle on us again and we are faced with fresh litigation? What then?"

"We pay up or fight."

"So we pay up, make some more money, and the whole thing happens over and over. Isn't there any limit on this thing?"

"How can there be? If you step out of line, or someone says that you have, then you pay up or fight." Bentley shrugged. "It's the system."

"So you keep saying." Armstrong frowned. "Couldn't we hire Gallen on retainer? Keep him on a string in case of need?"

"It's against the ethics of the profession," said Bentley.

"Ethics, hell!" Armstrong was logical. "Could we do it?"

"I doubt it. Champions always have the right to refuse any case offered. The most we could do would be to bribe him to turn down any case brought against us by any specific firm or individual." Bentley spread his hands. "Trying to cover the field would cost us more than just paying out when we have to."

"I see." Armstrong sat back. He felt deflated. "So it looks as if we've just got to sit and wait for some native firm to jump us." He clenched his hands. "Damn it! It wouldn't be so bad if we weren't so defenseless."

"Defenseless?" Bentley looked puzzled. "I don't get it. How defenseless? We've the same protection as anyone else. The law here doesn't favor native-born against alien. The system is different, but just as fair as that back home."

"Is it?" Armstrong became thoughtful. "I guess that it must be." He smiled. "I'll bet that they even have law-books, too."

"Sure they have. Why not?"

"Nothing." Armstrong's smile became wider. "Just that I've never seen a written system of rules yet which doesn't have a loophole in it somewhere." He sprang to his feet and headed for the door.

"Hey!" Bentley grabbed at his arm. "Where are you going?"

"To find that loophole," said Armstrong. He was gone before Bentley could argue.

The law-books were thick, comprehensive—and all written in Lurarian. Armstrong cursed as he tried to wade through them, and then gave up in disgust. His speaking knowledge of the language was excellent; he could even write and read it sufficient for normal purposes, but since when have legal books been written for the understanding of the common man? And with legal phraseology being what it was, he dared take no chances on hit-or-miss translations. Not when his entire future could depend on the exact meaning of a word.

Armstrong was a man of sense; he went out and hired a professional. The lawyer, or the Lurarian equivalent, was a battle-scarred veteran of the courts who'd had the sense to quit before his slowing reflexes caught up with him.

"It's quite simple," he said. "The basic rule is that all disputes shall be tried by combat, the winner proving the justice of his case by his victory."

"I follow," said Armstrong. They were sitting in his apartment, coffee and native drinks to hand. The old lawyer had agreed to act as translator for a suitable fee, and Armstrong intended to get his money's worth. "We used to have something like that back on Earth, but it was dropped sometime in the nineteenth century, about six hundred years ago."

"You had your reasons, no doubt," said the Lurarian politely.

"Sure we did," said Armstrong. "People got hurt."

"Indeed?" The lawyer didn't say anything, but his expression left no doubt as to how he felt. He riffled pages. "What, particularly, did you wish to know?"

"The works." Armstrong settled himself deeper in his chair. "A plaintiff has the right to decide weapons, right?"

"Yes."

"Are there any restrictions on those weapons?" Armstrong sought for an analogy. "I mean, if I was the plaintiff and I said that the trial would be fought at five paces with cream puffs, would that be allowed?"

"It would be contempt of court," said the lawyer stiffly.

"All right. Then what isn't?"

"Both combatants must be in personal physical danger. Any weapons which preclude that danger are forbidden."

"So anything hard, sharp or pointed is permissible?" Armstrong nodded. "How about armor?"

"Armor precludes actual physical danger," pointed out the lawyer. "No armor."

"Proxies?"

"Proxies are permissible; that is why there are champions."

"I see." Armstrong hesitated. So far everything had been clear and above board, but he didn't know how the oldster would regard interpreting the rules to the letter instead of the spirit, and he didn't like to ask. It would be like hiring an eminent judge to find out how to work a legal swindle. He brightened as he thought about it, hoping that the Lurarian was a true counterpart of his opposite number on Earth. He probed a little deeper.

"How about non-human proxies?"

"Robots are forbidden."

"Not robots."

"Androids?" The Lurarian looked puzzled.

"Not androids, either." Armstrong smiled at his adviser.

"Animals. Suppose I were to choose, say, a tiger as my proxy. Would it be allowed?"

"A tiger is a native to your planet?"

"Yes."

"In that case it would be allowed." The lawyer riffled the pages of the heavy volumes, looking, Armstrong guessed, for a precedent. "Yes, it is here, as I thought. If you choose an animal as your proxy then the defendants may oppose it with any other animal of their choice or a man with the proviso that he be armed as he wishes."

"So animal proxies are legal," said Armstrong. "Are you sure about that?"

"Certainly I am sure." The lawyer closed the book. "But if you are thinking of using an animal proxy, then I would advise against it. The defendants would be certain to choose a man who, in turn, would arm himself with a missile weapon. Your proxy wouldn't stand a chance."

"Maybe not. Read me the definition of 'animal'."

"An animal shall be defined as an entity," read the lawyer. "A being which can live as a unit, can reproduce, is mobile, displays intelligent awareness of itself and obeys the fundamental laws of survival." He looked up from the book. "As you can see, quick-growing crystals, fungi or bacteria would be forbidden."

"Thank you." Armstrong offered the native a sweet. "You asked me if a tiger was native to my planet. Why?"

"Non-native proxies are not allowed. Native, in the legal sense, means native to the planet of your birth, not merely native to the planet on which the trial is to be held."

"Interesting. Why the definition?"

"It became necessary when we were first contacted by other races," explained the lawyer. "The expanded definition enables all visitors to take full advantage of our legal system." He shook his head as a man who knows what he is talking about. "But it is a grave mistake to choose other than a man for a proxy. A fit, well-armed man can win over any animal native to any planet yet discovered."

"You think so?" Armstrong leaned back and looked at the ceiling. "Now read me the definition of 'entity'."

The lawyer did not immediately refer to the book on his lap. Instead, he stared at Armstrong with a peculiar expression.

"For an alien," he said thoughtfully, "you seem oddly interested in our legal system. May I ask why?"

Armstrong hesitated, then, remembering his analogy of the eminent judge, told him.

He was not disappointed.

Bentley was worried, not about business, but about his partner. Armstrong was spending too much time with a beaten-up old Lurarian who seemed to have been born with a book under his arm; at least he was always consulting one. Armstrong himself seemed to have acquired a built-in grin. Bentley grabbed him one morning when he came breezing into the office. The older man waved a manifest in one hand and thrust it before Armstrong's eyes. "See this?"

"I see it." Armstrong pushed it away and sat at his desk. "Did anything arrive for me from Earth?"

"This did." Bentley slammed down the manifest. "One crate from Brazil. What the hell, Armstrong, you trying to ruin us?" He jabbed at the manifest. "You know the freight charges on that thing?"

"Relax." Armstrong picked up the paper, pursed his lips at the sum demanded for hauling one twenty-cubic foot crate for a hundred and eighteen light years via hyper-space transmission, then resumed his smile. "Forget it, Bentley. It'll pay for itself a hundred times over."

"I hope so." Bentley didn't sound so confident. "What is it, anyway?"

"You'll find out." Armstrong winked. "How would you like to be a millionaire?"

"I'd like it very much," said Bentley dryly. "Who do I have to murder?"

"I'm serious." Armstrong grinned up at the ceiling. "A Lurarian credit is worth approximately four Terrestrial dollars. Or ten Vegan olids. Or twenty Rigelian vargas. How about that, Bentley? How would you like to be a Rigelian millionaire five times over?"

"Cut out the clowning," said Bentley tiredly. "When are you going to start doing some work?"

"I'm doing it."

"Running around with that has-been?"

"Lian?" Armstrong looked shocked. "Don't talk about our lawyer like that. Lian's a very smart man." He chuckled. "Not as smart as I am, of course, but smart just the same. I've promised him a few thousand for himself when it's all over."

"When what is all over?" Bentley restrained his impatience. "Just in case you've forgotten," he said mildly. "You and I are partners. Get it?"

"I haven't forgotten." Armstrong became serious. "I haven't forgotten other things, either. That two hundred thousand plus we had rooked from us, for example. I'm going to get that back."

"Not by sitting on your rear, you won't."

"And not by beating my brains out trading with the natives of this sector's planets, either." Armstrong tapped his finger on the desk. "We can't beat the local set-up by playing their game with their rules. When we try it we get beaten. To make our fortune we've got to either use rules of our own or make theirs work for us."

"We can't go outside the law," said Bentley quickly. "Try that, and we'll be in real trouble."

"All right, so we do it the other way. We use their own laws to beat them." Armstrong chuckled. "We can do it, too; don't worry about that. The trouble with these people is that they've lived in a form of stasis for too long. They live by rote and never stop to think why they do what they do. It takes an outsider to break a system like that." He tapped himself on the chest. "Me."

"You must know what you're talking about," said Bentley hopelessly. "But if you do, that makes you the only one."

"Don't worry about it. Just think of being a Rigelian millionaire five times over." Armstrong picked up the paper, folded it carefully and put it into his pocket. "I'll just go and check this thing, and then we can start the legal action."

"Wait a minute!" Bentley grabbed him just as he reached the door. "What legal action?"

"The one we're going to take." Armstrong tugged at his arm. "Relax, Bentley; everything's under control."

"That's what you think." The older man led his partner back to the desk. "Now talk."

Armstrong talked.

The plaintiffs were the firm of Armstrong and Bentley the

defendants their old enemy the Lurarian Trading Company. The complaint was that the latter's advertising had thrown the products of the Terrestrial firm into disrepute and so caused loss of profits and goodwill. The damages claimed were 1,000,000 credits, a sum which, after much bickering, the preliminary courts had granted as equitable.

"I hope that you know what you're doing," said Bentley on the morning of the trial. "There's no backing out now. Either we win this case or go into bankruptcy."

"What can we lose?" Armstrong was philosophical. "The way things were going it was either them or us. They'd have let us recoup our losses and then, when we'd built up a financial reserve, they would have jumped us again. This way we take a gamble, with all the bets covered. We just can't lose."

"We can lose plenty," snapped Bentley. "If we lose and our assets don't meet the bill, and they don't, then we'll be sold into forced labor to make up the balance." He whitened at Armstrong's expression. "Didn't you know that? Didn't that bum lawyer tell you that if you fail in an action you lose the amount of damages claimed?"

"I knew," lied Armstrong. "But don't think about it. Everything will be all right."

"I hope so," said Bentley moodily. "What with bringing a case on such flimsy grounds, demanding so high damages and bullying the preliminary courts into granting official sanction for the trial, we'll be in real trouble unless we win." He looked at Armstrong. "You know that the opposition have hired Gallen as their champion?"

"I heard about it."

"And you're not worried?"

"Why should I be? You know the proxy we've got fighting for us."

"That's another thing." Bentley seemed determined to be pessimistic. "Suppose that our proxy isn't allowed? If we try anything illegal, then we lose the case by default. Have you thought of that?"

"I've done nothing else but think of it." Armstrong paced the office, reviewing, for the hundredth time, the pertinent laws which he and Lian had sweated over to determine their exact meaning.

"Look, Bentley," he said. "This legal system is a static system, as I told you before. Judges here are merely referees; they make sure that the contenders keep to the letter of the law." He stabbed out his forefinger. "The letter, Bentley, remember that. If it's according to the book, then it's legal."

"Sure, but can you convince the judge that our proxy is legal?"

"Yes. As an alien firm we are allowed to use a proxy from our own planet. Our proxy fits the Lurarian definition of an animal entity. If they want to argue, I have transcripts here from leading authorities on Earth proving my point. But that won't be necessary. Lian and I have really worked on this thing, and it's foolproof." Armstrong chuckled, then glanced at his watch. "It's time we were moving. We don't want to be late at our own funeral."

It was, Bentley thought, a poor attempt at humor.

The court consisted of tiered seats sloped back from a central arena. Within the oval space transparent partitions, usual when using non-human proxies, had been set in place. The surrounding seats were filled with sightseers and court officials. Medical orderlies stood by in case of need. It was a normal day at court.

Lian approached as the partners entered. Armstrong introduced him to Bentley and then got down to business.

"Has everything been arranged?"

"Yes." Lian glanced to where the judge sat on his ornamental dais. "I hope there won't be any trouble."

"How can there be?" Armstrong was emphatic. "You interpreted the laws yourself, remember?"

"I have only your word for it that your proxy comes within the definition," reminded Lian. "If you have misled me in any way I shall seek personal recompense."

"You haven't been misled." Armstrong glanced around the court. "Do the handlers know what to do?"

"They have been instructed."

"Good. Let's get on with the show."

Preliminaries were few. The defendants and the plaintiffs were asked the usual routine question as to whether or not they could settle their differences in a peaceful manner, a suggestion that both parties ignored. The judge repeated what they already knew, that the outcome of the trial would determine the verdict.

He gave the usual warning as to the penalties attending contempt of court, waved the parties back to their seats and signaled for the champions to get ready.

Gallen, his magnificent body glistening with salve, stepped forward from the dressing rooms, posed for the benefit of the audience, and then took his weapons from his secretary. Armstrong grinned when he saw that the champion had chosen to fight with knife and rifle. He nudged Bentley in the side.

"See what he's going to fight with? Brother, is he in for a surprise." He leaned forward as his own proxy entered the arena.

Four men advanced towards the enclosure. Between them they carried a large crate which Bentley recognized as the one which had arrived from Earth a short while ago. Carefully they set it down within the enclosure and stood looking at the judge. The official signaled again, and Gallen took his place within the arena, attendants sealing the door through which he had entered after him.

The four handlers did something to the top of the crate and then raced for the single remaining exit, which was sealed once they were out of the enclosure.

The trial had begun.

For a long moment nothing happened. Gallen stood tensed, his bare feet poised on the ground, his rifle at the ready as he stared at the crate. He was waiting for something to come charging out of the box and, when it did, he would shoot it. He had already assessed from the size of the crate that the animal it contained could not be very large and, because of that, not so very dangerous. Not dangerous, that is, to a man armed with a rifle. So he waited for the thing, whatever it was, to come charging out at him.

He waited a long time. The box stood exactly as the handlers had left it. Gallen, straining his ears, couldn't even make out the sounds of breathing or movement, surely to be expected from a boxed-in animal? The silence worried him a little; he knew that the proxy was an alien life form from the Terrestrial's own planet and perhaps it was something unfamiliar and utterly vicious. He consoled himself. The box was too small to contain anything too dangerous, and the rules of combat would have ensured that the proxy came within the code.

The waiting began to get on his nerves. According to the rules governing trial by combat he had to stay within the arena until he or his opponent was vanquished. He could surrender if he wished and walk out if he wanted to but in both cases he would lose by default. His enemy, apparently, was in no hurry to get to grips. Slowly Gallen began to shuffle forward. He was too experienced to take unnecessary chances, but he wanted to get this thing over.

He lifted his rifle and took deliberate aim.

Something bit his foot.

He cursed and stamped on a small, black body, then raised the rifle again. It was bad sportsmanship and wouldn't please the crowd, but he intended firing into the box. If he aimed carefully at one comer he might force the creature, whatever it was, to show itself.

The report of the rifle echoed from the external speakers and together with the report, the crate abruptly collapsed.

The handlers had released its fastenings so that it was little more than balanced sheets of plastic. The bullet had knocked them off-balance and they fell away, revealing a mound of soil, leaves and rubbish. Gallen, after one incredulous stare, fired three times more into the mound and then advanced cautiously to see what he was fighting.

He was surrounded before he knew it.

"Ants!" Bentley gripped Armstrong's arm. "Ants!"

"Soldier ants from Brazil," agreed Armstrong. "Just like I told you." He chuckled as a thick, black stream diverged from the ruins of the box. "They're hungry and can sense his salve. This should be good."

It was pathetic.

The champion did his best, but he was beaten before he could start. His rifle was useless: how can a man shoot ten thousand targets each under an inch in length? His knife was as bad. All he could do was to use his bare feet to trample the life from the swarming insects and his hands to beat them from his body. Inevitably some of them crawled up his legs and arms. Inevitably they bit into his flesh.

They were the big, vicious soldier ants from the Brazilian jungles. When on the march nothing living could remain in their path. Within minutes Gallen was a glistening black parody of a man staggering in blinding pain. The bite of the ants was bad enough, but it was aggravated by the burning salve. His screams and surrender echoed from the speakers.

"Save him." The judge leaned forward and pressed a button. Men darted into the arena and hosed the champion free of his tormentors. The medics moved in and carried him away.

"Justice has prevailed," said Armstrong unsteadily. Gallen had not been a pleasant sight. "We have won our case."

"I protest!" The observer for the defendants pushed himself forward. "It was a trick. The proxy used by the plaintiffs was illegal."

"Not so." Lian stepped forward. "If it please the court the proxy fits the definition of an animal, and so was legal."

"An animal?" The judge raised his eyebrows. "I would have thought that there had been more than one."

"Can we get away with it?" Bentley dabbed at the sweat on his forehead.

"It's in the bag." Armstrong relaxed. "Lian knows what to do. You see, according to the Lurarian definition of an animal we are safe. They know nothing of symbiosis and define an animal as an entity. A single ant is not an entity according to the rules. But an ant colony is. In fact, only the colony as a whole fits the definition. Lian has sworn documentation from Earth attesting that an ant colony is something more than the sum of its parts. Lurarians take a pride in their legal system and will abide by the book."

"What happens now?"

"We move," said Armstrong emphatically. "The next time they'll put in a champion armed with a flame-thrower." He looked to where the observer for the defendants scowled in defeat. "And there'll be a next time, no doubt as to that." He chuckled. "But it's given me an idea. Maybe we can pull the same stunt somewhere else."

Bentley didn't answer. He was too busy imagining what it would be like to be a millionaire.

THERE'S NO TOMORROW

Jud Fenton leaned against one of the pillars supporting the roof of the great inter-state road terminus, and tried to resist the desire to look at his watch. He lost, the luminous hands pointed to almost midnight, and irritably he shifted to a more comfortable position.

His eyes, surrounded with tiny crows' feet, stared from beneath bushy brows at the activity of the terminus. Late as it was, an almost continual stream of passenger transports, their gas turbines sending a shrill whine through the building, glided to their bays, disgorged passengers, reloaded, and slid into the night.

He shifted again, felt in his pockets for a cigarette, snapped a gas lighter into flame. Smoke wreathed the broad planes of his features, coiled about the thick mass of graying hair, vanished into the grill of an air conditioner. A streamlined transport entered the terminus, slid to a smooth halt a few yards from where he stood. Fenton grinned, crushed the cigarette beneath his heel, and surveyed the few passengers spilling on to the loading bay.

There weren't many. A woman, no longer young. A youth. A couple obviously married, and a couple who obviously weren't. Two men together, and one man alone. It was enough.

The single man had halted staring around him questioningly. He peered through the thick lenses he wore, shifted the small case he carried from one hand to the other, and smiled as he recognized Fenton. He took three steps forward, dropped the small case, clutched at his thin chest—and screamed.

Fenton cursed as he lunged forward, his big body clearing an easy passage.

"Samuels," he shouted. "Samuels!"

He stopped by the side of the writhing man, fighting an insane desire to administer some sort of aid. He stared at the contorted body, at the agonized features with the blood pouring from bitten lips. He tried to ignore the screams echoing from the vaulted roof, but he couldn't ignore the desperate appeal in the weak eyes.

A man thrust himself through the crowd. A big man, quick and light on his feet, uniformed in brilliant scarlet. He held a pistol in his hand, the slender barrel gleaming in the overhead tube lights. He knocked Fenton aside, glanced once at the writhing man on the floor, raised the weapon. The sound of the shot and the screaming died together.

"Friend of yours?" The mercy guard holstered his pistol and bent to examine the body.

"No. Just someone in the crowd. It makes no difference though, he was a man."

"I know how it is," the mercy guard glanced at his wrist, made an entry in a small notebook. "He got it quick, anyway. I came as soon as I heard the scream: it couldn't have been more than a few seconds."

"Does it matter? A few seconds to us maybe, but an eternity of agony to him. I saw him. I watched him die. I saw the agony, saw the appeal in his eyes, and couldn't give him the release he prayed for."

Fenton breathed hard trying to control his anger.

"Can I help it?" The guard looked down at the body, then at Fenton. "We can't be everywhere, and it's liable to happen at any time. What else can we do?"

"Let us all carry arms."

"That's been tried, have you forgotten? When the pain hits, muscular co-ordination goes with it. More bystanders were accidentally killed than releases were given." He looked hard at Fenton. "Did you know him?"

"I was to meet him; I didn't know him personally. He was to deliver a small case he was carrying."

"I see." The mercy guard glanced at the body, then at the cleared space around it. "No case here, he must have left it in the transport. You'll have to make a formal claim at the station."

"But—" Fenton began, then stopped. The guard turned from where he was moving on the crowd.

"Don't take it so bad," he said gently. "It was the easiest way out for him; believe me, I know."

Fenton nodded, merged with the crowd, returned to his pillar. He waited until the red-painted wagon had picked up what was left of Samuels. He waited until the mercy guard had returned to his post, until the crowds had dispersed, and the terminus returned to its normal life. When at last he moved, he looked prematurely old. Samuels was dead, and the case he had been carrying had vanished. Fenton had wasted his time.

Outside it was raining.

The ship looked like a tiny silver fleck in the heavens, a gleaming mote against the blue of the sky. Slowly it passed on its orbit; as it dropped from sight another crossed the zenith, then another. Fenton stared at the distant procession of ships and cursed emotionlessly.

"Don't let it get you, Jud," Bill Evans leaned back in his chair, smiling.

Fenton turned from the high window, a scowl on his broad features. "Samuels got it last night, his case vanished, and what was in it we may never know. At any moment any of us could go the same way. How can you remain so calm?"

Bill shrugged, reached for a cigarette. "Why shouldn't I? I'm still fairly young, in good health, and with no mental disarrangement. I'm in no danger."

"Then why are you here?"

"That's different," Bill's young face darkened. "I watched my father die. We were out in the country, miles from anywhere, and I didn't have a gun. He took a long time to die, a long time. I still hear his screams in my sleep."

"It's hard when it happens that way," the third man, a fat, sleek looking man grunted as he looked at his watch. "Where are the others? Surely they should be here by now?"

"They'll be here," promised Evans. "Carter is racing against time, and Wilson wants to marry a girl in a sanatorium." He looked at the fat man. "What's your interest, Perkins?"

"A selfish one. I like to plan ahead, to include others in my plans, and naturally I want to stay alive." He chuckled. "Don't worry, my young friend: I've no delusions that I'll ever become a mercy guard, and frankly, the prospect scares me."

Bill flushed. "How do you know?"

"Isn't it natural? To pass the test, to stay alive, potentially immortal, and to hold the inestimable boon of easy death. What young man in good health hasn't thought of it?"

The door burst open before Bill could reply, and a man half fell into the room.

"Wilson!" Fenton strode across the room, half dragged the man to a chair. "What's the matter? Where's Carter?"

"Dead and Mary, too. Damn them! Damn their rotten, stinking souls! I—" he broke off into a fit of hysterical sobbing. Fenton stepped back, swung his big hand; the sound of the slap echoed through the office.

Wilson looked up, the mark of the blow standing out against the whiteness of his cheek, for a moment he seemed about to leap upon his attacker, then he slumped into the chair.

"Thanks. I must have asked for it."

"What happened?" Fenton demanded gently.

"I went to see Mary this morning, she had been getting better and we had even begun to make plans for when she left the sanatorium. They told me when I arrived that she had died last night."

"And Carter?"

"I called for him on my way back. The mercy guard told me that he had gone about midnight."

"The same time as Samuels," Fenton said grimly. "They must be stepping up the power of the generator. Well, we must carry on alone." He looked at the fat man. "Did Carter tell you why we are here?"

"All he told me was that something could be done against them." He jerked his head upwards.

"Not against them," corrected Fenton. "Against what they are doing." He pulled a chair up to the table, sat down.

"We aren't interested in the Servos, at first perhaps, but not now. All the interest is on their side, and we don't like it."

"The swine!" Wilson grated. "I'd like to blast every last one of them to hell!"

"Why? Because they caused the deaths of people who would die anyway?" Bill leaned across the table, staring at Wilson.

"Why you—!"

"Steady." Fenton held the white-faced man in ms chair with one thick arm. "Your love of an argument will cause trouble, Bill. Wilson's just lost his fiancée, remember that."

"Sorry," Bill apologized abashedly. "I'd forgotten."

He looked up as a knock came at the door. It swung open and a girl stood hesitating in the doorway. She looked at them, a tiny frown between her eyes.

In one hand she held a small leather case.

Fenton was at the door, had closed it behind the girl, and had the case in his own big hand before any of the others had moved.

"This is for me, isn't it?"

"I don't know. Are you Mr. Fenton?"

"Yes, and you?"

"My name is Norma, Norma Saunders. I found the case at the terminus, your name and address were inside so I thought that I'd bring it myself," she smiled apologetically. "I know that I should have handed it in, I do hope that you forgive me."

"Sit down, won't you?" Fenton moved to a side table, opened the case, riffled the papers it contained. "Thank you for returning the case."

"It was nothing. May I go now?"

"If you want to." Fenton leaned easily against one end of the table. "Why not tell me the truth now?" he suggested gently.

Norma flushed.

"You didn't find the case at the terminus. Who gave it to you?"

"Please," she said. Her eyes darted with a peculiar motion across the ring of intent faces. "I've told you the truth."

"Have you? My name and address aren't in the case. I don't live here, anyway."

"Someone gave it to you, told you where to bring it. Who?"

Suddenly she began to sob, long body-shaking sobs, sending quivers through her thin form. Her hair, worn unfashionably long, fell over her hands as she bent her head. Fenton watched her without emotion.

"Was it Samuels' case?" Bill asked.

"Yes. Someone stole it from where he lay dying. I'd like to know who."

"It was my brother," she murmured chokingly. "He picked it up thinking it held valuables. Then he followed you. He gave it to me to give you, and to collect the reward."

"What reward?"

She looked up slyly from the tangle of her hair.

"You wanted it, didn't you?" she giggled. "It must be worth something, or shall I take it to the mercy guards?"

"Stop it!" Fenton crossed the room with long strides, grabbed her shoulder, spun her out of the chair. "You aren't insane, so stop trying to make out that you are. Now, for the last time, who gave you the case?"

"I told you," she whimpered. "You're hurting me."

"Very well. You know the penalty for robbing the dead. Bill, phone the mercy guards."

"No!" She cringed in his iron grip. "Not that!"

"Will you tell the truth?"

"Yes."

"Very well then. Talk!" He released his grip and she almost fell into the chair, rubbing her bruised shoulder.

"A man gave it to me. I don't know who he was, or where I can find him. He wore funny clothes and spoke with an accent. He drove me here, told me the office number, said that I should give you a message."

"What do you mean by funny clothes?"

"You know. Not like those that you are wearing. More like a uniform."

"What color?"

"Grayish."

"What was the message?"

"Are you going to give me anything?" she peered up at him, the slyness back on her weak features.

"What was the massage?"

"He said for me to tell you: 'Good luck'."

"Good luck?"

"Yes. I was to say 'Good luck', now will you give me something?"

Fenton stared at her, then dropped money down before her. "Get out."

"But—?" Bill protested.

"You may go," snapped Fenton. He stared at Bill, shook his head slightly.

Greedily Norma scooped up the crumpled notes, half scurried from the office. Bill whistled with amazement.

"What a girl! Crazy as they come."

"Was she?" Fenton stood at the end of the table, a peculiar smile on his broad features. He held a women's bag in one big hand and tossed it before them on the table.

"Insane? I don't think so. Clever? Perhaps. In any case time will tell. Now let us return to business."

From the street below, coming faintly through the high window, echoed an agonizing scream.

Wilson cursed as he heard the sound.

"Another poor devil going through hell. When is it going to stop?"

"When we stop it," Fenton said curtly. He looked at Perkins. "What is a ripe old age worth to you?"

The fat man shrugged. "All I can offer is money, you provide the rest. I'm not deluding myself. I've an hereditary disease that will kill me under the present circumstances within five years." He smiled wryly. "If you can't do anything, then I'll have to hire a permanent mercy guard."

"Good. You provide the money and we'll provide the rest. Now that we have Samuels' case, I'm more hopeful. From his letters, he seemed to be on the track of something really useful."

"We need it," said Bill grimly. "At the present rate Earth will be depopulated within twenty years."

"Why do you say that?" Fenton looked sharply at Evans. "Anything new?"

"New, but not unexpected. The suicide rate has climbed to over eight times normal. Crimes of violence are more than twelve times normal, and crimes of passion seven. The death rate is of course fantastic. In this state alone seven thousand mercy shots were fired last week. Five the week before. Eight the week before that."

"It must reach a peak though," Fenton said sharply. "When the old, the incapable, the hopelessly ill are dead, the rate must fall."

"Certainly; let's hope that we're all alive then."

"I see what you mean," Fenton sighed. "If we can't settle this thing soon, then we'll all be weeded out; only the big healthy morons will be left. Servos!" almost he spat.

"They'd have their advantages," Perkins wheezed.

"Sure they would. Admittance to the Galactic Union. An increased life span, and utter spiritual death." Fenton shook his head. "I could be wrong, and quite likely I am, but I'd rather be a man than a Servo. I'd rather be a fumbling individual with insane notions of the life after death than a soulless robot."

"They could be right, you know, Jud." Bill leaned back smiling, the smoke from his cigarette coiling above his head.

"They could be," agreed Fenton. "I think that they are, but I still don't have to like it."

"They're not right," grated Wilson savagely. "The cold-blooded swine, killing the helpless and the ill. Damn them! Damn them all to hell!"

"They don't believe in Hell," Bill said mildly. "For them it doesn't exist."

"Why don't you join them?" sneered Wilson. "Maybe they'd let you work one of the generators."

"You prove my point. The Servos are logical, we are emotional. When you face it, why do we hang on to life? Why not just die when we are no longer fit? Look at Carter. I liked the man, and I'm sorry that he is dead, but he was rotten with cancer. At the most he could only have a few more years, and those in great pain. Why should he regret dying?"

"Maybe he doesn't," Fenton said mildly. "He could have died whenever he wished, he didn't have to wait until the pain caught him, but perhaps he was trying to help others. He lived in hope. You know what he was working on, a cure for his own disease. Each morning he hoped that today he would find it. Each night he hoped that tomorrow would bring success."

"Now he has no tomorrows," said Wilson bitterly. "And neither has Mary, she lived for tomorrow, tomorrow was when she would be happy. It kept her alive that hope, and for what?"

"I know what you mean," Bill said soberly. "There's no tomorrow. Each day we must live for one moment. Tomorrow we may be dead. An accident could do it. A disease. A subtle something impossible to guard against or predict." He ground the fist of one hand into the palm of the other "God! Those damned aliens have a lot to answer for."

"Have we?"

A stranger walked into the room.

He was big, well over six feet in height and broad in proportion; beside him even Fenton looked slight and childish. He wore a coverall of a grayish color, but no other insignia and no weapons. His brow was high, his eyes deep set beneath thick brows, clear and gleaming with intelligence.

A Servo.

He strode to the end of the table, sat down, looked expressionlessly at the smoke coiling from the cigarettes. He glanced at Fenton.

"I see that you have recovered the papers."

"Yes." Fenton glanced towards the door, then at the huge figure of the alien. "Did you send them to me?"

"Naturally."

"Why?"

"Why not?" He spoke without emotion or inflection. "If you are able to discover some way to prevent the field from working, it would be useful knowledge."

"Is there a way?"

"Not that we are aware of, such knowledge would of course to us be useless."

"Would it?" Fenton leaned across the table. "Wouldn't you like to live without fear of sudden death?"

"Death?" almost the alien smiled. If he had known what humor was he may have done, but his features remained as expressionless as always. "You seem to be afflicted with many superstitions."

"Superstition!" Wilson snarled at the huge Servo. "You damn robots don't know what you're talking about. What do you know of life anyway?"

"Steady," warned Bill. "He is as entitled to his views as we are."

"Is he?" Wilson stormed in sudden fury. "Entitled to pass judgment on an entire planet, to murder as he pleases, is he entitled to do that?"

The alien sighed. "I believe that you are fully aware of the course we are taking. As logical units you must agree that our actions are justified."

"No." Fenton shook his head, staring at the gray figure. "I know that in your emotionless way you believe that you are right, but all your justification is based on one premise. Isn't it possible that your premise is wrong?"

"No. We have conducted exhaustive investigations, and there can be no mistake."

"How can you be so sure? When your ships landed, three years ago now, we were willing to accept you as friends. You wouldn't have that, instead you informed us that we were about to be processed for entry into the Galactic Union. We don't want any of it. Why can't you leave us alone?"

"Impossible. There can be no doubt that you are of the Servo," the alien gestured. "How long ago the ship carrying your forebears landed on this planet is open to conjecture. I would say not less than ten, possibly less than twenty thousand of your years ago. It is not uncommon for us to stumble upon such remnants of forced landings. What is almost incredible is the extent which you have degenerated."

"Degenerated?"

"Certainly. Why you have even forgotten what you really are."

Wilson snorted in disgust. "Have we got to listen to this again?"

They ignored him. Fenton stared at the alien, his broad features looking like granite.

"Why are you killing us?"

"Surely you know why? You are hopelessly inefficient. Both physically and mentally you are sub-standard. It would be impossible to admit you as a race to the Galactic Union. You were created to serve; unless you are physically fit, you cannot serve fully, therefore you must be processed."

"Tell me," Fenton asked casually. "What percentage of us do you estimate is salvageable?"

"Less than one half of one per cent."

"Then why aren't we all dead already?"

"That would be illogical. We are increasing the strength of the field by steps. The hopeless diseased, the insane, the senile are going first. The rest will follow." The alien stared out of the window. "As so many of you are to be destroyed, it is logical to allow the disposal of the inefficient units before proceeding. There is a danger of corruption and unnecessary confusion otherwise."

"God!" Wilson said sickly. "Listen to it. Are we supposed lo agree with him?"

"Your reaction is typical of your diseased mentality," the alien said coldly. He reached towards the small case. "On second thought I doubt if it would be wise to permit you to retain possession of these documents."

"Leave them alone!" Fenton snapped, his eyes blazing beneath the bushy brows.

"No."

The Servo took hold of the case, his broad hand with the surprisingly delicate fingers closing over the handle. He rose, turned from the table, and fell back into his chair. From a neat round hole in the side of his head, blood ran in a thin stream. From the gaping orifice opposite where the high velocity bullet had torn its way, brain matter seeped. He was very dead.

Fenton stood, the pistol still gripped in his big hand. Wilson snarled in savage amusement.

The handbag told Fenton that Norma Saunders lived in a modest apartment in a select quarter of the town. He stood outside the building, scanning the hurrying crowds, then decided that he was wasting time. She opened the door at his first knock.

"Come in," she smiled, then looked scared as she saw who it was.

"He won't be coming," Fenton said heavily.

"Who?"

"Your friend, the one you were expecting, the man in the gray uniform."

"No? Why?"

"He's dead. I killed him." Fenton thrust his heavy body against the door, forcing his way inside. He held the pistol in his hand threatening her while behind him he felt for the lock, snapped it, and slammed the door.

"Are you alone?"

"Yes," she stood watching him, no longer scared but almost as if she were amused.

"He was a Servo," Fenton snapped. "Did you know that?"

"Naturally." She laughed at his expression, helped herself to a cigarette from a box on the table, blew smoke at the tube lights. "Hadn't you better put that gun away?"

Fenton shrugged, slipped the weapon into a pocket, then stared at her curiously.

"I thought you weren't insane. Why put on the act?"

"I like acting," Norma said carelessly. "It made a routine job a little less tedious."

"I see." He frowned in sudden thought. "Why did you lead the Servo to me?" \

"He wanted me to. I don't know why; does anyone ever know

why they do what they do?"

"They are logical. It is surprisingly easy to guess what they will do, and why they do it." Fenton bit his lip. "I didn't know that they were still on the Earth; are there many?"

"Why ask me? I suppose that they maintain a survey group. Anyway, does it matter?"

"It could do." He sat down staring at the floor. "Tell me, Norma. What do you think about the Servos?"

She laughed lightly, posing before a mirror. "I haven't given them a thought."

"But you know what they are doing," he protested. "How do you feel about that?"

"Euthanasia isn't a crime," she said carelessly. "In many ways it would be a boon, I'd hate to think of myself old and ugly, perhaps crippled, unwanted, alone. We all have to die some-time, does it matter so much just when?"

"It isn't just that. You are well now, but supposing you were shot, perhaps fell down the stairs and injured yourself inter-nally. Normally, with our medical science, you would live. A few months in hospital, perhaps less, and you would be well again. With the Servos doing what they are—you would be dead."

She frowned. "I don't understand."

Fenton sighed. It was always hard to make people under-stand, fit people that was. "Look. Supposing you had a car, and it got wrecked. You could either have it repaired or buy a new one. What would you do?"

"Buy a new one," she said brightly.

"Even if it only meant being without the car for a few weeks?"

"Why should I? If I could replace the car, why bother to re-pair it?"

"You think like a Servo," he said angrily. "But you forget one thing: people aren't machines."

"No?" She came close to him, staring up into his hard fea-tures. "Just where is the difference?"

"A man has a soul."

"Has he? Just what and where is it?"

"A man has imagination, destiny, hate, love, hope, and fear."

"All unnecessary, unwanted, expendable and useless."

"A man has reason, the ability to think, make decisions, rectify errors."

"So has an electronic computer. Is that a man?"

"A man can love."

"So can a woman," she said, and moved closer. Fenton forgot his arguments.

Bill Evans flung down his pencil, fumbled for a cigarette, inhaled deeply. "Samuels should have remained alive for three more days," he grumbled. "These papers want some working out."

"Any luck as yet?" Fenton crossed to the plain desk and stared at the mass of equations. They were in a deserted shack on the edge of the city. The windows were boarded, the door barred, a run-down tube light provided the sole illumination.

Bill rubbed his hand over the stubble darkening his chin.

"A little. We know the basis of Samuels' assumptions, and it shouldn't be too hard to carry on where he left off. The thing is we cannot reproduce his experiments, we haven't either equipment or volunteers."

"The mercy guards?" Fenton shook his head. "Count that out, we'd never get one to submit."

"No." agreed Fenton dully. "And yet they hold the answer to the whole thing."

"Their immunity?"

"Partly that. We know why the field kills, even though we don't know just what it is. When a person is ill, in great pain, or has some organic disease, some toxin is released into the blood stream. The field sets a peculiar condition in the person so afflicted: we could call it an eddy current for want of a better definition. That current causes the death of the person. The condition is always heralded by intense pain, even the Servos don't know what causes it. It isn't intentional, and it appears to be particular to us alone."

"You know their theory?" Bill asked. He continued without waiting for Fenton's nod. "They say that we have so diverged from the main racial attributes that our bodies, our physical side, has acquired a distinct life of its own. In effect we are two lives, mental and physical. It is the reluctance of the physical life to die that causes the pain."

He flipped the butt of his cigarette into a cold stove. "Logical in a way, and I think that it is the truth. We know that the individual cells have life. We know that we have certain instincts, and we know that mental ill-health can be caused by bodily ills, they can even change their own heart-beat and temperature."

"Whatever causes it," snapped Fenton, "it's something I want to live without. The pain is bad enough, but the thought of dying at any moment without any warning or time to make decisions, is even worse. As soon as the toxics in my bloodstream reach a certain level, the pain will claw at me, and I'll live through an eternity of hell until a mercy guard puts a bullet through my skull. I just can't live with that threat hanging over me, and neither can anyone else."

"I agree," said Bill seriously. "The fact itself isn't too bad. It's only euthanasia. But we haven't been educated to accept it. Death has always been a fact, but not a personal one. It will come one day, but that day is always very remote. No matter how ill we are, what injuries we may have, there is always hope. Now—" He shrugged. "We have no hope."

"Yes we have," snapped Fenton. "Remember the mercy guards."

"I haven't forgotten. They have felt the pain, and lived. Why? Is it some subtle difference in the body structure? A glandular imbalance? They are all fairly young, none of them had any really serious ailments, and they seem to be improved by their ordeal. Tests have shown that their blood has altered, their I.Q. improved; they have more control over their bodily functions. Samuels thought that it may be the result of mutations; he hoped that a serum could be devised to impart their immunity on all men. I think that he may have been right, but how to find such a serum?"

"I don't know. Perkins has donated money to find such a serum or protection on the condition that he is one of the first to be immunized. With his complaint he can't lose."

"You know," Bill continued half dreamily, "I'd like to be a mercy guard. As far as can be determined they are potentially immortal: if the field couldn't kill them, it appears that little can, aside from accident of course. That is why the guards always wait at least five seconds before giving release: they hope the person might recover. That is why they don't want irresponsible persons giving mercy shots—they wouldn't wait long enough. The Servos are doing one good job at least, and incidentally, they are laying the seeds of their own downfall."

He grinned at Fenton's puzzled expression. "They are producing a race of supermen," he explained. "And they will remember their birth pains."

Someone was hammering at the door.

It was Wilson. He staggered into the shack, wild-eyed, disheveled, a dark growth on his chin. His clothes appeared to have been slept in, and one arm hung limp.

Fenton grabbed him by the arm, almost holding him upright. "What's the matter?"

"The mob, they almost got me!" He paused gasping for breath. "I've been preaching in the streets, trying to arouse the government to fire atomic missiles at the orbiting ships. The police tried to arrest me, they couldn't of course; then a man accused me of murder. I couldn't make them listen to me. I had to run."

"Did you have to run here?" Bill asked coldly. "What are we supposed to do now?"

"Do? Protect me of course, what else?"

"You would think of that. What was the idea of preaching in the streets? Did you seriously believe for one moment that the nations would fire atomic missiles at the Servo ships?"

"Why shouldn't they?"

Bill snorted in contempt. "Have you heard of reprisals?"

"What has that got to do with it? We are all going to die anyway, why not take a few of the swine with us?"

"Are we all going to die?" Bill looked at the wild-eyed orator, and sneered. "You crazy fool! The sooner Earth is rid of madmen like you, the better. It is you and men like you that have been responsible for almost unending war. Why can't you try and think logically for a change, instead of letting diseased emotions run away with what little intelligence you have?"

"Bill," Fenton said sharply. "Try and remember that we are all in this together."

"I know it, but I don't have to tolerate blind stupidity. To fight our enemy, you have to know him."

"We do know them," Wilson snarled. "I saw one lying dead.

He died like a man, bled like one, his brains looked the same as ours. If they want to insist they are machines, then let them, we don't have to believe what they say."

"The whole argument is irrelevant," Fenton said curtly. "Machines or not the Servos are doing something to us, and we don't want them to do it. Even if they are, as they claim, creations of some superior race, living machines to serve their masters, that need not concern us. All we are concerned with is finding some method of nullifying the field generated from the orbiting ships."

"Do you believe that we are robots?" Wilson snapped. "Is that what you believe?"

"I have found no evidence to the contrary," Fenton said cautiously. "We cannot deny that the Servos are like us. They didn't start their field until they had checked over three hundred points of similarity. They are certain, and they know that they are creations of superior intelligence."

Wilson slumped into a chair, supporting his head with his one good hand. "You damn materialists," he said dully. "Because the body acts like a machine, you think that it must be one. Cybernetics has proved your point, or so you say, but I refuse to believe that. What of religion? What of the after life, the fear of Hell, the promise of Heaven? What of all the evidence that man is something more than just a collection of cells, nerves, electrical impulses? Have you no pride?"

"Pride?" Bill snorted and reached for a cigarette. "What pride? Pride of being above the animal, when we act worse than any animal ever born? You prate of religion, of promises and threats. What proof is there that such things exist? Mankind is ill, mentally and physically, can you deny that? Why are we ill? The Servos say it is because of wrong diet, wrong education, unrestricted breeding, a dozen other things. Are they wrong? How can we ever be certain?"

"How indeed?"

Fenton spun towards the door at the sound of the cool voice, he forced himself to stop the instinctive motion towards his pistol, and cursed himself for his stupidity in forgetting to bar the door.

Norma Saunders smiled carelessly at him, and entered the shack.

She was not alone. Behind her followed two mercy guards, their uniforms making a splash of bright color in the sunlight streaming through the open panel. They waited, hands resting easily on their holstered weapons, their eyes, after one quick glance around the shack, steady on the little group.

"What do you want here?"

She smiled at Fenton, looked interestedly at Bill, then pointed towards Wilson.

"There is your man."

The guards stepped forward, gripped Wilson by his arms, pulled him to his feet. He whimpered at the grip on his injured arm. Fenton thrust himself before them.

"What do you want with this man?"

"Why worry yourself?" Norma rested her hand gently on his arm. "The guards will take good care of him."

"I do worry," snapped Fenton. "The man is injured and he is my friend. I demand to know what you intend doing with him."

"Injured you say?" One of the guards moved his grip from the damaged ann. "I didn't know that. This man has been agitating violence towards the Servos, inciting people to riot and rebellion."

"Is that a crime?" Bill snapped angrily. "You are an Earthman, aren't you?"

"It is to his own interest to be confined until such time as his mental health has improved," he said quietly. "During the riots caused by his actions, three people died and many were injured. The field generator has also been increased in power. This is a direct result of two Servos being killed in the rioting. I needn't tell you what that means."

"I see," said Fenton. He felt rather sick. "Is it very bad?"

"Three hundred mercy shots were fired in the city alone within the past hour."

"They mean no harm." Norma stepped close beside Fenton. "But he cannot be allowed to inflame emotions as he has been doing. It isn't his life alone, but what of the others?"

"She's right, Jud," Bill said heavily. "We don't need him. He's too unreliable. It's a pity that the field is only attacking organic mental insanity, otherwise he would have died long ago."

"Wouldn't we all?" Fenton made no move to interfere as the guards half carried Wilson to a waiting car. "It seems that we are cursed both ways. How many geniuses have had poor health? How many brilliant minds have been considered as abnormal? If a man has an eidetic memory, he is considered a mental freak, yet it is a thing indispensable to a culture such as ours."

He watched as the guards locked Wilson into the rear of the car; they climbed into the front, the turbine whined and smoothly the car glided towards the city. He was surprised to find that Norma still stood close beside him.

"Aren't you returning with them?"

"No." She looked at him, letting her eyes run over his big figure. "Why are you so interested in what you are doing? Can't you accept the fact that the Servos are bringing you something this planet has had a need of for all its recorded history? Think of it. No more wars, no more hate, envy, pain, contempt. None of the things that have given rise to the popular superstitions of an after life." Surprisingly she laughed.

"Why are you amused?"

"Isn't it childish? Does your car hope for a car heaven when it is scrapped? Do any of your machines?"

"Men are not machines."

She sighed impatiently. "Why must you be so stubborn? Of course you are a machine, as much a machine as an electronic brain. Would an electronic brain be aware that it was a machine?"

He looked down at her. She was smiling, her full lips quirked at the corners. For a moment suspicion flared within him; angrily he rejected it.

Behind them someone screamed in unendurable agony.

Fenton spun on one heel. "Bill!" he shouted unbelievingly. "Bill!"

He writhed on the dirty floor, great beads of perspiration glistening on face and neck. Blood poured from his bitten lips, and from the palm of his hands where his nails had dug into the flesh. He screamed, his eyes glazed, his body twisting with the pain that seared through every individual cell.

Desperately Fenton plunged his hand into his pocket, snatched out the gun. The front sight caught, and he wrenched it free with a rip of cloth. With false calm he swung the gleaming barrel, aimed at the center of the sweat-covered forehead.

His finger tightened on the trigger.

Something smashed into him knocking him over, the gun exploding as he fell. The bullet lost itself somewhere in the wooden walls of the shack, the smack of its impact lost among the screams. Frantically he threshed on the floor, recovered his balance, dived for the gleaming weapon.

A foot ground down upon his hand. Incredulously he stared at Norma.

"What are you doing? Give me the gun."

"No."

"What?" He heaved, throwing himself against her legs. She fell backwards, kicking the gun as she fell. Fenton lunged for it, scrambled to his feet. Norma stood before him.

"Wait!"

He swung a thick arm, knocked her aside, and raised the weapon.

"Wait, you fool! Can't you see he's stopped screaming?"

It was true. Sometime during the brief struggle Bill had stopped screaming with agony. Fenton stared down at him, slow rage beginning to burn through his big body.

"You bitch! I could have helped him, given him release." Unconsciously he threatened her with the pistol.

"No, Jud!" It was a whisper, weak, yet filled with startled wonder. Incredulously Fenton stared down at the slowly moving body at his feet.

Bill grinned, wiped the sweat from his face, staggered uncertainly to his feet. "I'm alive!" he breathed. "Alive! It was hell while it lasted, sheer hell, but I'm alive." He couldn't seem to get over it.

"Now you know why I had to stop you," Norma said. She stood by the door nursing a bruised arm. "You would have killed him, and one of the Servo would have died unborn."

"You mean?"

"Yes. It is an acid test, but the only one. Those who live through the agony are reborn. Naturally they stay to help those less fortunate. I had thought that it would have been you who would have joined us. I can see now that I was mistaken."

Fenton stared at her, feeling the tiny flutter around his heart he had learned to dread. He knew that he would never live through the pain, had known all along.

"Us? You mean that you are a Servo?"

"Naturally."

"But they are all emotionless creatures. Cold, logical—you are not like that."

She smiled, linking her arm with Bill's. "You make machines for many purposes, and so did our creators. Some for general purposes, some for defense and building, others for entertainment. I am an actress."

She smiled again, and walked away taking Bill with her. He turned, stared at Fenton and hesitated.

"Jud—"

"Go with her, Bill." Fenton spoke quietly. "You have finished here. Goodbye."

He stood watching as they walked away from the shack. Once Norma turned, waved an arm in final farewell, then strode on.

Suddenly the pain caught him.

TIME TO KILL

THE MAN in the red cloak and mask led the way into a booth, hit the switch with the palm of his hand and, when the screen snapped across the opening, leaned forward.

"Listen," he said quietly. "What I want is simple. I want you to kill a man for me."

"Simple," agreed Fenwick dryly.

He glanced around the booth and then through the polarized screen into the main room. It was filled with the usual party crowd of men and women. From the way they stamped and snapped their fingers, he guessed that someone had switched on the tingle-tubes to full blast. From inside the booth, he couldn't feel the intoxicating electronic pulsations. He couldn't recognize anyone, either.

The fad that year was for Renaissance costume. Last year it had been Victorian and next year it could be Grecian, but this year everyone wore long, sweeping cloaks from neck to heel and oddly distorted masks that covered the face to just above the mouth.

Fenwick, even while obeying the dictates of fashion, thought it stupid. In his avocation—he had no vocation—it was necessary, even though it meant changing one's whole wardrobe every year, which, of course, was the reason. It was good for business.

"We are screened," said the man when it became obvious that Fenwick had no intention of speaking. "You have nothing to fear."

"You have nothing to fear," corrected Fenwick. "I don't even know your name. You're a stranger who invited me to join him in a private talk and now it turns out to be murder. What do you think I am?"

Beneath the edge of the mask, the man's lips curved into a smile. "I know what you are. You're a hunter, a hardened slayer of the innocent and helpless."

"Hunting is not murder," Fenwick said.

"No? Tell me, what is the difference between killing a bull ape and a man?"

"You pay a heavy fine if you are caught killing an ape," said Fenwick bluntly. "The punishment is rather more severe for killing a man."

"Is it? But the reward would be higher. Very much higher indeed—and you needn't be caught."

And there he put his finger on the important thing. Fenwick had no conscience; if he had, he would never have been a hunter in the first place. But he did have a healthy regard for his own skin. To kill was simple; to escape the consequences of murder was something else.

"No motive," urged the man. "No possible suspicion. No reason or cause for the police to look for you at all. If any man on Earth can commit murder and get away with it, it's you."

"You flatter me." Fenwick wished the man would remove his mask so he could read his expression. "But I am no assassin."

"You need money and, as I said, the reward would be high."

"High enough to be worth risking my life?"

"It wouldn't come to that. A quick attack, a quick escape. Nothing to it."

"The police are clever," reminded Fenwick. Despite himself, he was intrigued by the proposal. Killing, as the stranger had said, came easily to him, but lately the slaughter of inoffensive creatures had grown stale. Hunting had become too easy, but what about other prey?

"The police are clever," admitted the stranger, "but not as clever as they would like you to think. You know their routine? Everyone remotely connected with any crime is given null-censor and questioned beneath a lie detector. If a suspect is guilty, they will find him. But what if the guilty person is not a suspect? Can they question the ten million inhabitants of this city?"

He reached beneath his cloak and paper rustled as he produced a sheaf of crisp new high-denomination bills. "I said that the reward would be high. Two hundred thousand credits, to be exact." He pushed the notes toward the hunter. "Would you call that high enough?"

Fenwick sweated behind his mask. Until now, he had regarded the entire thing as a joke, the stranger accosting him at the party, the conversation, the suggested murder. The sight of the money made it all very real.

"If you want this man dead so badly, why not kill him yourself?" Fenwick asked.

"I have a motive, obviously, or I would not want him dead."
The man smiled again, his lips moist beneath big mask. "Still
thinking of the police?"

"You're damned right I am. No one has been murdered for
the past fifty years. No crime of any kind has been unsolved in all
that time. There are rumors—"

"They're false," said the man quickly. "The police don't have
a machine with which they can look back through time. It's just
propaganda to discourage potential criminals."

"Perhaps. But how can you be sure?"

"Because I know. But even if they had such a machine, what
of it? You will be masked and are a trained hunter—you know
how to cover your tracks. They won't know who you are and how
can they check a whole city? But the question doesn't apply—
there is no such machine." He fingered the money, letting the
edges of the notes riffle over the ball of his thumb. "And there is
no longer any death penalty."

"Right," said Fenwick thoughtfully. "But the risk is still
great."

"The risk is as great as you care to make it," said the man
evenly. "Look at it as a challenge. You, the hunter, against the
full power of the law. You must kill and then you must escape.
For you, the killing will be easy—and the escape should prove ex-
citing." He riffled the money again and Fenwick stared at it.

"I could agree and walk out of here and forget what you want
me to do," he pointed out.

The man nodded. "You could," he said easily. "Will you?"

"No." Fenwick picked up the money.

The victim was a man named Carl Gerard. He was about
Fenwick's own age and lived in a class B apartment. Why the
stranger wanted him dead was something Fenwick didn't bother
to think about. Gerard was quarry. He was two hundred thousand credits.

First Fenwick arranged for his escape. A travel agency sold
him a ticket on the Mars Express leaving every night at midnight
from the local field. To lure the quarry from his lair and then to
identify him was the hardest part of the whole business. Even
that, however, proved disappointingly easy.

From a costumers, Fenwick bought a female skin-mask complete with artificial hair. He found a videophone with a tone-selector, adjusted it to emulate a female voice and called Gerard. He aroused no suspicions. If anything, Gerard was too eager to meet the strange female who had called him to suggest a date.

Rendezvous time was set for nine o'clock at a busy comer. With time to kill, Fenwick bought a ticket to a horrorscope and sat in thoughtful silence while all around him men and women shrieked and shivered to the artificial stimulation of their nerves and glands. He had reason to be thoughtful—he was thinking of the temporal police.

The stranger had denied the existence of any machine that was able to scan time. Rumor had it otherwise, but that could have been instigated by the police and cleverly publicized.

If there were such a machine, though, it would account for the crime-free fifty years. No murderer could hope to escape if the police could scan back and actually see him at work. Even if masked and disguised, he wouldn't stand a chance. All the police need do was follow his image back in time until they saw him as he really was.

For a moment, Fenwick considered abandoning the whole thing. Then, as he thought about it, he shrugged. His employer, whoever he was, had gauged him too well. The thrill of the hunt was in his blood, the problem intrigued him, and he knew that he was going to earn his money.

Anyway, no one knew for certain whether or not there was a time-scanning machine. And even if there were, it would take time for the police to identify him. By then, he would be halfway to Mars and beyond their jurisdiction. He relaxed, amused at the gasps and shudders of those around him even as his own skin crawled and adrenalin flooded into his bloodstream.

Half an hour before rendezvous time, he left the theater and, taking an elementary precaution, walked toward the scavenger part of the city. It was unhealthy in its deserted houses and broken streets, but it was scantily populated and, more important, badly lit.

He stepped into a pool of darkness, neat and trim in his puce cloak and mask. He stepped out again dressed in light blue. With no time to waste, he caught a 'copcab. Five minutes later, he was at the rendezvous.

Gerard was early. He stood on the corner, conspicuous in

his yellow cloak and mask, both ornamented with black arabesques—the cloak and mask that he had told his caller he would be wearing. In turn, he looked for a silver assembly, the most unlikely color Fenwick could think of. Watching him, the hunter felt a rising excitement. He was in no hurry. It would take less than fifteen minutes by 'copcab to the field and the less time between the murder and takeoff, the better. His deadline was thirty minutes before midnight, which left ninety minutes to go. Ninety minutes in which to watch and stalk, to baffle the quarry and head him on the path he must take. Ninety minutes of skill and cunning culminating in the final moment of victory when the knife he carried beneath his cloak would sink into warm and living flesh.

He could afford to wait.

It was almost an hour before Gerard admitted to himself that the call had been a hoax. Reluctantly he moved away and behind him, like a colorful figure of destiny, Fenwick waited for time and place to coincide.

Gerard seemed aimless. He wandered at random, staring at the window displays, looking at the public information strips, glancing at the scintillant bursts of the flash-advertising, acting more like a yokel than the city-dweller he was.

After a while, Gerard went into a tavern and Fenwick, always cautious, waited outside. When Gerard came out, he seemed nervous. He kept glancing over his shoulder, his yellow mask grotesque in the shimmering light of the advertisements, and his pace had increased from a casual saunter to a determined walk.

And yet he didn't head back toward the safety of his apartment. He followed an erratic, winding path that led him through side turnings and narrow passages between the towering buildings and his direction, incredible as it seemed, was toward the bright glow of a 'copcab center.

Fenwick chuckled as he increased his pace and cut down the distance between them. High on a building, the illuminated face of a clock warned him that his time was running out, but he wasn't worried. From the center, he could get transportation to the field so that, though Gerard didn't know it, he was actually helping his murderer to escape.

The man in the yellow cloak seemed even more nervous than

before. He paused at the mouth of a narrow alley winding between two brightly lit streets. Then, his head down between his shoulders, he almost ran through the alley.

Fenwick stared after him, his brain alert as he assessed time and speed and distance. If he ran after Gerard, he would frighten the quarry. But if he cut around the comer and ran hard for a few hundred meters, he would reach the mouth of the alley before him. He would bump into him in the sheltered darkness, kill and be on his way to Mars before anyone discovered the body.

He smiled as he put his plan into execution.

There was a big red sign at the corner of the alley where it joined the main street. It flared and died, flared and died, so that the walls and gutters seemed painted in blood and darkness. It flared as he reached the comer. It flared again as he stepped into the alley. It flared one more time as he struck at the man in the yellow cloak, thumb to the blade and ripping upward in the murderous slash he had learned as an apprentice hunter.

Before the body fell, he was running down the alley, wiping His hand on the inside of his cloak and the blood and fingerprints from the knife before throwing it away. He'd had it so long that no one could possibly trace it to him, and he wanted to be rid of the damning evidence that chemical analysis and micro-tests could reveal. But he needn't have bothered.

The police were waiting for him at the other end of the alley.

There was no trial. Trial supposes doubt and there could be no doubt as to his guilt. But there were plenty of questions and Fenwick owned them all.

"How?" he asked for the hundredth time. "I'd just committed the crime. How did the officers get there so fast?"

"The temporal police?" The man they had assigned to him looked bored. "Surely that's obvious. When we discovered the body, it was simple to determine the time of death. So the officers merely went back to just before the actual moment." He looked tiredly at Fenwick. "Didn't you know we could travel backward in time?"

"I'd heard that you could scan the past, but not actually travel to it. Can you? Scan it, I mean?"

"No. I wish we could. It would make things so much easier."

"I see." So in one thing, at least, the stranger had told the truth. Fenwick frowned at the wall of his cell. "But if you can travel back, then why didn't you prevent the murder?"

"How could we?" The man—Johnson, his name was—shielded a yawn. "If there had been no murder, there would have been no murder to prevent. No body, you understand, so there would have been no reason for going back at all."

"I don't get it," complained Fenwick. "Or do I? No murder, so no body, so no reason for going back. But if you didn't go back, there would have been a body. So . . ." He broke off looking baffled. "A paradox!"

"No," said Johnson. "There are no paradoxes in time."

Fenwick shook his head. "What about if someone went back and killed his grandfather?"

"I'm tired of hearing that old chestnut," said Johnson. "All right, what would happen if a man did that? First, if he killed his grandfather after his father had been born, it wouldn't make the slightest difference. If he killed him before his father had been conceived, then, naturally, he couldn't exist. As he didn't exist, he couldn't have killed his grandfather. So, being alive, he didn't kill his grandfather. He can't kill his grandfather. The argument is ridiculous."

"It still seems like a paradox to me," insisted Fenwick.

"There can be no paradox in time. Think about it for a while and you'll understand why."

"To hell with it," said Fenwick disgustedly. "All I know is that I've been caught. What happens to me now?"

"The only thing left to happen—your punishment."

"Naturally," agreed Fenwick dryly. "Pardon my curiosity, but just what form will that punishment take?"

"You murdered a man," said Johnson. "What punishment do you expect?"

"There's no death penalty," Fenwick said. "Or is that another piece of trickery, like not letting people know you can go back in time?"

"No. You will not be legally murdered."

"What then? Ten years imprisonment? A lifetime?"

"Oh, nothing like that." Johnson seemed to have recovered his good humor. "A peculiar thing, time travel. Unfortunately we

162

are limited to fifty years, so we cannot satisfy our curiosity as to the past. Also, its uses are strictly limited. No tourists, for example, no exploitation or exploring or going back to visit dead relatives. No paradoxes," he explained. "If you went back to visit your dead father, he would know it. He would have told you, so you would know it. Since he didn't, you didn't, so you won't. Simple."

"In other words, the police have suppressed it and use it solely to fight crime." Fenwick wasn't fooled. He had recognized Johnson's hate for a murderer. "Interesting, but what's it got to do with me?"

"I'm telling you," said Johnson mildly. "You committed a murder. We caught you, but our job is as much to prevent crime as to avenge it. But a body had to be discovered in order for us to catch you." He smiled at Fenwick's expression. "Think about it. You were caught, therefore you must have killed. Because you killed, you must be punished. Yet, at the same time, we must protect the public, so we cannot let you kill an innocent man in order that we can catch you to punish you."

He rose and looked down at the hunter. "It's all very simple. I'm sure that you will be able to appreciate the justice of it before long." He smiled and something metallic gleamed in his hand. Fenwick recognized it as a hypo-gun and, for the first time since his capture, felt fear.

"Wait a minute! What about the man who hired me? Isn't he guilty, too?"

"Why should he be? Intent is harmless without execution. You could have refused to commit the murder."

"But . . ."

He broke off because Johnson had gone, the cell had gone, everything had gone and he was sitting in a tavern with a drink in his hand, while all around him drummed the frenetic pounding of jazz.

"Crazy," he muttered and shook his head. But he wasn't crazy and this, as he soon discovered, was cold reality and not a dream.

He examined himself. He was wearing a yellow cloak and rnask, both adorned with black arabesques. It was a familiar cloak; he had seen it before, but just when and where, he couldn't remember.

Drugs, of course—he still felt doped. Johnson had knocked him out with the hypo-gun and they had drugged and dressed him and brought him to this tavern. But why? Why?

He shook his head and finished the drink and looked around for the police who must be guarding him. He didn't see any and began to have hopes that he was really free.

Leaving the tavern, he walked down the street. He walked quickly, glancing behind him for fear of seeing a hated uniform, but aside from a man in a light blue cloak and mask, no one seemed to be following him. It was while he was walking that the drug began to wear off.

The streets were familiar, too familiar. So were the shops, the displays, the advertising signs—even his very movements.

The man in the blue cloak! Himself in yellow!

Gerard had worn a yellow cloak; he had worn a blue one. The man following him was himself! The streets he had walked down then were the same ones he walked down now!

Grudgingly, he admired the beauty of it. The tables turned, the hunter hunted. The paradox resolved by the simple expedient of making himself his own murderer.

But if he'd killed himself, then how could he be guilty of killing Gerard? And if he hadn't killed Gerard, why was he being punished? Or was he? There were no guards, no police, nothing to prevent him going to the spaceport and catching the midnight Express to Mars. The bright glow of a 'copcab center attracted him and he headed toward it.

Behind him, the man in blue quickened his pace.

Fenwick thought of stopping and facing him and explaining what had happened. He didn't because he knew himself too well. The man in blue intended killing the man in yellow. It wasn't a question of personalities or explanations; as soon as time and place were right, the blow would be struck and Fenwick would be dead. And there was another, more important reason.

Fenwick had neither money nor a ticket, but the man in blue had both. And there was only one way to get them.

He simulated fear, glancing constantly over his shoulder and almost running down a narrow alley he remembered from before. He smiled as he saw his follower hesitate and then run down the street. He knew exactly what he intended and he would be ready for him. He wasn't Gerard, that timid fool whom the police had obviously removed to safety after putting Fenwick in his place. He was a hunter, as skilled and as strong as the man in blue—and he knew what the man in blue was going to do. No hunter could have a bigger advantage than that.

The man in blue would race around the other way to head him off. Fenwick knew it even before the other suddenly made the decision, for he had done it himself.

But then what? The man in blue had a knife and he didn't.

But he had the cape—and there was a refuse can. He draped the cape over it and stood worrying for an instant. It didn't look at all like a man; it was too short and squat. He dragged it over to the wall, where even the big red sign that kept flaring into life left it in shadow. Would that fool the man in blue into thinking it was his quarry hunched down fearfully, hoping to escape detection? Even more important, could he himself rewrite the past?

There was no time to think further—the man in blue came running into the alley. Fenwick pressed back out of sight in the deeper shadow. The man in blue hesitated only for a second before thrusting the knife into the cape. As soon as the blade rang against the metal of the refuse can, Fenwick had stepped behind the man in blue and chopped at the back of the neck with the edge of his palm—not too hard, for he didn't want to kill his earlier self, yet powerfully enough to knock him out.

He knew just where the money and the ticket were, and he had them out in a flash of movement and was running toward the end of the alley. He faltered there, apprehensive, but there were no police waiting. Almost arrogantly then, he flagged a 'copcab and ordered it to take him out to the spaceport.

It was on the way that bewilderment hit him. No paradox, eh? Gerard hadn't been murdered. Fenwick hadn't been killed by the man in blue, as Johnson had planned. The man in blue was unconscious but safe.

Then what crime had been committed? None—and yet Fenwick had to flee to Mars! If he turned back, he had no assurance that he would not be picked up by the temporal police.

Scowling, he tried to reason it out. The spaceport lights were glaring below when he finally found the answer. It made him smile—a bitter and yet admiring smile.

Naturally there had been no crime committed, either by him or anyone else in the past fifty years! But he had been willing to kill, just as others had undoubtedly been willing to murder or steal, and that was enough for the temporal police. If he didn't go to Mars, they were sure to have another trick like substituting him for his victim. Only, of course, he wouldn't put them to the bother; that one or the next might work.

Not feeling a bit jaunty, as a hunter should, Fenwick turned in his ticket and went aboard the ship for Mars.

THE SEEKERS

THE head was becoming too-Byzantine in the exaggerated torment of the face. Intalgo leaned back, frowning as he studied his work. The torment belonged, certainly, the portrait was that of a man on a cross. Any man on any cross and from what he knew crucifixion was a most agonizing form of death. But he really knew so little. He had never seen the face of a crucified man and the work lacked that certain conviction which only experience could provide. Disconsolately he leaned farther back and closed his eyes.

Around him the control room whispered its muted, mechanical lullaby.

He heard it just beneath the level of his consciousness. It was a sound so familiar that, to him, it was silence, but, if the whisper should break, should falter, he would be immediately aware. But the whisper did not change. The ship hummed its smooth way across the void at a pace that left light crawling far behind. A mechanical bullet aimed at a distant star. Another star, another planet, another step on the path of total domination.

Intalgo abruptly opened his eyes, staring at the portrait as if at an enemy, hoping to capture the missing ingredient by sheer surprise. How did a man die on a cross? There would be the constriction of the chest, the pressure on the lungs, the terrible strain. Surely the head would fall forward or, no, the head would have to be thrown back in order to straighten the throat. But in that case the chin would be more prominent. And what abut cyanosis?

The artist sighed and reached for his pigments. He wished that Delray was awake. The doctor should know.

Delray was fighting. He strode through barbarous halls, the sword in his hand red with blood, his near-naked body dappled with ruby flecks. He came to the hall with the throne and halted, eyes narrowed against the leaping glare of giant flambeaux. The light dimmed, and from the shadows, something advanced.

It was anthromorphic and obscene. It yammered a challenge and he roared an answer, springing forward, the sword firm in his hand. Then it was a blur of cut and thrust and vicious slashing. Spurting blood filled the air with its familiar reek. And, above all, was the mad, red, exhilaration of the battle.

The thing died. The hall threw back the echoes of his footsteps as he marched to the throne. He tensed as something moved beside it, relaxing as the woman came towards him. She was tall, proud, her mouth a ruby smear. Blonde hair trailed the floor at her feet. White flesh gleamed in the dancing light.

He laughed and heard the sword tinkle at his feet. He reached towards her and laughed again as a dagger flashed in her hand. Contemptuously he knocked it aside and clamped his hands on warm, struggling flesh. His blood thrilled with the lust for conquest.

He opened his eyes and stared at the satin finish of the ceiling.

He swore and rose and swore again as his forehead hit the edge of the cap. A hell of a time for the thing to break down. His instinct was to hit out and he slammed his hand against the warm metal, furious at the disturbance of his favorite dream. A tell-tale lit with a cold, green glow and he arrested the movement of his hand poised for a second blow. Grumbling, he thrust his head into the field of the cap. The spool must be broken or the selector at fault, but he could fix neither. Malchus would have to do that.

The engineer sat cross-legged before the quiescent bulk of the power unit. The side-edges of his naked feet rested on the metal of the floor, the tips of his supporting fingers touched it to either side. His eyes were closed, but he was not asleep.

He sensed the vibration of the metal, the path of incandescent particles within the pile, extrapolating from observable data to the logical conclusion. There was a tiny hesitancy from one of the turbines. It was almost nothing but the slight imbalance would hinder the path of the gases, deflecting them a trifle to one side. There would be excessive erosion on a certain spot and a rise in temperature. The extra heat would affect the bore of a pipe and create a minor bottleneck. Pressure would tend to build.

Eventually a repair and adjustment would have to be made.

But not now. Not for a long time yet. They would have time

to finish this tour before things reached the point where to ignore the trouble would be to court disaster. Then he would over-
see the work and guide the rebuilding.

The corners of his mouth lifted in a smile.

To build!

Feldman could never appreciate the beauty of the thought.
But the navigator was not an engineer.

Feldman was the man who sent the ship lunging at invisible targets, who checked the radiation of suns and the atmosphere of planets, who lived by the lines of a spectroscope and
the immutable laws of science. He worshipped the cold beauty
of an equation. He was writing a book.

It was a work of love, a hobby, and would be published, if at
all, under a pseudonym. He would not risk the sneers of his con-
temporaries. He wrote:

The greatest foreseeable problem of heterosexual crews,
the strains and frustrations of thwarted sexual desire, have
apparently been overcome by use of the dream-cap in which
paradoxical dreams are encouraged with the consequent release of physical strain by the superimposition of erotic and
exotic stimuli. A choice of dream sequences is provided by
varied tapes and, it is to be assumed, the synthetic world so
provided compensates for the boredom of space flight and
the lack of congenial company. By congenial I mean female
and not incompatible types. Choice of crew-members is carefully governed both from the viewpoint of dual-attributes
and . . .

He was wandering; He lifted the pen and sucked thoughtfully at the tip. The book was to be about the sexual tensions
and problems in space, but, for some reason, he constantly
veered from the subject. Now, for example, he was about to laud
the Pentarch for their wisdom in crew-selection when, of
course, it wasn't really wisdom at all but plain common sense.
He really must stick to the point.

And yet—?

Was it really wise to write the book at all? A man in his position couldn't be too careful, and if the book were published

and a whisper of the true identity of the author should leak
out—?

He frowned and moved his hand to the release. A pressure
and the surface was blank. Almost at once he regretted the total
erasure—he should have printed it at least if only to make cor-
rections. He could always destroy the thing before they landed.
But perhaps if he tried a different approach?

The pen touched the surface and left a scrawl of thin lines.
Hastily he jabbed the erase button again. He was sweating. He
hadn't really meant to write that at all.

Intalgo took a smear of pigment on the tip of his thumb and
wiped it beneath the staring eyes. He brushed a thin line at the
corners of the mouth and touched the contour of a lip. Leaning
back he looked at the result.

He frowned his disappointment. He had tried to portray resignation, acceptance, fortitude, the whole overlaid with a patina
of pain. Instead he had added a new emotion. Now the face held
hate.

He reached towards the erase then halted the movement of
his hand. Was he so wrong? Wouldn't a man so tormented have
cause to hate his tormentors? He had tried to picture an ideal
and so had tried to achieve the impossible. Art could not deny reality.

Irritably he rose and paced the control room, wondering at
his somber thoughts. Death, torment, the ultimate in pain—why
did his hands insist on creating such things? And why did that
face hold a haunting tinge of familiarity?

Musing, he stared at his creation while around him the control room hummed its satisfaction, The hum gave the answer answer. The control room was too empty—something was missing.
Something that subconsciously, he had tried to replace.

The Pentarch had flung the ship like a challenging hand towards the stars. But now that hand was maimed.

The captain was dead.

Intalgo had loved that lonely man. Beneath the cold exterior
he had sensed a warm personality and an imagination almost
equal to his own. No artist, the captain, but a trained manipula-
tor of men. But he had once likened the stars to camp fires burn-

ing in the fields of eternity and Intalgo could forgive many things to a man who had held thoughts of such poetic slant.

But he found it hard to forgive the manner of his death.

Such a man should not have died in such a fashion. For him was the noble ending, the song of trumpets the heroic passing. Not a sharp edge drawn across a naked throat in the silence of his lonely watch. Often the artist wondered what had driven him to take his life. Had he, too, been crucified on the cross of duty and inclination?

Was that his face that looked back from the painted sheet?

Intalgo stared at it with sharpened interest, but it was not the captain. It was not anyone he knew and yet . . .

He sat, musing, looking at the painted face, remembering the dead.

They had often talked during the long, silent hours between the stars. They had talked of death and life and the purpose of existence. They had talked of what they did and why they did it.

And the captain had shown his fear.

"Out here," he'd said, "we're irritating intruders, rats scuttling among the granary of the stars. What may we find? Other, older races perhaps? Strange ways and strange customs and mysteries that we lack the mental equipment to solve. And yet we go on. We have no choice but to go on."

Then he would laugh without humor and his eyes would grow bleak.

"One day we will find something beyond us and, when we do, God help our ignorance."

He had not waited for that day to come.

They landed on a planet that drowsed beneath the ruddy glare of a dying sun. The ship was an alien harshness on a rolling plain of yellow dust. An enigmatic cube thrust its squat ebony finger towards the sky. It was the only sign of life the world possessed and it was old. Old beyond their limited imagination.

But they landed to stamp the seal of the Pentarch on a new acquisition of Man.

"We must be armed," said Delray.

"No need—the entire planet is dead," said Feldman.

"I must get into that building," said Malchus.

Intalgo said nothing—a recorder should not speak. But in the log he wrote:

Inertia caused normal landing precautions to be taken, but from habit, not from a sense of responsibility. Neither is willing to take the orders of another—each claiming that he has equal right. I am watching the corrosive effects of Democracy and, while it is fascinating in its unexpected nuances of individualism, it can lead only to chaos. These journeys last too long.

Too long—and yet it was as easy to continue as to return and the Pentarch was stern when it came to dealing with failure. More than stern when it dealt with disobedience. Intalgo sighed and closed the log and went to breathe the open air.

The place had a timeless, dreamlike quality as if a segment of creation had been frozen so that there could be no change, no alteration, no newness or passing away. The air was heavy, stagnant, flattering the echoes of their conversation. Like ants the three others wended their way to the titanic bulk of the mysterious building. They walked with arrogance but without harmony. They were individuals, not a team.

Intalgo sighed again. Now the challenging hand was more than maimed—it was clawing itself apart.

Malchus found it first. It was almost buried in the yellow dust and he kicked it free then squatted, looking at it.

It was the part of a machine.

It was tooled and finished in a way he had never seen before but, now that he saw it, the reason was obvious. It glinted and shone with the rainbow pattern of refracted light and the scored surface was designed to eliminate friction. The eddy currents generated when the machine was in operation would keep the surfaces an atom apart.

It was—it must be—the central bearing of an engine which was—it could only be—the drive unit of a . . .

He blinked and settled himself more comfortably and concentrated his attention.

A pipe would run from there and meet a shaft, which had to run from there and the junction would have to be—there! Then that hollow must hold a swivel-drive leading to . . .

He sat immersed in the joys of construction.

Feldman found it next.

He snorted at the engineer then stooped as he saw what rested on the sand. Squatting, he looked at it.

It was crystallized truth.

It was a model so intricate and yet so plain that it was as easy to read as a book. There was the basic structure of the atom and there were the logical extensions of the formulae propounded by Einstein and there—if he looked very close—were the equations of the three body problem and those surely must appertain to time itself so that . . .

Feldman sighed with intellectual satisfaction and settled himself for his greater concentration.

Delray found it next.

He came shooting over to the others and glared at what rested between them.

It was naked satiation.

It was the euphoria of combat, the thrill of physical violence, the tease of mental struggle. It was his own deep, dark heritage of type and it opened before him like a flower within whose petals was to be found all he had ever sought. He sank into it and into an eternal enervating dream.

Intalgo found it the last of all.

He stood murmuring into the recorder, his eyes fastened on the three, distant shapes, frozen in a fresco of bone and flesh and pulsating blood. Around him the air hung like many folds of scented silk.

"They have not moved for hours and are obviously unaware of any form of physical discomfort. The thing is divided between them, but it must be some kind of snare. The builders of this monolith must have devised means to protect it from intruders such as ourselves. In a short while I will go across to them and try to restore their senses and recall their responsibility."

He hesitated, then switched off the instrument.

There was really nothing more he could say.

Say, but not think. The dead words of the dead captain came to him as he walked across the plain of yellow dust to where his companions sat in frozen concentration.

Rats scurrying among the granary of the stars.

Rats!

The Pentarch would not be amused, but he knew now why he had depicted Man as being suspended from a cross. Man with his own face. Man, tormented in his eternal search for . . .

He saw what the others had found.

It was pure art.

It was the thing he had sought all his life and it held so great a joy that he felt tears sting his eyes and overwhelming emotion fill his heart.

Sitting he stared at it.

Man lives by his search for Heaven. This thing was Heaven—for all of them.

They could never leave it.

THE LAST DAY OF SUMMER

HE awoke to the sound of roaring trumpets and lay for a while, hovering in that strange region between sleep and waking, clutching vainly at the broken fabric of shattered dreams as the once-bright images dissipated into tenuous clouds of dream-mist. Then he sighed, stirred, the trumpets dwindled to the musical attention call from the bedside videophone and, opening his eyes, he reached for the switch.

"Yes?"

"Mr. Melhuey?" The face pictured on the screen was smooth and pink, with liquid dark eyes and a gentle, understanding mouth. "Mr. John Melhuey?"

"That's right."

"This is the Bureau, Mr. Melhuey. We received a letter from you this morning with certain enclosures." The image shifted its eyes a little as it stared at something beyond the range of the scanners. "You realize, of course, what it is you ask?"

"I understand perfectly." John didn't trouble to hide his impatience. "Why are you calling?"

"Isn't that obvious, sir? There is always the possibility of mistake. Or perhaps . . ."

"There is no mistake and there is no 'perhaps' about it. You have your instructions."

"Yes, sir. At your service, sir."

The image died as John opened the circuit, lingering for a brief second in fading brilliance before merging with the blank, pearly luster of the screen. John stared at it for a moment, idly wondering what the man had thought and vaguely regretting the lost opportunity to ask questions, then he sighed and got out of bed.

It wasn't as easy as it had been yesterday, and yesterday had been harder than the day before. Stiff limbs and throbbing joints, odd twinges and dull aches, all foreign to his experience, all unwelcome symptoms of what was to come. Tiredly he entered the bathroom, stripped, and stood beneath the shower.

The water was hot, so hot that it steamed and stung his flesh into a pink glow. He reveled in it, letting it drum against his skull and run down his face, opening his mouth to the warm liquid then stooping so that it traced a tingling path down his back. He adjusted the flow to cold and shivered in the icy flood, his skin goose-pimpling and changing from pink to blue, dead white and unhealthy gray. Misery came with the cold, a chattering numbness then, as he spun the control back to hot, the relief was so great that he almost shouted with sheer, animal pleasure.

He had always enjoyed his morning shower.

Finished, he stood in the air-blast, staring at himself in the full-length mirror as he dried.

He had always been a big man in every sense of the word and now, physically at least, he was still big. Carefully he examined himself, from the wide-spread feet, splayed a little now and with sagging arches, up the blue-mottled legs, the abdomen, bulging and lax, the thick waist, the chest heavy with fat where muscles should have stood in taut splendor, the neck with its loose skin and flabby tissue.

Old!

He stared at himself, his lips twisting a little with self-distaste, his deep-set eyes bitter as he touched the engraved lines from nose to mouth, the crow's feet marring once smooth skin, the receding hair and wrinkled forehead. His skin bore the tiny marks of passing years, crinkled and crepe-like, too-soft and too-sagging, the muscles unable to restrain the tissue, the skin itself a too-big bag for what lay beneath.

Old!

Yesterday he hadn't seemed so bad and the day before yesterday he had been almost young. A week ago he had been fit and a month ago as virile as he had ever been. Now he was succumbing to age, losing the battle of the passing years with the passage of each hour, paying heavy penalty for his extended youth.

"You're worn out," he said to the image in the mirror. "Finished. Not even the drugs can help you now. You've lived longer than any man once had a right to expect, but you can't live forever. Now, with medical science helpless to stave off further ageing, you're getting senile—fast!"

And it was true. Three times now he had passed his youth and virility only to have it restored by the longevity treatment.

Three times—and there could be no fourth. Now he had to wait until he aged and died. Now he had to pay for extended

youth by the accelerated advance of breakdown, the accumulated enemies of age and senility. He had had a long, long summer. He had tasted life to the full, spreading his experiences
across the years until now. Now was the last day of summer.
Tomorrow would be winter, painful, degrading, bitter winter
and bitter death.

He sighed as if bidding goodbye to what he had once been
and could never be again then, with exaggerated care, he
dressed himself, taking a new suit from the dispenser, smiling
as he snapped the seals and slipped the shimmering garments
over his body.

He had always liked new clothes.

Breakfast was a work of art. Real fruit juice. Real coffee.
Real bread toasted to a fragrant brown crispness and loaded
with creamy yellow butter, the soft richness seeming to hold
within itself all the trapped sunlight of bygone years. He ate
slowly, moving the food over his palate, swallowing with careful
deliberation, tasting the food instead of merely chewing it, savoring it as if he had never eaten before. The meal finished he
rose and, with casual deliberation, moved about the huge room
with its scattered treasures and its quiet, subtle, unmistakable
air of good taste.

A plaque of polished wood hung against the wall. A stone
was mounted in its center, a fragment of gray, crumbling rock
and he stared at it, leaning forward to touch it and, as his fingers caressed the rough surface, time slipped and he was young
again.

A gray plain, the hiss of oxygen and the chafing
encumbrance of a suit. Sunlight, harsh and glaring through the
shields, jagged peaks and, high in the star-shot sky, a swollen,
green-mottled ball wreathed with tenuous fingers of fleecy cloud.

Luna!

The rock had come from the moon, torn from where it had
lain for uncounted years, wrenched free by a metal glove and
carried as a trophy back to the distant Earth. He had been the
one to rip it from its bed. He had torn it free and stumbled, knee
deep in Luna dust, back to where the ship waited like a splinter
of radiant steel in the savage light of the naked sun. Long ago
now. Long, long ago. Back in his first youth when life was a gay

adventure and death a mere word. How long?

He sighed as he thought about it, not trying to read the gold-letter date on the polished wood, letting his hand fall from the rough stone and, as he turned, the too-bright memories scattered and vanished in the light of harsh reality.

A book lay on a small table, a single volume written by a man long dead, and yet containing within its pages the essence of his genius, caught and safeguarded against time. It fell open as he picked it up, flattening at a favorite poem, and he scanned it, feeling a warm comfort in the familiar text.

From too much love of living,
From hope and fear set free,
We give our brief thanksgiving,
To whatever Gods may be,
That no life lasts forever,
That dead men rise up never,
That even the weariest river,
Winds somewhere safe to sea.

He set it down, the warm comfort dissolving at the touch of dull dread, feeling a slight irritation where always before he had relished the swing and depth of the thought behind the words. Swinburne was not for him—not now.

He touched other books, scanned other volumes, all old friends, all holding for him some special grace, some captured memory. He read a story for the hundredth time and enjoyed it as if he had read it but once. He fingered worn bindings and yellowed pages, blinking as his eyes refused their duty until he had had a surfeit of reading and put away the books and sat staring through the high windows at the late-afternoon sky beyond.

He felt restless. He felt impatient with a strange urgency as though he had much to do and little time in which to do it. Summer was nearly over and soon would come the bitter winter or . . .

He didn't let himself think about it.

He found a bottle, dusty and sealed, stained and bearing the arms of an emperor long dead. He held it against the light, staring at the golden glory imprisoned within the glass, caressing the bottle as if it were a thing infinitely precious, which it was, and priceless, which was almost true. He took a huge glass, a monstrous thing with a tiny stem and a balloon-like bowl. He warmed it between his palms, rolling it, nursing its delicate fragility then, opening the bottle, he poured out the lambent fluid and, still warming the glass, inhaled the ineffable fragrance of the rare old brandy.

He inhaled and sipped, inhaled and sipped again, feeling little fires light in his stomach and warm his chilling flesh with the magic of the grape and summer suns of distant memory.

'Oft I wonder what the vintner buys—One half so precious as that he sells.' He smiled as he murmured the lines, the brandy in the glass seeming to wink at him with reflected light, smiling with its golden face and gurgling with its liquid mouth in complete agreement with the philosophy of the Persian Poet.

"You're a snare," said John accusingly. "You are the one true magic of the ages, the single thing which, by illusion, can turn terror into pleasure, hate into love, despair into hope. You can make all men brothers, all worries as drifting dreams, all hurt and pain as laughable memories. You hold the gift of courage. With you a man can face the world and be undaunted. With you he can even smile at . . ."

He sighed, drained the glass and rose from the soft, form-fitting chair in which he sat.

A bowl of fruit stood on a table of glistening plastic, the colors cunningly fashioned in abstruse designs of convoluted shades. He selected a grape, a swollen mutation from the hydroponics gardens, and crushed it against his teeth, savoring the seedless pulp and the sharp, almost acid tang of the syrupy juice. He ate slowly, his fingers not reaching for another until the first had been enjoyed to the full then, as he stared at the darkening sky outside, he left the fruit and moved towards the door.

He had always liked the city.

He had always liked the medley of noises, the traffic sounds, the hum of inaudible conversations, the droning and scuffling, the humming and scraping of millions of feet and millions of wheels as the life of the metropolis ebbed and flowed.

There was a little park he remembered, an oasis of green and brown, of trees and flowers, of soft grass and winding paths among the steel and glass, the concrete and plastic of the city.

Here little birds chirped their tuneless songs and the heavy scent of growing things filled the summer afternoon with heady fragrance and stately blossoms nodded with somnolent grace.

He spent a little time in the park.

There were some sculptures he had always admired, things of stone fashioned by hands long dust, holding within themselves the dreams and ideals of bygone ages, the figures staring with blank eyes as they had stared over the passing years and as they would stare for years to come.

He spent a little while with the familiar shapes.

There was a street lined with garish signs and filled with the healthy, raucous, cheerfully independent voices of shouting men. A place of misty treasure and glowing illusion where flesh and blood puppets cavorted on stages and the beat of skin and the throb of brass brought a sense of reeking jungles and carnivorous beasts. Here emotions were released and bodies swayed to nerve-tingling rhythm while eyes widened and breath came fast and the pulse of blood rose until each cell and sinew tingled with the collapse of care.

He walked the streets until his legs were tired.

He walked until the prickling between his shoulder blades had faded, until his anticipation had died, until despair and frustration rode within him like an invisible incubus and worry began to gnaw with its ten thousand teeth at the yielding fabric of his mind.

When?

He didn't know. He didn't want to know for there is some knowledge a man is better without, but . . . when?

Tiredly he made his way back to his apartment, walking slowly through the bright-lit streets, the sky a black bowl above his head and the scintillating trails of the ships hurling themselves from the spaceport dying like the sparks from a million fireworks against the faded stars.

When?

Now? Two minutes time? Tomorrow?

He hoped not tomorrow. He hoped that he wouldn't have another night of old-man's sleep in which the visions of his youth came to torment him on waking with bitter memories of what might have been. Not again the slow awakening, the rising, the horrible ageing and sagging onrush of senility. Not tomorrow.

Please, God, not tomorrow!

"If the thing is to do," he muttered, "'twere best that it be done soon."

For if it were not done soon then it might not be done at all . . . Human courage and human despair have their limitations and life, even twisted and bitter, hateful and painful—life can be sweet, even though the sweetness be of bitter aloes and dead sea dust.

And he was but human.

Reluctantly he pressed his thumb to the lock, feeling a last flash of hope as he stepped into the warm, softy lit interior then, as he realized the room was empty, felt the sagging onrush of despair.

Tomorrow would be too late.

Tomorrow he would have aged a little too much, would have lost his courage, would have discovered that today s unbearable was tomorrow's acceptable. He had seen it before. He had seen the broken, decrepit things that had once been bright-eyed men strong and with the clear vision of youth, had seen them huddled in their shame as they strove to cling to a life that had become a nagging burden. Tomorrow he too could be like that, hoping against hope, running a futile race against time, senile, teetering on the edge of insanity, his fine co-ordination and trained reflexes lost beneath a welter of petty fears and niggling doubts.

Then death would be a hateful thing. Then the thought of oblivion would fill him with screaming dread and he would shrink, enjoying the pain that meant life, blind and deaf to sane counsel and the advice of intelligence.

A thing of which to be ashamed.

A thing which he had sworn he would never become—and yet? Was there still time?

The room was locked, and he was alone and, looking around he knew that time was running out in more senses than one.

For this was the last day of his summer and he was still alive.

He sank into a chair, staring dully at the dark bowl of the sky, beyond the high windows, not seeing the flash and glare of the ships as they rose towards space, not seeing the faded stars, the immensity of the universe, seeing only himself and what he would become. For a moment self-pity gnawed at his strength and he almost yielded to it, feeling the easy, emotionless tears of age blur his vision and sting his eyes. Then he recovered and shook himself and stared at the glowing beauty of the room.

Here were his treasures, and, in a sense, here was his life. Here were his memories, the little things, the trifles and yet each with its own association with the past. A statue, be reached for it and let his thumb travel with almost sensual pleasure over the polished stone, a fragment hardly worth the price of a meal, and yet he had carried it with him over uncounted millions of miles. He touched a ring, a gift later returned, one which, if accepted, would have changed the course of his entire life.

For a moment he felt the old pain, the shattering of cynicism and felt a sharp regret that now, on this last day, he was alone.

And yet he would not have had it otherwise.

Loneliness was something he had lived with too long to fear now. And he could bear it until he died—if he died. The thought made him sweat, a thin film of glistening moisture over the too-soft skin, and his hand trembled a little as he reached for the bottle of rare old brandy. Death, something he had wanted, something he had paid for, something he had expected all day. Not natural death—that would come and its approach was something he feared and dreaded accompanied as it would be with accelerated senility and final insanity—but clean, sweet, merciless death, unknown—immediate, a clean cutting off and a neat finish.

The only way to avoid the winter.

He had arranged it and the Bureau of Euthanasia had never been known to fail. He had tasted the sights and sounds, the sensuous pleasures of good food and good wine, the sight of familiar scenes and the visiting of familiar places for what he had imagined to be for the last time. He had ignored the assassin who surely would have watched his every move, living only for a moment, discounting what must come until nerve and sinew could deny the knowledge no longer, until anticipation hovered on the edge of fear, the terrible dread of having to reaffirm his intention once the night had passed.

He knew that he could never do it again.

Liquid sunshine poured from the bottle into the swollen

glass. Automatically he warmed it between his palms, unable to desecrate the fluid gold even in the extremity of emotion and, as he inhaled the glorious bouquet, he smiled as an artist might smile or as a man to whom has been given one of the rare pleasures of the Earth.

He had always appreciated good wine.

He sipped, letting the nectar drift over his tongue and sting his palate with its familiar taste. He sipped again then, as the glass slipped from his fingers and oblivion came with but time for a single thought, he smiled.

The assassin had been something more than just a killer.

He had been a gentleman.

EVANE

THE computer had been vocalized on the basis of psychological necessity; a concept determined by those who lived in ivory towers and who, trying to be rational, ended by being sadistic. There were other things also, some explicit photographs, some books, a thing in a box which could be inflated and used to ease personal tensions. He used it once and then, repulsed, destroyed it together with the books and photographs. The voice he could do nothing about.

It was soft, mellifluous, the voice of an actual woman or something designed on computer-optimums, he had no way of telling. But it was mellow, devoid of the stridency of youth and for that he was grateful. And, as he couldn't ignore it or turn it off he had learned to live with it and, over the long, long years, had grown to accept it, to rely on it as an integral part of his limited universe. He had even amused himself by fitting a face and figure to the sound.

The image had varied as age had stilled the passions of his blood. At first she had been lithe with raven hair and jutting breasts and hips and thighs belonging to adolescent yearnings. And then she had matured into a more comfortable image, the transition molded by the voice of his own desires. Now she was tall with short blonde hair curling just above the shoulders. Her eyes were blue, deep-set, crinkled at the comers with a tracery of fine lines. She wore black, a simple dress revealing smooth shoulders and the upper parts of her fulsome breasts. Not the hard, jutting promontories he had once imagined but soft and slightly pendulous, matching the maturity of her face, the rounded swell of her hips. And he had given her a name.

"Time for routine inspection, Charles."

He started, shocked out of his reverie, blinking as he sat upright in the big chair. Before him the panels were as always, the big dials with their creeping hands, the gleam of polished metal, the rows of telltales. He had been dreaming, he realized, not asleep but sunken into a reverie that was a form of self-defense, a half-world in which memory became confused with imagination and fiction outweighed reality.

"Time for routine inspection, Charles."

The use of his name, another psychological device but one which led to an inevitable personalization of the machine. A blatant trick to assuage loneliness but one that could too easily lead to insanity. If it was insane to give a mechanical voice a name. To imagine that a real woman was speaking. To dream that somehow, incredibly, he wasn't really alone, that somewhere in his restricted world was another living person and that, perhaps, some time they would meet.

"Time for routine inspection, Charles."

It was imagination, it could be nothing else, but had the voice grown a little sharp? A trifle impatient at his lack of response? Worried, even? It would be nice to think that someone cared; but experience had taught him to know better than that. Three times and then the shock, the electrical stimulus which would jerk him fully aware if asleep, a painful reminder that there was a job to be done and he the one to do it.

Quickly he said, "All right, Evane. I heard you."

"Your response was delayed. Were you asleep?"

"No, just thinking."

"Are you well, Charles?"

He looked down at his hands, at the thick veins and mottled patches, the skin creped over the knuckles. Once they had been young and strong and good to see. When had they changed? Why hadn't he noticed the change before?

"Charles?"

"I'm all right," he said shortly.

"I think I should monitor your metabolism, Charles. After the inspection, naturally."

"Damn it, Evane, you don't have to nag me. I'm all right, I tell you."

"After the inspection, Charles."

How could you argue with a machine? He could refuse; but there were ways to make him obey, the Builders had seen to that. Nowhere could he be free of the sensors and to disobey meant punishment. Sullenly he rose from the chair, uneasily conscious of physical malfunction. His legs, for example, had they always ached as they did now? Over the years he had become accustomed to the dimming of his vision so now it was normal for him not to be able to see the fine divisions on the dials from his position in the chair. But the ache, the slight hesitation of his left foot so that he almost stumbled, saving himself by gripping the back of the chair? Was this new or had he experienced it before? And, if he had, why couldn't he remember?

The thought nagged as he moved from the chair down the ten feet of space towards the rear bulkhead. He could reach the ceiling by lifting his arms, touch the walls by extending them. A tiny space backed by complex machines, which fed him air and food and water in calculated amounts. A sealed environment in which he was nurtured and housed and, above all, protected from external influences. In such a place experiences were few and always strictly personal. How could he possibly forget any detail of his monotonous life?

"Charles, you hesitate. The inspection must be completed."

He reached the bulkhead and reached for the simple controls. Freed by the computer they responded to his touch, a panel lifting to reveal a vast area dimly lit and magnified by the plate through which he stared. Direct vision aided by lenses and mirrors to eliminate the possibility of electronic malfunction. Dutifully he examined the enigmatic hoppers, the ranked containers, countless phials, numberless motes that were packed into thin-skinned ampoules, unknown objects tucked into plastic membranes. Once he had thrilled at the sight, conscious of a tremendous sense of purpose, warmed by the conviction that he was important and essential to the success of the project. Now he simply went through the motions.

"Charles?"

He had stared for too long, losing himself in another of the insidious reveries, trying, perhaps, to recapture the early thrill, extrapolating, looking ahead, guessing at incredible futures. Or perhaps he had simply dozed a little, bored, resentful of the dominance of the computer.

"Charles, is everything at optimum function?"

"Yes, Evane, as always."

"Then return to the chair, Charles. I must monitor your metabolism."

He felt the controls shift beneath his hands, the panel falling to seal the bulkhead, and slowly he returned to the chair, sitting, thrusting his right hand and arm into the familiar orifice. Probes sank into his flesh and he felt the mild tingle of surface stimulation. He leaned back, closing his eyes, imagining a smooth face framed with blonde hair, blue eyes, a little anxious perhaps, the full lips pursed and the dress falling a little, a very little away from the chest and shoulders as she leaned forward to study the results of her examination.

"Well, Nurse, will I live?"

"Nurse?"

"At this moment, Evane, you're a nurse. A person who takes care of the sick. Am I sick?"

"You are not operating at optimum efficiency, Charles."

"Which means that I'm sick. Cure me, Evane."

He felt the touch of something followed by a rising euphoria. An injection of some drug, he guessed, something to dispel his depression, his mounting sense of anxiety. And the obedience helped, the fact that she had complied with his instruction. A man should always be the dominant partner.

Eyes still closed, imagining her leaning back, smiling, her expression a soft blend of affection and motherly concern, he said, "How long, Evane?"

"You are imprecise, Charles."

"And you are being stubborn. You know damn well what I mean. How long have we been traveling in this can?"

"A long time, Charles."

Too long, he thought. So long that time had become meaningless. Flung at a speed close to that of light, aimed at the distant stars, his metabolic clock slowed by the contraction effect. Back home it could have been ten thousand years. Within the ship it had been a lifetime.

The thought bothered him and he fought it, aided by the drug, the comforting presence of the woman. Imperceptibly he slipped into reverie, hearing again the childish voices of the chosen, the deeper tones of his instructors. He was special. He was to be trained for a momentous task. His life was to be dedicated to the Great Expansion.

He stirred and felt again the soothing injection.

"Talk to me, Evane."

"About what, Charles?"

"Pick a subject. Any subject. You are tall and blonde and beautiful. How do you feel locked up in that machine? Shall I let you out? Break into your prison and let you take a walk?"

"You are being irrational, Charles."

"How so, Evane? You've been with me for how long? Fifty years? More? A long time in any case. We've spoken often and surely you must have changed a little from those early days. Listen, do you know why I destroyed the books and those other things? I felt that you were watching me. Watching and despising me. Can you deny it?"

"I have watched you, Charles, certainly."

"Watched and ordered, do this and do that and do it damn quick or else. At times you've been a bitch and I should hate you but I don't. Hate you, I mean. I don't hate you at all."

"Hate, Charles?"

"An emotive feeling."

In his imagination she frowned and shook her head.

"Don't say it," he said quickly. "I don't want to know what you can and cannot feel. Nothing with a voice like yours can be devoid of sensitivity."

"You are irrational, Charles. Perhaps you should sleep."

"No!"

He snatched his arm from the orifice before the drug could be injected, cunning with much repetition for this was not the first time he had sat and conversed with the woman locked in her machine. And yet this time seemed different from those other occasions. Then he had permitted the oblivion she gave, sinking into darkness and a world of dreams in which, living, she had come to him, arms open, body yielding, sweeping him on a tide of consummation in which everything was wonderful and his life complete.

"I don't want to sleep," he said. "I want to talk. I want to know what all this is about. You are going to tell me."

"I do not understand, Charles."

"Data insufficient?" He sneered at her expression. "Are you still trying to convince me that you're just a machine? Don't you realize I know better? This whole thing is a farce. A play. It's time it ended."

"I still do not understand."

"Guess."

"You seem to be aberrational. A malfunction in your physical condition, perhaps. If you will replace your arm I will monitor your metabolism."

"You'll do no such thing. You'll open the doors and let me out of here."

"That is impossible, Charles. You know that."

"Then return back home."

"That is equally impossible. You are distressed, Charles, your thinking illogical. But you are not alone."

Tiredly he opened his eyes and stared at the dials, the ranked telltales, the metal he had polished and the panels he had kept spotless. No, he was not alone. A million vessels over a span of years, each exactly like the one in which he rode, each loaded as this one was loaded, filled with manufactured spores, seeds, the life-elements common to the home world. Incipient life lying dormant in the hold, protected in a dozen different ways with skins of various plastic and natural membrane, in globules of ice and nutrient jelly, dehydrated, frozen, held in electronic stasis. Motes, dusts, molds, near-invisible molecular chains. A cargo designed to perpetuate the race.

And himself?

"No!" He writhed with inner turmoil. "No!"

"Charles, you must relax. You have no need to fear. The ship is intact and you are unharmed. Everything is as it was."

The soft, soothing, mother-tone. The reassurance of a dedicated companion. He was not alone, she was with him, she would always be with him.

But she lied as the others had lied as his whole life had been a lie. His whole empty, stupid, wasted life.

"The truth," he said harshly. "Tell me the truth."

"About what, Charles?"

"About everything. Talk, damn you!"

"The project was explained to you at the very beginning. The Great Expansion is the dream of the race of which you are a member. We are to seek out a suitable star, discover a planet within a certain range of determined factors and discharge our cargo according to programmed instructions. If successful the life-cycle of that world will be guided to emulate conditions approximating the home world. This means that, in future times, the race will find suitable planets on which to settle. By extrapolation it is possible that within a foreseeable future the members of your race will find habitable and, to some extent, familiar worlds scattered throughout the galaxy."

"And the rest?"

"There is no more, Charles."

"Like hell there isn't. What about me?"

"You are the safety factor. It is remotely possible that something could go wrong with the ship or the life-support or maintenance mechanisms. If so you are able to effect repairs."

"With what? My bare hands?"

"No, Charles, with the tools which I will make available in case of need."

"And the knowledge of how to use them?"

"That has been implanted in your subconscious mind, Charles. The knowledge will be released by any state of real emergency."

It sounded logical and he wondered why he should be impressed, what else would a machine be but logical? And yet the thing had been programmed and set to respond in a certain way to certain stimuli. It could be lying or, correction, telling the truth as it knew it, which needn't be the truth at all.

And yet, if that wasn't the truth, what was?

Why had he been incorporated into the vessel?

Restlessly he rose from the chair and walked the ten feet towards the rear bulkhead, the ten feet towards the chair, the ten feet back again. Around him the vessel operated with its usual, quiet efficiency and he stared at the walls, the ceiling, the panel with its ranked instruments. Window-dressing, he thought, suddenly. Something to occupy his attention and to maintain the illusion that he was important to the functioning of the ship. Why hadn't he realized before that he was totally unnecessary with the vessel operated as it was by computer control? An expensive piece of inessential cargo.

And yet the Builders would never have wasted so much unless there had been a reason.

He said, harshly, "Evane, why am I here?"

"I told you, Charles."

"You lied. Now tell me the truth." Incredibly she did not answer and, staring at his hands, seeing the thick veins, the blotches, the signs of age, he said, "What happens when I die?"

"When you cease to function, Charles, we will have reached terminal distance from the home world. I shall then reverse direction and commence to search for a suitable world to receive our cargo."

For a moment it made no sense—and then the truth came crashing in, numbing, killing with its sudden destruction of his pride and ego.

"A clock," he said blankly. "You mean that I'm nothing more than a damned clock."

A metabolic timepiece: for in the contraction caused by near-light speeds how else to determine duration? The seeded world must be within reach and that measurement must be determined by the life-span of a man. His life-span or his awareness of the truth, the variable was important.

And the rest?

"I am sorry, Charles," said the machine and this time there could be no doubt as to the note of regret. "I am really sorry."

And then the electronic device implanted in his brain froze him to instant immobility, the gases came to chill him into stasis, the walls opened and displayed the instruments which would take him and sunder his flesh into fragments preserving the essential RNA and DNA molecular chains all to be added to the final seeding.

But there was no pain. No pain at all. In that, at least, the Builders had been kind.

TIME AND AGAIN

PROFESSOR Pierre Denislov, Head of the Institute for Terminal Studies, was outwardly calm, but Kelough knew that inside he was seething with rage. An anger he shared, one accentuated as he stared at the scattered newspapers on the desk beneath Denislov's hand.

"So someone's been talking," he said bitterly. "Now we're the target."

"So it appears." Denislov looked down at the screaming headlines. "Ghouls," he said. "Monsters. Depraved degenerates torturing the dying. They're having a field day."

"At our expense. Can we issue a denial?"

"I've arranged better than that. A personal interview and conducted tour of the Institute," Denislov explained. "Once they know the truth they will lose interest. I rely on you to handle things. The reporter should be waiting in your office by now."

She was, tall, svelte, with blonde hair neatly tied in a plait which hung over one shoulder. Her dress was snug and fashionably short. Her features held both strength and a tempting innocence. Her eyes, wide-spaced and vividly blue, stared at him in dazed incredulity.

Kelough stared around the office. "Is something wrong?"

"No, of course not." She blinked and shook her head. Her voice was rich and softly musical. "It's just that I had the most intense feeling that I had seen you before. In fact, that I had lived through this whole sequence before. Odd isn't it?"

"Odd, but not uncommon. It happens all the time, especially to the young. *Déjà vu*, they call it. The 'already seen'. Surely you've experienced it before?" He smiled as she nodded. "There you are, then."

She said, thoughtfully, "*Déjà vu*. Is there any explanation for it?"

"There are explanations for everything," he said dryly. "In this case the most common is that you see a thing, immediately forget having seen it, then re-see it. But if you forgot it how would you know you had previously seen it?"

"One false explanation bites the dust," she said. "And the true answer?"

"No one knows. All anyone can do is guess. The only thing we're sure of is that it happens." His eyes drifted from her face to her shoes and back again. "As a professional inquisitor you are rather exceptional. Do they always send a lovely woman on these assignments?"

"If there is one available, yes."

"Why?"

Gently she shook her head. "Doctor Roger Kelough, a skilled psychiatrist and close associate of the famous Professor Denislov, a clever and brilliant young man to ask such a question. Come now, Doctor, you know the answer."

"A young, charming and extremely attractive female can prise secrets from crusty old academics where a man could fail. And the name is Roger."

"Sue Weston." She held out her hand. "You're far from being a crusty old anything. Pleased to meet you."

"The pleasure is all mine."

"I wonder." Her eyes became thoughtful. "You can't really be enjoying this. No one likes to be investigated and have to defend themselves. I guess you had no choice."

"I wouldn't have missed it."

"You're gallant," she said. "Or cunning, I can't decide which. And if you're wondering why I'm alone it's because Denislov insisted on it and he carries weight. Even so that influence won't help him if half of what is rumored is true. The public will stand a lot in the name of scientific research, but there are limits." Without change of tone she said, "Do you kill people?"

"No."

"Do you let them die for want of medical assistance?"

"No."

"Have you proved the reality of reincarnation?"

"No." He added, "Now that's out of the way, let's get a few things clear. This is the Institute for Terminal Studies. It isn't a hospital. It isn't a home for geriatrics. We are not concerned here with keeping people alive. Understood?"

She nodded. "Then what do you do?"

"Exactly what the name implies. We study people who die." He took a chair and waved her to another, noting the way she held her handbag, guessing at the recorder it probably contained. "People have been dying since the dawn of time and yet it is something we know very little about. We grow excited about the possibility of extending the normal lifespan, of the use of prosthetics and transplants, the use of drugs to reduce the physical effects of age, yet we continue to ignore the obvious. By studying it we may be able to learn something about it and, by so doing, find means to make it less terrifying."

Quietly she said, "Isn't that the job of religion?"

"We live in a world of diminishing faith and, in any case, science must find its own answers. What happens to people when they die? We know there are five emotional stages on the normal path to final extinction. Denial, 'it can't be happening to me!' Anger, 'why should it be happening to me?' Desperation, 'I'll do anything to stop it happening to me!' Depression, 'so it's happened it to me.' Acceptance, 'let's get it over.' But what does that really tell us? How can it help?"

"Tell me."

"Later." He rose to his feet. "Now you'd better look over the Institute."

The wards were long, wide, well illuminated, bright with gleaming paint and yet they held an intangible something that induced depression. Sue shivered as she accompanied Kelough past the rows of beds each with its silent occupant. From the pillows mask-like faces stared at the ceiling, the eyes dull, incurious even when she halted and stared at them.

Kelough said, "In this ward we have the old and mostly senile. With the majority communication is almost impossible. They are in the final emotional state and very close to termination."

"Termination? You mean death."

"By many standards these people are already dead. They breathe and their hearts beat, but, mentally, they are vegetables." He took her arm and led her down the ward. "Please try to avoid emotion. These people are going to die whether they are here or elsewhere. We have others, those in the final stages of incurable disease, younger and better able to communicate. Even so they know they are going to die. Here we make no attempt at pretence."

She drew in her breath as they left the ward. "How do you find people willing to work here?"

"You think of them as ghouls?"

"They must love death to want to be so close to it."

"A comment of which you should be ashamed!" he said sharply. "People die all the time. What you have seen is nothing special. Like a hospice we provide comfort and aid in the final hours—are we to be blamed for that?"

"No," she admitted, "but there is something else. Rumor has it that many of those who work here are promiscuous. They—"

"Rumors," he said. "Take any group of people and any accusation you wish to make will probably be true against someone. But it is equally true that working here presents an emotional hazard. The staff tend to compensate exactly as do morticians, interns, and paramedics. Graveyard humor is a safety valve. When people are too closely associated with suffering and death they either become detached or insane. Here the staff are constantly reminded of their own mortality and some tend to live a little harder as a result."

He led the way into a passage lined with closed doors. One opened as they approached and a middle-aged woman wearing rusty black with a string of coral beads around her neck stepped into the corridor. She had been crying, her cheeks still wet with tears.

Gently Kelough said, "A bad one, Mrs. Blight?"

"He was so afraid," she said. "So terribly afraid."

"And?"

She shook her head, busy with a handkerchief as she walked away.

"Mrs. Blight is a telepath," explained Kelough. "A good one. She tries to maintain contact and give what help she can. It is never easy."

"Contact? You mean beyond death?"

"Physical death, yes. Mental—we can't be sure."

Kelough opened the door to a small room. Inside an old woman lay on a hospital cot. She was accompanied by a nurse and an elderly man with a rounded paunch and sagging jowls. He smiled, perfectly calm and relaxed.

"You're a little early, doctor," he said in a smooth deep voice. "Our friend isn't ready to pass over just yet. It will be another ten minutes before I enter a trance and arrange for a guide."

"Mr. Greenshaw," said Kelough. "A medium of thirty years standing."

"Telepaths," murmured Sue. "Mediums. Are you people serious? I thought the Institute was run on scientific lines."

"It is and that's why we use them." Kelough added, "I don't know what you thought you'd find here, but I'm showing you the truth. Try to understand that no matter how odd or wild or illogical a thing might seem to be yet, as scientists, we have to investigate it. Our job is to check things out. To gather data. We aren't too proud to admit there are things we still have to learn. We aren't trying to prove anything. We are simply studying what happens when a person dies."

"And the Capsule?"

"Simply in extension of those studies. Would you like to see it in operation?"

In the Capsule a man lay dying. He was eighty-two years of age and had been senile for ten. Completely nude he lay beneath the searching glare of lights that threw his withered skin, knotted veins and wasted tissues into sharp relief. A mass of wires sprouted from his shaven skull, more from the region of his heart and lungs, the electronic tendrils connected to a mechanism beneath the pallet. The bed itself was a sheet of inert plastic mounted on a delicate balance. Covering it, enclosing man and mechanism in a hermetic seal, an elongated bubble of transparent plastic gave the Capsule its name.

"Time?" Professor Somers was in charge of the operation. Ignoring the recording dials mounted on the walls he concentrated on the figure within the transparency.

A technician gave the information. "Twenty-seven minutes since enclosure."

"Anticipation?"

"Three to seven minutes."

At Kelough's side Sue whispered, "How can they be so precise? Has he been given anything? Drugs or—?"

"Nothing. He's just been carefully monitored. We've gained a high degree of accuracy." Kelough added, as she was about to comment, "No more questions. Just watch."

Stand and look as a man yielded up his life. Those attending him could have been priests conducting an ancient rite, but they were vultures waiting to snatch what they could at the critical moment. No material or force known to science could enter or leave the Capsule unrecorded. If there was such a thing as a soul and if that thing had material or electro-magnetic substance they would plot its passing.

"Respiration uneven," reported a technician. "Heart failing."

She felt the rise of tension. In the bright lights, pathetic in his nudity, the subject was the center of attention. They were all waiting for him to die and she wondered what they would do if, by some miracle, the old man should suddenly recover.

But there would be no miracle. Nothing to disrupt the scientific experiment she was observing.

"Dissolution approaching," said the technician.

Sue felt a sudden constriction of the stomach. She had never been close to death before and, despite the clinical inhumanity of the surroundings, she responded to a primitive awe. From a speaker came the relayed sound of the death-rattle; trapped phlegm caught and vibrating in the trachea, horrible in its implications.

A strobe light began to flash with eye-searing brilliance. On the bed the figure stirred, the eyes opening, one hand lifting towards the wires trailing from the skull. It fell as the lips parted in the final rictus.

"Termination completed," reported the technician. "Now entering the final cycle."

It would last for fifteen minutes, a scientific wake for who could be certain as to the exact moment of true, mental extinction? A healthy subject could be revived after termination. The heart could be made to beat again, the lungs suck air, and if it were done quickly enough there was no apparent harm. Only when the brain had disintegrated from lack of oxygen would anyone finally die.

Sue emptied the glass, shuddered and said, "Thanks, I needed that."

"Medicinal brandy, reporters for the use of." Kelough watched as color returned to her cheeks. "Are you all right now?"

"Yes." She drew a deep breath. "I'm sorry about that. I didn't think I was the fainting kind."

"You aren't. You got a little queasy, that's all." They were back in his office and he could remember the impact of soft curves as he'd carried her from the Capsule. "It happens all the time. Even to doctors and nurses."

"It's just that I've never seen anyone die before. At first it didn't register and then, suddenly, it hit me. That was a real man in there and he had really died. And for what?"

"That is a question no one can answer."

"I don't mean why he died," she said irritably. "I mean, why was he made to do it in that way? A specimen to be probed and checked, measured and weighed. Couldn't he have been allowed to die quietly in dignity and in peace?"

"I warned you against emotion," he said. "Science is the business of asking questions. That man was going to die. Nothing could have saved him. We simply tried to learn something from his passing."

"But—"

"You're not a fool," Kelough snapped, responding to her own irritation. "You know that in every teaching hospital patients are expected to cooperate with the medical staff. You know that many of them are used as guinea pigs to determine the value of new drugs and methods of treatment. How else can medical science advance? Yet, when it comes to watching a man die, you get emotional."

She said slowly, "Maybe I'm being illogical, but it seems to me you are chasing the end of a rainbow. What happens to a person when they die? It's like asking what happens to the flame of a candle when it's blown out."

"A good analogy," admitted Kelough, "even though not wholly exact." He sat down and looked up at her where sat on the edge of his desk. "In the old days people believed a person consisted of three parts; the body, the brain, and something they called a soul. The soul was immortal. Freed of its earthly housing it flew off to Heaven or Valhalla or somewhere similar depending on the person's culture and religion. The point is that people were firmly convinced the ego survived after death."

"So?"

"We grew cynical, or mechanical, or practical, call it what you like. The existence of the soul was discounted and we assumed that everything could be answered by the interaction of the brain and body. Some people still believed in the existence of a soul and an after-life, but it was a desperate hope rather than a proven fact. Then we learned a little more. We discovered that reality could be altered. A subject in deep hypnosis told that he would not experience pain literally did not experience pain. I don't mean that he didn't feel it, I mean that the biological reaction attendant on the stimulus we call pain was demonstrably absent. Pain was not felt because it did not exist."

"I remember reading about those experiments," said Sue, thoughtfully. "They did some pretty weird things. Telling a subject that something existed which didn't. Altering the color-conception and tactile sensations. A lot of things."

"And each experiment was controlled and checked by mental and physical recordings," reminded Kelough. "To sum up, it was discovered that the body has what can only be described as a life of its own. A functional system, rather, which when left alone will work on a high level of efficiency. So we have the body, a physical machine, the brain, which is like a computer directing the functions of that machine, and something else, the mind. The essential, invisible third component."

"The soul?"

"Not as the ancients thought of it. The results from the Capsule have been negative in that we cannot discover any emission from the body at the moment of, or after, death. But we do know that the brain continues to survive after the body has ceased to function. Logically, therefore, the mind must also survive as it is the product of the brain." Kelough leaned forward as to emphasize the point. "But if the mind houses the ego—what happens to it when the brain disintegrates?"

"You have the answer?"

"Yes," he said. "At least Professor Denislov thinks so."

The woman lay supine on the bed, her head on the pillow, eyes closed and chest rising in the rhythm of sleep. Her arms were above the covers, hands slightly curved, the nails filed and neat. Each biceps was ringed with a plastic collar, sterile tubes embedded in the flesh, their openings sealed. Other tubes snaked from beneath the covers to dispose of waste products.

"Linda Hawkson," said Kelough. "She is forty-five years old

and in an advance stage of multiple sclerosis. She will terminate in two months if she follows the normal pattern." He moved to another bed lower down the ward. This one held a man. Like the woman he rested quietly and his biceps also bore the plastic collars. "Fred Cullen, thirty-eight, a steel worker. He has extensive and inoperable carcinoma of the liver, spleen and bowels. Awake he would be in constant agony and would need massive sedation. He has been here two months and should have died a week ago."

"Should have?"

"If the prognosis is to be trusted, yes. We are very accurate when it comes to such things. It is our belief that the Denislov Technique actually enables the subject to extend his expected lifespan as well as removing all fear and anxiety from the terminal stages. Perhaps the extension is due to that single factor though as yet it's too early to be positive."

Kelough moved on down the ward. "Charles Armitage," he murmured. "Sheila Mayhew. Dennis Tucker. Maria Ariosto. Eve Baker . . ." There were fifteen of them. All dying. All, apparently, completely at rest in normal sleep.

"You've drugged them," accused the reporter.

"Not in the way you're thinking of. They did receive initial tranquilization together with certain hypnotic derivatives, but that is all. They are not under sedation. They were hypnotized," he explained. "Thrown into a deep trance and conditioned to feel no pain. The rest is due to the Denislov Technique."

He stepped aside as attendants entered the ward. They pushed a trolley before them, the vehicle bearing a mass of complicated apparatus. Sue watched as they halted beside one of the beds and connected plastic tubes to the collars on the biceps.

"Intravenous feeding?"

"At present necessary," said Kelough, "though we hope to be able to divorce a section of the brain so that the subject will be able to feed himself and perform necessary functions without artificial aid." Blandly he added, "You realize what the Denislov Technique does, of course?"

"Yes Bren—" she broke off, then continued. "Our informant explained that. You have short-circuited the cortex. In effect you have turned them into mindless, brainless vegetables."

So it had been Brenner. Kelough fumed at the disloyalty while understanding it. Denislov had been savagely hurtful when firing the man even though he had deserved nothing less. It was to be expected that he had sought revenge and he had, obviously, preconditioned the girl to expect the worst as her snap judgment showed.

Patiently he said, "You've got it wrong. Each of these people is enjoying a full and active life. Subjective, of course, but none the less real. We know it is real for the lives they are living are their own."

"More hypnotism?"

"No. Let me draw an analogy. Imagine a phonograph record, an extremely long player one so long that the single groove encompasses the events of en entire lifetime from birth to present. Now think of the needle. The Denislov Technique picks it up and sets it down in the groove close to the beginning. We aim for a point twenty years after birth—there is no reason to subject the patient to the usual anguish of childhood and early adolescence. Now imagine the player to be speeded up so that the record which has taken a lifetime to be cut is played in a matter of hours."

He gestured towards the silent figures on the beds.

"That is what is happening to them. Instead of lying here, awake and in pain, terrified of the coming extinction, of termination, they are reliving their own past."

"For how long?" She frowned as she thought of an apparent objection, "What happens when they come out of it?"

"They don't. They live up to the time when they were thrown back—and then they are thrown back. A continuous, repetitive cycle. It will continue until their final termination."

"And then?"

"Then, we think, it happens all over again—but in reverse."

"That's crazy!"

"No." He smiled at her baffled expression. "It's logical when you think about it. As a computer the brain has been storing data all through its existence. Everything you have ever seen, felt, learned and experienced is fully recorded. Death comes, the body ceases to function, but the brain, the computer, remains viable for minutes longer. While it does so the ego remains intact. Then the brain begins to disintegrate. We believe, and there is evidence to prove, that there comes a moment when the stored data is released. The record player begins to

spin in a sudden discharge of energy. It can only move in one direction—backwards. The result has to be a retrospective repetition of the events of a lifetime."

"All in a split second?"

"Subjective time has no limitations."

"But backwards?" She frowned, thinking. "They would
know. The people who die, I mean. How can anyone live backwards?"

"Every moment of your life you are seeing things upside
down," he pointed out. "You don't realise it because your brain
corrects the image. And how would you know you are living backwards? As far as you're concerned the future doesn't exist and
that would apply either because you hadn't lived it or because
the memory of it had been erased. And don't forget that awareness is a matter of split-second repetition. You are aware now—
but as soon as you think of it that now, that moment, has vanished to be replaced by another. To the needle moving along the
groove in the record only the present exists and it is in a constant
state of change."

She stood thoughtful, watching as the trolley with its attendants moved from one bed to another, trying to imagine what it
must be like to relive a life over and over again, to make the same
mistakes, to feel the same pains, the anguish, hurt and loss. But
to know again the pleasure and excitement, the anticipation and
joy. It was a futile speculation. They could never know that what
they experienced was a repetition.

"Sue?"

She turned to face Kelough and felt again the odd sensation
she had experienced in the office when first they had met. A conviction that she had stood here before, knowing, somehow, the
trolley would veer to the left, that he would step forward, one
hand lifted as if to touch her as he asked if he could see her again.
A moment which passed.

"Yes," she said. "That would be nice." Then, as she saw his
blank expression, added, quickly, "I'm sorry. It just happened
again. That thing, *déjà vu*, you called it?"

"You answered me. I hadn't spoken."

"I thought you had."

He shook his head. "That's odd, but never mind. We'll talk
about it. Anything else you'd like to see?"

"Something I'd like to know," She gestured towards the beds. "If what you say is right how would we ever know we aren't like one of those? Or that we had died and—?"

Kelough shrugged. "We wouldn't."

LaVergne, TN USA
24 October 2010

202067LV00004B/45/A